"I was *horrible* to you," Desiree said.

"You're a good person who's scared to make connections, who's been in one too many bad situations in life." As he dipped his head, his eyes widened with sincerity. "You haven't heard that enough, have you? That you're every bit as good as you say I am."

"Look." She licked her lips, stared at the buttons on his shirt. "You're not saying all this or...doing all this because..."

William waited as she strung the words together, pushed them out.

Her pulse wasn't right. It just wasn't. "...because you have some kind of feelings for me. Are you?"

He didn't answer right away. Then, almost down to a whisper, he said, "You know what I wish?"

She began to shake her head then stopped. She did want to know.

"I wish you could've lived here," William said, "instead of wherever it was you come from. I wish you'd have run here...whoever it is you ran from."

She closed her eyes. *God. Who* says *things like that?*

W9-AON-614

Dear Reader,

I'm thrilled to give you my seventh book for Harlequin and my first for the Harlequin Romantic Suspense line! If some characters in *Hunted on the Bay* seem familiar, it's because they have appeared as secondary characters in other books. But *Hunted on the Bay* is special because not only is it a standalone story, but I also get to introduce you to Desiree Gardet.

Desiree is new to the bay. She feels she might even belong there. But the past has come back to haunt her in the worst way. Fortunately, those secondary characters I mentioned and the hero of the story, William Leighton—who might just be the world's last good man—aren't going to give her up without a fight.

The thing I love most about family sagas is just that—family. Finding home is a theme I revisit often in my books because I believe that it is vital to every character's journey. I'm pleased to say that after years of searching, Desiree has found home and family. Read on to find out how she, William and the others help her fight her demons so that she can finally embrace both.

I hope you enjoy *Hunted on the Bay*!

Sincerely,

Amber

HUNTED ON
THE BAY

———

Amber Leigh Williams

HARLEQUIN
ROMANTIC
SUSPENSE

If you purchased this book without a cover you should be aware
that this book is stolen property. It was reported as "unsold and
destroyed" to the publisher, and neither the author nor the
publisher has received any payment for this "stripped book."

Recycling programs
for this product may
not exist in your area.

ISBN-13: 978-1-335-73837-0

Hunted on the Bay

Copyright © 2023 by Amber Leigh Williams

All rights reserved. No part of this book may be used or reproduced in
any manner whatsoever without written permission except in the case of
brief quotations embodied in critical articles and reviews.

This is a work of fiction. Names, characters, places and incidents
are either the product of the author's imagination or are used fictitiously.
Any resemblance to actual persons, living or dead, businesses,
companies, events or locales is entirely coincidental.

For questions and comments about the quality of this book,
please contact us at CustomerService@Harlequin.com.

Harlequin Enterprises ULC
22 Adelaide St. West, 41st Floor
Toronto, Ontario M5H 4E3, Canada
www.Harlequin.com

Printed in U.S.A.

Amber Leigh Williams is an author, wife, mother of two and dog mom. She has been writing sexy small-town romance with memorable characters since 2006. Her Harlequin romance miniseries is set in her charming hometown of Fairhope, Alabama. She lives on the Alabama Gulf Coast, where she loves being outdoors with her family and a good book. Visit her on the web at www.amberleighwilliams.com!

Books by Amber Leigh Williams

Harlequin Romantic Suspense

Hunted on the Bay

Harlequin Superromance

Navy SEAL's Match
Navy SEAL Promise
Wooing the Wedding Planner
His Rebel Heart
Married One Night
A Place with Briar

Visit the Author Profile page at
Harlequin.com for more titles.

To Jerry Lee, WriterDog extraordinaire and the world's best Papa Dog.

We love you, always.

2005–2022

Chapter 1

Desiree Gardet didn't give a damn if the neon sign flashing over the entrance to Tavern of the Graces was off. She'd waited to see its light burn out. She'd waited for the last customers to straggle out into the night and for the proprietor to flip the placard to Closed.

She'd waited a week. She'd wanted a slow night to commit this, her first crime: theft.

It's not theft, she consoled herself, eyeing the single car in the graveled lot. *Not really.*

She'd chosen a Tuesday. Because the pace of life seemed slow and subdued here on Alabama's Mobile Bay on Tuesdays. Or *slower*. Nightlife wasn't exactly hopping on the Eastern Shore outside tourist season.

Desiree flipped the collar of her black vest so the high points obscured what little of her face the trapper-style hat did not. She kept her head low and ventured into the dim parking lot. Her feet felt heavy, leaden inside her boots. That could've been the long wait in the shadows. Or it could be that her feet knew the same thing her head did—that this plan was flat-out stupid.

Her hands weren't shaking, she assured herself. And her breath puffing in a cloudy haze didn't hitch as she approached the car.

There were cameras. She'd pinpointed them the first night she'd cased the place. She kept to the shadows, tilting her face out of the light. From the corner of her eye, she sized up the double entry doors.

She'd watched the man who owned the place. It would've been too risky, venturing inside. Bars had never been her scene. Nevertheless, she'd watched him—the tall, lean stranger with messy blond hair and wondered, *How'd you wind up with my mother's car?*

Her breath came faster as she closed the distance to the Pontiac Trans Am. In the streetlight's beam, through the pluming of her breath, she could see it. The license plate was custom. They hadn't replaced it. It bore the letters she'd chosen: Mercy.

Her heart stumbled hard on the downbeat. She felt relief in droves.

She couldn't back down. No matter what Mercedes Gardet would've thought of her pride and joy busting into the old family vehicle and double-timing it for I-65 north, Desiree had come too far to stop.

She'd ventured here for a reason, to this quiet place, the impossibly charming small town of Fairhope. *Too* small for her to remain secure in her anonymity. She'd come to take back what was hers.

The car hadn't been at Bracken Mechanics like she'd thought. It'd taken her days to trace it to one William

Leighton—the owner of Tavern of the Graces, one of the more high-profile bars in the area.

She'd toyed with the idea of confronting him face-to-face. She'd failed there before with James Bracken, the owner of Bracken Mechanics. The car had been in Bracken's name, after all, and had been since Desiree's mother passed on. Right around the time the car mysteriously vanished.

There was a connection there—between Desiree's mother and James Bracken. One Desiree had contemplated exploring while she was here on this wild, impulsive, completely uncharacteristic Southern venture. In the end, she'd chickened out. Sometimes things were best left as they were.

Usually for her, connections led to misery.

Though Desiree was one step away from the part of her mother's legacy that she'd lost. One step closer to unlocking memories, mislaid or buried—bitter and sweet. One step closer, she felt, to Mercedes in general.

She touched her hand to the flat of the beat-up cab. "Hi, baby," she whispered. Doubling over, she shined her penlight through the back window, then the driver's. Clean. Somebody had cleaned her up. New upholstery. Fresh paint, too, Desiree noticed, taking a closer look at the exterior.

Fumbling in the front pocket of her vest, she felt for metal. Using the light to guide her hand, she put the key in place. *Please don't have changed the locks.*

She pushed the key home. Desiree sighed tumultuously. "Mary Mother, full of grace…" she chanted as tumblers ground and the mechanism gave way. Dancing on frozen toes, Desiree yanked the door open.

Behind the wheel, she shut the door and hit the locks.

"Start," she willed, fitting the key into the ignition. "Start, please."

The alternator skipped before turning over. Desiree didn't know whether to feel more relieved or wary. She glanced over her shoulder at the tavern doors, then scanned the parking lot.

She swallowed. Her throat was incredibly dry. Still, she yanked her seat belt into place. Then she shifted gears and, placing her hands at ten and two on the wheel, she began to back out slowly. Gravel crunched under the tires.

She was *so close*.

Who'd miss this old clunker, really? Sure, somebody'd put some work into her...

Don't feel guilty. The car was all that was left of the real-life Mercy. No matter what the will had stated, it belonged to Desiree.

I'll send this Leighton fella a thank-you card. Without the nom de plume, of course.

"Bye-bye, sleepy town," she muttered as she put the car in Drive. Her foot eased off the brake.

It mashed down, bringing the car to a jerky stop, when she saw the man standing in the headlights. Lean enough to be a lamppost. Messy head of fair hair. Arms crossed over a gray sweater worn under the collar of a checkered shirt. The undershirt's tails stuck out the bottom of the sweater. Up close, she saw a straight-line jaw, strong and critical at the base of a narrow face. He stared. She stared back.

I'm dead, she thought fleetingly as he moved, gradually, from the front of the car to the driver's door.

When his knuckles rapped on the window, she cursed. Obediently, she rolled it down and fought the urge to collapse in on herself like a burned-out star on the edge of stability.

William Leighton bent down to peer at her, one hand braced on top of the driver's door. He studied her until she began to sweat even more underneath her vest and turtleneck.

Finally, the corner of his thin mouth moved ever so slightly and his voice came to her, moving past the pulse against her eardrums. "Well," he drawled. She saw movement under his top lip that was the slow, considering sweep of his tongue over his top teeth. "You don't look like a miscreant."

His casual tone caught her off guard. She couldn't look away from him any more than she could take her hands off the wheel.

His shook his head slightly and straightened. "You best get out of the car, Miss…"

She could lie. In fact, she *should* lie. But her true name came to her more naturally than air. "Gardet," she mumbled.

"Miss Gardet," he said formally.

Strange. It didn't sound like an accusation. When he popped the handle and swung the door open, he offered a long, finely tapered hand.

Desiree considered her options. She could attempt to flee. He wasn't being forceful. The chivalry struck her as odd. She had no doubt that whatever his manner, whatever she decided, he'd alert the authorities. He would turn her in, and—just like that—she'd be ruined.

Images tumbled fast through her mind, as if the fissured glass she habitually sieved the past into had upended completely. *A ruin—all over again.*

She couldn't run. Even with her heart banging, nerves

crawling, she knew she wouldn't try to evade him. His patience didn't help matters, nor the offered hand. Like a refined date at the end of a pleasant evening.

A voice came to her, whistling on the chill breeze through the open window. *Leave the car and take the man's hand,* chère.

It had been some time since Desiree had heard Mercedes's voice in her head. So long that Desiree had thought, in all the twisted byways and techniques she'd used to cope with life, she'd funneled it out by mistake. The novelty of it was enough to propel her into action even if the soft command made no sense.

Take the man's hand? Nuh-uh, Mama.

Still, she turned off the car. Leaving the key, she took a moment to rub her hands across the wheel, the leather cracked and cold under her palms. Leaning forward, she pressed her brow to its hard surface. "I'm sorry," she whispered, rife with regret.

Chapter 2

William brought her to Hanna's Inn, the three-story white bed-and-breakfast presided over by his second cousin, Briar Savitt, and her family, because it was next door to the tavern, its quiet rooms made him feel at home and it made more sense. He had no idea whether this stranger—Miss Gardet—would be more trouble than she looked. It was after hours under Cousin Briar's roof; her guests were tucked into the pristine parlor or their cozy beds, and any disruption wouldn't at all be fitting. He knew that.

However, the tavern was empty, whereas Hanna's provided some backup if it were needed. Briar's husband, Cole, was retired from the police force. Cole's instincts about people were rarely wrong. It was the man of the house who showed them in by way of the private kitchen, where William quickly relayed the story and pulled out a chair for Miss Gardet.

She stared at the seat for a full minute before glancing from him to Cole and back.

"It's a chair," Cole informed her. "Not a bomb. You can take a seat." He exchanged a glance with William and asked, "What do you need me to do?"

William took a long breath. It filtered slowly out through his nose. Their *friend* still hadn't sat down. "I'm not sure yet."

Cole took stock of Gardet's stiff posture, the way her eyes jumped from one part of the room to the other. They were dark eyes. Inkpots deep enough to wallow in, William thought…

Cole cleared his throat. "Reckon we should call out to the Farm?"

William wondered briefly what the people who lived across town at the Carlton farm might have to do with this. Then the connection clicked. "You think he might know something about this?"

"It was his car, wasn't it?" Cole reminded him.

The woman flinched. William saw the tension volley through her, from her neck to her toes. She went motionless. Did she stop breathing, too? William scratched his scalp through hair gone curly with this wild December weather they were having. "Would you mind? I think the lady and I could both use some coffee."

"Want me to ask Briar to join you?"

Briar. William wondered if his cousin's gentle spirit was what it would take to move Miss Gardet to an explanation. He left that possibility for later. "I don't want to disturb her, too. And I know my way around the kitchen."

Cole gave him a single nod. "Holler if you need us."

No sooner had the door swung shut than she whirled

on William. "Why don't you just call the police—have me arrested?"

"That's what you want?" he asked out of genuine perplexity.

"That's what anybody else would do in your situation." She looked him up and down, trying to size him and his intentions up in one gulp. Confusion blipped across her glassy eyes. Her jaw was all but humming with nerves. When she spoke, though, the words were crisp. "I won't try to stop you."

A rare criminal, this one. William moved farther away from her around the table to the coffee service Briar kept in the corner closest to the swinging door. "If it makes you feel better, I haven't ruled it out yet, Miss Gardet."

"You need to stop calling me that."

"Why?" he wondered, swiveling his attention to her again. When her lips firmed in refusal, he guessed. *It unsettles her, being addressed properly.* He reached for a ceramic mug printed with the inn's logo and sighed, picking up the carafe, too. "Coffee?"

"No, thanks," she said rigidly.

That was wise. She was jumpy under her wariness. William helped himself. He was going to need java and plenty of it to make it through the rest of this night. Going back to the table, mug tipped to his mouth, he found the coffee to be strong and warm enough to liven his spirits. Instead of sitting, he leaned against the countertop farthest from her, scanning her as he sipped. He ran his tongue over his lips. "You'll have to forgive me. My mother comes from a long line of Southern belles. She or any of her kin wouldn't take kindly to me addressing a lady less than formally."

"Your mother's not here," she pointed out.

He glanced quickly at the kitchen door and raised both brows. "I don't know that for sure, do I?"

She frowned. It caused a downward crease at the corners of her eyes. "You're afraid of your mother."

He didn't deny the charge. "I take it you're new here, so I'll clue you in. I haven't met the man who isn't afraid of my mother. If he's out there…" He tipped his head to the side and dipped his free hand in his pocket. "Well, he damn well ought to be."

"That doesn't speak well of her."

"On the contrary," he said, and he smiled, because when she wasn't causing him embarrassment, the thought of Olivia Lewis Leighton did bring William pride. The smile faded when Gardet's eyes rose to the ceiling as if seeking help. Then she slid loosely into the chair he'd pulled out for her, the move not so much acquiescence as surrender. She placed both hands on the table in front of her and looked at them numbly.

William studied her. Vulnerable, he noted, and well beyond the point of trying to cover up the fact. Lowering the mug to his hip, he cleared his throat. "If you don't take to me calling you Miss Gardet, you could always offer the alternative."

Her throat moved on a swallow. "Desiree," she said mutedly. Her shoulders settled against the back of the chair and seemed to sink. "My name is Desiree."

Vulnerable she might be, but her voice remained an even alto. Butter smooth. William couldn't pick up any trace of an accent. He'd learned many things as a full-time bartender. One was tracing a person's origin by his or her dialect, distinguishing between the brassy notes from the North and the more fluid intonations of the South.

Desiree had either been schooled out of her local lingo or she wasn't willing to give herself away. Whatever the reason, it made her even more mystifying.Car thieves normally didn't wear fur-trimmed hoods or matching suede vest-and-boot combos. He caught the flash of a slender wristwatch in the low light from the stove. *That didn't come cheap.*

Had Desiree Gardet walked into Tavern of the Graces, he'd have pegged her as the classy type. The way she held her sweet knob of a chin. The way her jaw stayed parallel with the tabletop even as her posture caved in defeat. Her shrewd inkpot eyes. Her skin was a few shades darker than a summer tan, though only just, which implied her biracial heritage. She'd have picked a table in the corner, ordered a glass of red and contented herself in solitude. She had a solid leave-me-alone vibe that could curtail any attempt at conversation.

He'd have noticed her, William mused. He noticed everyone in his bar. But his attention would've strayed to her once, again and repeat. Why was she alone? Did she have anyone at home?

Why the hell had she tried to steal his car?

A knock clattered against the door to the kitchen. William saw Desiree's hands jump toward one another so that her fingers overlapped. Her shoulders straightened. Any more on guard and the points of her jacket could've been mistaken for shoulder pads. Her eyes bounced to the door then to him. In the dull light of the stove, he swore he saw her nostrils flare. Like prey the second before it bolts.

Something shifted across her face. It took him a moment to realize that he was seeing repressed terror. Knowing who waited on the other side of the door, William couldn't fathom it. He slid his mug onto the corner of the counter.

He turned the knob and pulled the door wide, greeting James Bracken with a nod. Like Cole, William had known the man all his life and trusted few others. There was no blood relation between the Leightons and the Brackens, but that did't make them any less close. James's wife, Adrian, Olivia Leighton and Briar Savitt had been thick as thieves long before anyone else had joined their tight circlet.

James wasn't just a member of the circle; he was a pillar of the community. As a family, the Brackens had a hand in several entrepreneurships—Bracken Mechanics, Carlton Nurseries, a flower shop called Flora…even a pet business James shared with his daughter-in-law called Bracken-Savitt Aerial Application & Training.

The man had an armload of tattoos. He flew planes and owned a spiffy car collection. And, despite his rough past, he'd managed to build an exemplary legacy for himself and the family he doted on. To say William and his twin brother, Finnian, had looked up to James from the time they were tots was an understatement. He was the cool uncle figure they'd tried and failed to emulate.

"William," James greeted, unzipping the front of his jacket. Above the line of his full, peppered beard, his nose and cheekbones were pinched pink from the wind. "Everything all right at the tavern? Cole said there was a situation."

"The tavern's fine," William said. He waved in Desiree's direction. "Just enjoying some unexpected company."

James seemed to realize there was someone else in

the room. His eyes narrowed on Desiree. "I don't believe I've had the pleasure…"

Desiree didn't move to introduce herself. She stood, remote, her full mouth drawn tight and her lips pale. William cleared his throat. "This is—"

James released a heavy breath before William could get the rest of it out. "Mercy."

Desiree jolted.

James moved forward a step.

Desiree moved back. The man paused, weighing the status quo and Desiree's caginess. "I'm sorry," he said with his easygoing grin. "You look exactly like someone I used to…"

William jumped in when he trailed off. "Cole thought there might be a connection." At the turn of James's head, William spilled the beans. "She tried to take the Trans Am."

James's eyes homed in on Desiree again, studying her a little more pointedly. "You're her daughter," he said after a silence.

"How would you know?" Desiree asked.

"Well, you're too young to be her sister," James noted. "She didn't have relatives. She didn't seem to have anyone. But you could be a carbon copy of her. At least what she was when I met her."

The corners of Desiree's mouth creased as they drew down at a sharp angle. A blip of heat flashed across her face. Her voice heightened with authority. "You don't know anything about her."

"I knew enough," James asserted. He dragged the ball cap off his head. "She passed away. Ten years ago. Right?"

"Eleven." The lines around Desiree's mouth deepened. "It'll be eleven years this Christmas."

"I'm sorry," James said, holding the cap in his hands. The bill bent farther between his large palms. "I didn't know she had children."

Desiree was tight-lipped on that point. "I came for what's mine."

James frowned. "The car."

"Yes," Desiree said. "Isn't that why you sent for me?"

James shook his head. "I'm not sure I know what you mean."

"The newspaper," she said. "You sent me an article from the newspaper with the address of your garage."

"You're mistaken there."

"Here." With brusque motions William was sure were meant to disguise the quaver in her gloved hands, Desiree dug into her vest pocket. She pulled out a square of folded paper and thrust it at James. "You didn't send this to my home address a month ago?"

William told himself that this was between James and the newcomer, but his eyes strayed to the article James unfolded. There it was, in bold letters: Local Business Owner Arrested for Explosive Materials.

William knew some of James's troubles. No sooner had the Trans Am come into the man's life than trouble had taken over. The police had been tipped off about explosives at Bracken Mechanics. They had searched the garage to find the makings of an IED in the trunk of the car. James had been arrested. In the end, it all came back to a rival family, the Kennards, who had wanted to frame James to settle old scores. Apparently, in the swamp where the Kennards lived—or had until a police raid over the summer—morals were lean and grudges were long.

"That's from the *Courier*." William noted the small type at the bottom of the page.

James scanned the headline, the mug shot of himself. A muscle in his jaw flexed. His thumb passed over the bleed marks from the reverse side. Turning the clipping over, he revealed the address to Bracken Mechanics written in large letters.

"You had to have sent it," Desiree insisted. "Who else would?"

James shook his head again. "Desiree... Is it all right if I call you Desiree?" She shrugged in a jerky motion, and he went on. "I didn't know of your existence until tonight."

"You had to," Desiree said, the skin of her forehead steepling. "Or a member of your family—"

"The only people who know of my connection to your mother are my wife and son. My wife wouldn't have done something like this without my knowing, and my son has been overseas for the better part of two months on navy business."

"Then how...?" Desiree firmed her lips together. "I don't understand."

James scanned the clipping again. "I'm not sure I do, either."

William looked to Desiree. "If you thought James sent you this, why didn't you go to the garage? Why did you try to *steal* the car?"

That threw her off. He saw a flash of awareness before she quashed it, leveling her chin again. "It's like I said. The car's mine. My mother gave the car to me when I was sixteen. Whoever found it should have returned it to me."

James folded the clipping slowly along the worn seam. "There's not much I know about the circumstances of the latter years of Mercedes's life," he said thoughtfully. "You're right about that. But I do know some ten years ago a lawyer showed up here with the title and a copy of her will stating that for some reason the car was bestowed on me. Mercy and I hadn't spoken since I left Florida, so I just assumed she left it to me because I was the one who gave it to her in the first place. I didn't choose to look any further into it, because the car went missing."

"Yes—*he* took it," Desiree said under her breath.

"The lawyer?" William wondered out loud.

Desiree blinked, as though she'd misspoken. "No." She frowned at William. "It doesn't matter. What matters is that she never should've bequeathed it to anyone but me."

"So why would she do it?" James pressed.

"I don't know!" Desiree said, her frustration at its peak. "Because she was sick? Because she wasn't thinking clearly? It doesn't make any more sense now than it did then."

James watched Desiree as the puzzle spread across her countenance, limned in frustration. He lifted two fingers to his mouth, scrubbing his knuckles across his upper lip. "And you figured since I leased the car to William, you'd…swipe it out from under his nose?" He scanned Desiree from tip to toe. There wasn't much censure there, but there was bewilderment. "If that's the case, then you're no more Mercedes's daughter than I am your father."

Desiree stilled completely. Her tone dropped. "It wouldn't have been that much of a loss then, right?" Her brow arched. The muscles in her temple trembled slightly to keep it in place. "The car's not worth much—to you. Or you," she added to William.

William lifted a shoulder. "Still my car, even if it is a rental," he muttered, reaching for the carafe again.

"It's still a crime," James reasserted. "Or would have been, had he not caught you at it."

"So have me arrested," she said. "Why're we even having this conversation?"

"Because I owe Mercedes Gardet a debt," James said. "One might even say a life debt, as she saved mine. And she would've wanted better for you."

"I make my own choices," she stated. "I've been on my own for over ten years. Whether she'd have approved or not, this was my decision. Now, either do what anybody else would've already done and call the cops, or let me go."

William eyed James uncertainly. He didn't see that the man had much choice…

A small, enigmatic smile slowly climbed the contours of James's rugged face as he passed the clipping back to Desiree. "I think we can do better than that."

"What do you mean?" Desiree asked, taking the newspaper cautiously.

"I mean…" James thought it over, then nodded in decision. "…that you should stay."

"*Stay?*" Desiree asked, stricken.

"Yeah," James said. "It's the off-season. I'm sure Briar has a spare room here at the inn…"

"Who says I can afford it?" Desiree asked. "Who says I want to at all?"

"I'll cover the expense if necessary," James supplied quickly.

"I'm not a charity case," she told him, blunt.

"No," James said. "But until we—the three of us—solve the matter of the Trans Am and this—" he indicated the clipping held between her fingertips "—I'd say you'd best make yourself comfortable. Consider Fairhope your home away from home for the next week or more."

Desiree gaped at him. "What you're telling me to do…it's impractical!"

"And boosting a car wasn't?" William ventured. "Sure, you may be a practical person, but you gambled once. Bet again, but *with* the house this time. It might just get you what you want…without the hassle of a warrant."

"Is that a threat?" Desiree wanted to know.

"If you need to know anything about me, darlin'," James said plainly, "it's that I don't make threats. I'm more in the business of promises. Once, I promised Mercedes I'd do what was right in life, just as I'm sure you did. Let's see if we can't give her what she wants—together."

Chapter 3

The following morning, Desiree was under the impression that they were all insane. James Bracken. William Leighton, who despite nearly having his ride stolen out from under his nose hadn't argued when James suggested she take a room at Hanna's Inn for an indefinite sojourn.

Sure, the Savitts' place was miles ahead of any jailhouse by way of accommodations. Desiree had gone to bed and woken up in luxury. Yet luxury didn't make sleep easier.

James had volleyed her mother's name too casually for comfort.

Luxury didn't wipe away any of the assumptions she could draw now that she'd met the man. She could only hope James hadn't drawn the same conclusions she had practically from the time the lawyers had read Mercedes's will…

Desiree had enough to worry about without assumptions. What was James's endgame? What did she have to do to get out of this cutesy little town? Could she avoid coming face-to-face with William, whom she knew very well she couldn't look in the eye?

And how was she supposed to get past the swarm of hens roosting around the breakfast table? They all looked around when she came through the swinging door of the kitchen.

There was Briar—William's soft-spoken cousin with the empathetic eyes who'd helped her settle in. There were two other older women at the table. The first with a curly mass of silver-tinged blond hair thrown into a messy bun. Her heart-shaped face wasn't without a set of piercing peepers. Her mouth pursed as she blew steam from the mug cupped in her hands. The second woman's study of Desiree wasn't as plain with curiosity. This one's stare brimmed with trouble. It tossed Desiree back to twelfth-grade physics and what must've been the look on her face when she flipped through her textbook for the first time. This one, with cropped hair that was red once, Desiree guessed, looked away before any of the others.

The gaggle was completed by two younger women, more Desiree's age—late twenties. The one with a red rope braid falling down her back had a face full of angles. The other could only have been the troubled older woman's daughter. Though she was dressed the opposite, her pronounced makeup and black wardrobe setting her apart. Neither of them reached for the other, but Desiree could see the solidarity between mother and daughter in the way the younger leaned slightly toward the older.

The room was too quiet for the crowd, nearly too big for the circular table in the kitchen's center. Desiree didn't have to guess this congregation wasn't a regular Wednesday morning occurrence. They were gathered here for one reason and one reason only—to size up the life-size physics question in the room. To determine whether it was going to upset the balance in what Desiree could only imagine were perfectly normal, lovely lives.

Briar seemed to remember herself as innkeeper. She rose from her seat. "You're awake. Wonderful."

Desiree placed her hand on the jamb, wondering if it was too late to retreat. "I know you said breakfast is usually served in the dining room. I thought it'd be quieter in here."

"Not likely," the woman with the messy bun drawled.

Briar cut her gaze to the woman quickly before returning her warm hostess smile to Desiree. "We'd be happy to make a place for you. Won't we, ladies?"

The one with the rope braid nudged her chair over to make room. Chair legs shrieked across the wood flooring in response. It was answered by the movement of every other chair around the table as each woman took turns inching chairs around to make room for the one Briar brought out from behind the pantry door. "Please have a seat," the innkeeper invited. "Tea or coffee?"

"Ah…" Desiree didn't move. This was bound to be the inquest of a lifetime. "I won't be intruding?"

"Not at all," Briar said.

Desiree wanted to draw some measure of trust from that earnest face but couldn't manage it. "Coffee would be great. Thanks."

"Have a seat," the messy blonde said.

Desiree planted herself on the checkered cushion. Briar promptly gave her a fresh cup of joe and announced

to those assembled what they already knew. "This is Desiree Gardet. She's taken the Bayview Suite."

Taken. Desiree frowned over the coinciding image of
the Trans Am. Knowing the reference to her wrongdo-
ing wasn't intentional, she tried to smile as Briar iden-
tified the others.

"This is my daughter, Harmony Savitt," Briar said of
the fire-engine redhead.

"Savitt-Bracken," Harmony rebutted quickly. She
pulled a face. "Mom's still not used to my marital status."

"It'll take a while for any of us to get used to it," the
woman in black muttered.

Harmony peered at her. "You say that because I married your brother."

Briar gestured to the one in black. "This is Mavis
Bracken. I believe you met her father, James, last night."

Oh God, Desiree thought with a flare of panic as
Mavis swung her insouciant gaze back to Desiree.

Briar went on with the next bombshell. "To her left
is her mother, Adrian."

The troubled one. Desiree fought the urge to look away
as Adrian offered a ghost of a smile. "It seems you and
my husband have some history."

Desiree didn't want to go over this again. "It seems,"
she responded, trying to sound polite and noncommit-
tal at once.

"He owes your Mercy a great deal," Adrian went on
in an even tone that showed nothing of the portents her
dark eyes held. "All of us do," she added, glancing briefly
at Mavis.

Mavis only hummed in answer. Not knowing quite
how to respond, Desiree lifted her hands to her mug and
lifted it for a testing sip.

"And last," Briar said, "my cousin Olivia Leighton."

The messy blonde was a Leighton. Desiree carefully lowered the mug back to the table. Which made her...

"William's mother," Olivia informed her, as if reading Desiree's every thought. By the curve of her mouth, she found the situation amusing.

She was the only one. Especially when Desiree recalled how William had spoken of his mother the night before. What should she say to a mother who inspired such loyalty, fear and pride in her full-grown son? She took a quick glug of coffee and raised the linen napkin from the table to her mouth when it scalded. She wasn't just in over her head here. She was drowning.

She couldn't count on any of the hens to throw her a lifeline. Determined to hold her own, she set her coffee down to cool. "I—"

"Beignets," Briar said, placing a plate in the center of Desiree's place mat. "I made them this morning."

"Um, wow." Desiree stared at the plump heaven cakes. They were sprinkled with just the right amount of powdered sugar. The smell hit her like a fist in the stomach, and she closed her mouth as it filled with saliva. She hadn't thought she was hungry. Neither had she counted on beignets.

"Pipin' hot and sweet as sin." Mercy grinned as she set the basket in the center of the table with a flourish.

Desiree dived in despite the warning, her adolescent fingers moving wax paper aside greedily so she could get at the offering. Most Sundays thirteen-year-olds spent sleeping in. She'd gotten up as soon as she'd heard the first sizzle of grease, a clear indication that Mercedes was up and dropping the first beignet into the FryDaddy.

She licked her fingers clean, still tasty with sticky

citrus from squeezing orange juice. The sound of Mercedes's full laugh brought her head up. Her mother was trying to hide her amusement behind her hand. Mercy touched her top lip. Desiree swiped her forearm across her nose and mouth, pulled it away and saw the powdered sugar.

"Mmm-mmm," Mercy said with a shake of her head. She tossed a napkin across the table. "What would them boys at Boarden Prep think of you now?"

"Don't care," Desiree boasted. She left the napkin on the table and reached for more pastry. "If it came down between men and beignets... I'd take beignets every time."

Mercy cackled until she wheezed and wiped her eyes on her sleeve. "Lord, child. If only that were true for both of us. We'd be in for less trouble..."

Desiree blinked in rapid succession. She glanced from her plate to the strangers around the table and fought the sweet ache swelling to a painful boil. Breathing carefully, she swept it aside. No way she was about to tear up. Not in this company. Not in any company. Not even her own. "I'm sorry," she said after a hard swallow. She pushed the plate away, quelling memories and the tasty temptation in one swoop. "I'm not really a breakfast person." She pushed the chair back and stood. Zeroing in on Adrian, she said, "If you could give me some direction as to where to find your husband this morning, maybe we could get this mess straightened out."

"It's Wednesday," Mavis answered for her mother. "He'll be at the airfield."

"Right. And where is that, exactly?"

"Half an hour's drive," Mavis replied.

Desiree had relied on public transportation to get her

from Wichita to the coast. No sense in taking the set of wheels she'd bought and paid for legally when she planned on stealing another. "Are any of you going that way? I could tag along."

"It's Wednesday," Mavis said again.

Desiree lifted her shoulders. "So?"

Adrian sent her daughter a weary glance before cluing Desiree in. "It's training day at BS. James will be in the air with his aerial application students for the better part of the day."

Desiree choked back a curse. She looked to Olivia. "What about William? I noticed on the sign that the tavern isn't open on weekdays until the afternoon. Is he around?"

Olivia grinned. "Monday through Wednesday mornings, he's normally up to his own extracurriculars."

Whatever that meant. Desiree puffed up her cheeks then expelled the air. "Okay." She sought Adrian again. It might be a long shot, but she asked anyway. "Did you send it to me—the clipping from the local newspaper with the address for the garage? James said you wouldn't do that. But…"

"But you think I might have done it anyway," Adrian finished for her. "He's right. I'm sorry. Last night was the first time I've heard your name. And, you should know, I advised him to sell the car once his name was cleared."

Mavis nodded in agreement. "It's got bad juju written all over it."

"Not to me," Desiree said. She stopped to check her tone. She leveled with Adrian again. "Maybe…since you're James's wife…you and I can hash this out."

"You think so?" Olivia asked, content again in her amusement.

"Yeah," Desiree said. She nodded to herself. *This could work.* Adrian struck her as a sensible woman— one of the more sensible hens at the table. Sometimes, a sensible woman could get things done faster than a ludicrous man ever could.

Adrian pressed her lips inward before answering. "It's not my place, I'm afraid."

"But...you're his *wife*," Desiree reminded her.

"We share a life," Adrian gave her, "and have for the better part of forty years. But before, we made our own—independent of one another. He's revealed to me the truth of those years, as I've given him every truth I have to give about mine. But his were his. The time he spent with your mother meant a very great deal to him. You being here now, even under the circumstances, *means* something to him. It'd be best if you and me— and everybody else," she added, giving a pointed look at the others—Olivia and Mavis in particular, "let what's to be be."

The goose is just as crazy as the gander. Desiree frowned at her then at Mavis, who frowned right back at her. Desiree lifted her hands to her face and scrubbed.

Someone touched her arm. She jerked in surprise.

Briar lifted her hand at Desiree's disquiet. There was an apologetic bend to her smile. "I have some mini quiches left over from yesterday's brunch. I could heat those up for you, if you prefer. It won't take but a minute."

Desiree had to get out. "Thank you, but no. I'll get something. Later. Excuse me."

She went out the door she'd come through the night before. The screen slapped shut behind her. The sun shined off the water, throwing diamond pinpricks in her eyes. Squinting, she followed the sound of waves sliding on sand.

It arced, the Eastern Shore. She could see the line of piers, the struts from sea-battered docks sticking out of the waves like sawteeth. There were those that sagged and those like the Savitts' with new Trex composite boards and wicker chaises. Desiree had forgotten her vest, but she crossed her arms over her chest and trudged from the sand to the deck, hunching her shoulders and braving the stiff gale. It was cooler under an empty, ice-blue sky than Desiree would've imagined this far south. She'd forgotten the wintry bursts that could sneak in on the subtropical zone.

Wherever she'd been as an adult—and she'd been places—she'd remained a thin-skinned, born-and-bred Floridian. Winters spent in the northern portion of the United States had proven that. She'd often found herself dreaming of Daytona beaches. The salt of the marshes. The fluid glide of the great blue heron. The explosive burst of Cajun crawdads on her tongue. She'd dreamed of January days that didn't make her feel like her face was going to fall off. She'd dreamed hot molten dreams of summer afternoons that melted asphalt, that easily made one believe in hell on Earth. The languidness of those days.

Then she remembered other things about Southern life. Things that had chased her away, from state to state until she'd charted a course farther and farther north, landing in Chicago. She'd left a trail of jobs and identities behind her.

Some people ran screaming from their demons. She'd ghosted hers, hiding behind new names, new looks, in new and bigger cities until she'd lost touch of the Southern girl she'd left behind what seemed like a century ago.

Desiree ducked under the roofed section of the dock. There she sheltered from the chill. She toed the line of a crab trap submerged below the gray surface of the bay, then looked across the choppy water to the shadow of Mobile to the west. She wasn't a city girl. But cities were safe. In a city, she could fade into the wallpaper; she was just another survivor crashing through life.

She closed her eyes. The smell of the turbid bay and the Gulf beyond, the fish that lived below the tideline… it overwhelmed. She'd stayed away from water, keeping to the Midwest She'd wanted to forget who she'd been— the idealistic girl with big musical dreams. She wanted to forget how close she'd come to achieving them. The price she'd paid. The mother she'd lost and the less-than-worthy men they'd let into their lives…

Who had sent her the clipping? If it wasn't James or Adrian, could it have been their son in the navy? Was there some way she could contact him personally? Or should she just run back to Wichita?

What was to stop them from contacting her again? Could she really change her address, her identity *again*? The thought exhausted her, more than the chaotic confrontation the night before…more than the inquisition of hens around the breakfast table… She thought of moving boxes and DMVs and shook her head. She couldn't… She just couldn't go through all that mess again.

The man was dead. The one who had chased her from Florida, all the way up the Eastern Seaboard, to Chicago… He was dead. She shouldn't have to do this anymore. She shouldn't have to cut and run again…

"If it came down between men and beignets... I'd take beignets any day of the week."

"Lord, child. If only that were true for both of us. We'd be in for a lot less trouble..."

Damn it, Mama, Desiree thought. *I couldn't agree more.*

The phone in Desiree's back pocket vibrated. She pulled it out and frowned at the unknown number on the screen.

Something in her gut said no. Don't answer.

The phone continued to buzz. She pursed her lips.

The nightmare from her past couldn't follow her anymore. She hadn't received a strange call in twelve months. She had ended that part of her life.

It was probably one of her clients calling. Normally, they reached out through text or email. But occasionally they did call.

Desiree took a careful breath. Then she made herself press the Answer key. "Hello?" she said after raising the phone to her ear.

She heard a click. Then...nothing.

She took a quick peek at the phone screen to make sure the call hadn't been dropped. "Hello?" she said again, seeing that she was still connected with the person on the other end of the line.

She was answered this time – in a chilling whisper. "Burn."

Her lips fumbled. Her heart dropped. "W-What did you say?"

Her phone beeped. The call had ended.

Still, Desiree kept the phone to her ear, frozen in fear. It was over. She knew it was over.

Then how...

She scrubbed the heel of her hand over her brow to stop panic whirling on the other side of it. "It's not real," she chastised herself.

She was just imagining it. The call had been real, sure. But there had been static. Nothing more. No one had told her to...

Burn.

"I'll take you."

Desiree bolted abruptly from her thoughts and turned back in the direction of the inn. Mavis Bracken stood, outfitted in black against the white vista of the main house and its stunning gardens that were somehow resplendent on the far side of the year. Her nose was pink, throwing her silver nose ring into distinction.

She looked like Adrian, sure. Built small. Round face. But her strong jaw and chin marked her as James Bracken's daughter, all right, and that made Desiree more ill at ease than the wary way Mavis had watched her over breakfast.

"What?" Desiree asked, doing her best to silently slow the scared, bucking bull that was her heart in her chest.

"I'll take you to the airfield," Mavis said again. "Harmony's co-owner there, and she's got to be at work within the next hour. Dad usually breaks for lunch. You're most likely to catch him in the hangar with Seb, the mechanic. Those two old grease monkeys normally take that time to jaw over mechanical problems."

Desiree shook her head. Her mouth was dry. She swallowed, hard. "What about Adrian and her 'Let It Be' refrain?"

"I'll worry about Mom later," Mavis told her. "To me, the whole thing is simple—you came for something. A car. When you get it, you'll leave. Am I right?"

"Yes," Desiree affirmed. "The sooner, the better."

"We agree, then," Mavis said shortly, sealing the deal. Her hands linked. The fingers of her right hand went to the fourth finger on the left and the band circling its base. It held a single red ruby. "My family...they've been through a lot this year. My brother came home and got engaged. My dad almost went to prison for something he didn't do. Both my parents nearly lost everything—their reputations, their livelihoods... Then Kyle shipped off again with the SEALs. His and Harmony's wedding in September was good medicine for all of us. For the first time in a long time, everything went right from start to finish. I want the same next month for me and Gavin. No hang-ups, no complications. No worries."

"I'm not here to steal your thunder," Desiree said.

"It's not about thunder," Mavis claimed. "It's about family and security and making everything right for Mom and Dad, as much as for Gavin and me."

Desiree scowled. "I'm not saying that what I did last night was right, but I went about it the way I did to make as few waves as possible. I don't want to be here any more than you want me here."

Mavis's brow creased. "You know, normally I'm good at reading people. No matter how hard I try, though, I can't get a bead on you. I'm not sure what that says... For all I know, you could be everything Dad says Mercy was—who sounds awesome, by the way."

Desiree nodded slowly. "But you still don't want me here."

"Just be clear about your intentions. And don't try to screw over William again. He's a good guy. Probably the most decent guy I know."

Desiree fought the urge to roll her eyes. Despite Wil-

liam's show of chivalry the night before, Desiree could
no more plant the label *decent* on him—or any guy, for
that matter.

"Before we go, is there anything you need?" Mavis
asked. "Cole thinks you've been here over twenty-four
hours. You don't have a vehicle. Where's your luggage?"

"At a motel about a mile south," Desiree admitted.
She was still holding the phone. Her hand was still damp
around it.

"I know the place." Mavis took a step backward.
"Come on. We'll round up Harmony, stop by for your
things and get you to Bracken-Savitt Aerial before noon."

"Ridiculous!"

"Humph?" William roused from the sleepy haze he'd
blessedly sunk into. His wool plaid jacket had kept him
cozy in what he liked to think of as the sweet spot between the west-facing side of the tavern and the brick
wall his parents had added a few years before his mother
unofficially retired as tavern keeper. Not only did the
wall offer an intimate enclosure for those who preferred
drinking outdoors and an incredible view of the sunset—
the wall gave off a fair bit of solar heat. Only too inviting
on a wind-battered afternoon like this one.

Inviting. Like the dark eyes of Desiree Gardet. Even
when they were shooting daggers at him, he'd found it
difficult to look elsewhere...

In the space of a few hours, he'd seen her anxious, irritated, near petrified and perplexed. Now, as he watched
her pace the lawn between the piazza and the sandy
shore, he saw something new, and despite her intriguing
set of ink-dark peepers, he could hardly say she looked
inviting.

She looked livid.

There was no hat on her today. Her hair was swept up. The wind teased the coils, and her angry gait made them bounce. Last night she'd looked kempt. She'd dressed and carried herself like someone who was well composed. While the vest-turtleneck and black pants combo was the same as the night before, she didn't look as together.

She looked real. The distinction struck him, then drew him as much as the warm brick wall beside him. She scrubbed the flat of her palm across her temple, failing to flatten the worry lines there.

Come here. The invitation was mute but clear. He wanted her to sit with him awhile by the warm piazza wall. He wanted her to tell him her troubles. Not because he was a bartender. Not because the mystery of her confounded him and most everyone he loved at present. Because he wanted to help her.

Maybe, somewhere along the way, she'd learn to trust. Seemed to him it'd been a long while since Desiree Gardet had had reason to trust anybody.

You can trust me. He knew it. The woman in question was a long way from that realization and not likely to come around to it before her time here was up.

She pivoted to face the tavern. She started in his direction then stopped, seizing on his sprawled form. She shifted back in reflex. He read *retreat*, plain and clear, from her expression with half the lawn between them. The anger grounded her. It climbed onto her russet features. That was good, William reckoned, even as she gunned for him.

He sat up slowly, placing his elbows on the arms of the Adirondack chair, and watched her come. Why wasn't she wearing the gloves from the night before? Or at least something to cover her ears? Beyond the piazza wall, it was far too brisk to be without.

"How long have you been sitting there?" Desiree demanded.

He reached up to tug at his earlobe. "Let's just say I was here first."

"You could have said something."

"I could've," he granted. When her eyes widened, he added, "You looked like you were having a lively enough chat with yourself. Didn't want to interrupt."

"Oh, that's great," she said. "You sat and watched me yammer at myself for five minutes."

He pursed his lips. "It was more like ten."

She rolled her eyes. He fought a smile. The levity would've been harder to fight if there wasn't still worry under all her ire. If she wasn't shivering with cold. He released a sigh. "Come here."

"E-excuse me?"

"I said, 'Come here.'" He tilted his head at the neighboring chair. When she eyed him, he explained, "I can hear your teeth chattering. The wall's blocking the wind. You can hunker down better on this side of it."

"I'm fine," she told him, even as she threaded her arms over her middle.

"Hmm," he said by way of argument. "You aren't a Northerner."

"Why do you say that?"

"You don't like cold."

"Does anybody?"

"Maybe," he said, thoughtful. "People are crazy for all kinds of reasons."

"It takes crazy to know it."

He smiled and glanced around the vista. "Crazy's common as corn around here, Miss Gardet. Though, if I'm certain of anything, it's that it's the same everywhere else."

She scanned him from head to toe. He felt it. Her nose crinkled unsatisfactorily. "Were you sleeping out here?"

He made a noise. "Guilty."

"Who sleeps outside a bar in the middle of the day?" she charged. "Aside from hogs and drunkards?"

William chuckled low. "The owner."

"You're not drunk, are you?" she asked, wariness doubling.

He didn't have to look to know his button-down shirt was wrinkled. He'd pulled it out of the clean laundry this morning. The pile had been on the floor for days. It was routine, simply pulling what he wanted out instead of hanging it up—much less ironing. He didn't have to reach up to know there was a nice growth of gold-tinged stubble growing like a curse across his jaw. He'd slept later than he'd bargained and hadn't had time for shaving before leaving his apartment early that morning.

Her assessment might've been fair, even if it was bold. It was easy to think the worst when you'd seen the worst in most everybody. "I'm not drunk," he said evenly, hoping she'd see truth where it was plain.

When she chose to remain in the wind, he struggled with patience. He rose quickly, pausing a minute when his lower back gave a protest. He stopped to stretch it, raising his arms and twisting a bit. Then he moved toward the tavern.

"You're walking away?"

"You can come, too," he said over his shoulder.

"Where?"

"It's warm inside. You can stop shivering there, and

I can prep for business hours." He paused to take the keys out of his pocket, happy he'd remembered them. He'd been knocking on Briar and Cole's door more and more of late. He blamed sleeplessness. Without looking back to see if she had followed, he unlocked the door and opened it.

She'd come farther than the piazza at least, he saw when he turned. There was indecision on her face. He swung the door wider, holding it high in silent invitation.

Desiree glanced from him to the inn. There was nobody who'd ventured outdoors, but the distance from the tavern to Hanna's was small. She looked back at him then through the tavern door, licking her lips as she bounced on cold toes.

"There's hot cocoa." He raised a brow.

Her mouth parted slightly. She cursed, ducked her head and picked a direction.

Chapter 4

Not what she expected. Desiree looked around Tavern of the Graces as the lights came up, one after the other. Not what she'd expected at all.

It was more than the roadside dive she had imagined. The lights, the woodwork, the beam structure, the bar itself... It was a classy aesthetic most wouldn't associate with drinking establishments. She did a slow turn. "This is...nice."

"High praise," he said as he unraveled his green scarf. He tossed it behind the bar. "If I'm not mistaken, that's the nicest thing you've said since we met."

She liked his drawl too much. It rivaled the strum of a well-worn guitar. Acoustic. Raw. No need for accompaniment, just the essence of the instrument itself. Wood, strings, the glide of key changes, the strum of rough fingertips. She shrugged at the lure of it.

"Can I take your coat?" he asked.

She crossed her arms over it. "I'm fine."

Holding up his hands, he took a step back. "This way," he invited, folding up a small hatch on the far right side of the bar.

Were bars usually this clean? The tables were high, stools stacked on top. The floors shined. The walls gleamed. There were recessed lights everywhere, but the centerpiece was a stunning wine-barrel chandelier. Around the walls, she'd expected to find mounted buck heads or fishing trophies. Instead, the walls had been carved to mirror the history of the Alabama Gulf Coast.

The bar curved smoothly around both sides. Behind it gleamed shiny gold handles, two dozen or more. Behind those, a vintage mirror to complement the amber hue of the chandelier. "This isn't what I expected," she said out loud.

"What did you expect?"

"The smell of cheap beer and cigarettes," she admitted. "The aura that hangs in the air after a bad date." He sent her a frown over his shoulder. She shrugged. "That's the extent of my bar knowledge."

"I take it you do your drinking at home," he said.

"Preferably."

"And where's that for you?"

She raised a brow at him in answer. He lifted a shoulder and grabbed his scarf where it'd fallen. "You don't drink alone, do you?"

She followed the curve of the bar, running her hand over the wood. Solid. Almost warm feeling. Then she ducked through the pass-through. On the business side of the flattop, she felt like an intruder. "Maybe."

"And the mystery continues."

"The less you know, the better."

"Why do you say that?"

"Because I'm gone." Desiree was more than aware of her promise to Mavis Bracken—and her own dogged commitment to it. "As soon as I get what I came for."

He sidestepped any mention of the Trans Am, opening the swinging doors into the hallway beyond the tavern. "You don't plan on trying us out during business hours? The atmosphere's better when the tables are jammed and there's a live band onstage. Wednesday's ladies' night, which means open mic and dollar mojitos."

"It's a shame I left my feather boa and fiddle at home."

He chuckled as she paused, scanning the hall beyond the doors. "You play the fiddle?"

She realized the mistake too late and pressed her lips together. Glancing back at the barroom, she deferred by asking, "How long did it take you to put all this together?"

"The tavern's been in my family for three generations," he explained. "My grandparents built it before my mother was born, and my great-grandfather did most of the woodwork. They passed it on to her when they retired. It was only recently that she decided to take a step back and let me take over."

Desiree wondered briefly if he'd taken over the family business because he'd wanted to or out of obligation. The margins of tradition and obligation weren't far apart, especially when they existed inside the realm of a town as off the map as this one. Then she looked more closely. That foreign flash in William's hemlock-green eyes was, again, pride. Pride in the establishment his mother's family had built. Pride in the work it took to keep it alive. Pride that she had seen what he saw from the moment she walked in—something that was well loved and cared for.

Desiree studied the carving of a long battleship on the wall closest to her. It was so detailed, she could see the rivets, the worn marks on the bottom of the hull where it'd been kissed by waves. She couldn't trace her own family beyond Mercedes. She didn't know her father's name, much less his family history. Not having roots of her own beyond the marshlands on the east coast of Florida and the mother she'd been forced to let go of, Desiree found it almost intimidating to be with William under the roof his predecessors had refined.

What was it like to feel that…grounded to something—a place and its people, past and present? His sense of self was complete. He knew exactly who he was and where he came from, where he belonged and likely where he'd be for the rest of his life. She didn't want to envy his roots, or him, but Desiree struggled against a stream of longing for something…

Something more constant.

She swallowed. "Don't you ever worry? About failing them if you don't succeed?"

William pulled a face. "I don't plan on finding out."

"But even sometimes the best laid plans…" She trailed off as his smile disappeared into a contemplative line. She was being unkind to him—this man who'd been kind to her when it would've been wiser not to. "Never mind."

He tilted his head toward the hall and took the lead. "Back here."

Desiree followed. There wasn't much she knew about the people of this town. Her face-to-face with James Bracken in the hangar at noon hadn't done anything to answer the questions she had about him, what he was to her mother or what he was to her. She didn't know how to read beyond the smiles of Briar Savitt, Olivia Leighton or James's own wife. Even if she'd spent time with the younger women, Mavis and Harmony, Desiree still wasn't sure what to make of them. She did know, however, that William Leighton was not an unkind man. She'd known it the night before. She'd just been too conflicted to admit it.

Kindness wasn't near as common as crazy. Neither was courtesy.

Keys jangled on a large ring as William took them from his pocket. He flipped through them before he found the one to fit the lock on the first door to the left. He pushed his shoulder against it and turned the handle. "Jamb sticks a bit," he excused. He reached in to switch on the light. "I've been meaning to get Cole to fix it, but there's always something for a handyman to do at the inn, especially now that they've expanded." He lifted his hand in indication. "After you."

Desiree sighed. "Look, you don't have to do this every time."

"What?" he asked with an innocent blink.

Jeez. Not only was he chivalrous. Chivalry was so ingrained in him, it was involuntary. *I'll bet his middle name's Ashley Wilkes.* "Hold the door," she indicated. "It won't hurt my feelings if I'm second into the room."

One side of his mouth slid into a canted half smile that suited him as much as the wrinkled button-down shirt and khaki slacks that fit him fine but were frayed slightly around the cuffs. A tiny dimple showed itself on his left cheek. "Humor me, then," he suggested.

He wasn't going to stop, she realized. Her heart picked up pace. Was that panic or attraction?

She no longer knew the difference. How sad.

Quickly, she went through the door. There was a couch squatting low to the ground. It looked clean and comfortable enough for a siesta. An L-shaped desk with a rolling chair was set up with a computer, several labeled binders, a stack of unfiled paperwork, a printer/fax and phone. Above the wide-screen monitor, there was a large painting of midnight blue seas and an old ship sailing under the wicked white sickle moon.

William nudged into the room close at her back. She jumped a bit, smelling him for the first time. Last night, she hadn't noticed the spicy hint of cologne or deodorant that clung to him. She turned sharply toward him as he uttered "Excuse me" and moved to the corner behind the open door.

"Oh," she said at the sight of the small kitchenette. There was a counter large enough for a sink and portable burners. She watched him open the cupboard, where he grabbed an envelope of cocoa powder and a small pot. "Oh," she said again. He hadn't been lying about the hot cocoa.

He filled the pot under the faucet before setting it on a burner. Turning the element on high, he took two mugs off a hook. "Marshmallows?"

"I…" She couldn't remember the last time she'd done this. Cocoa. Companionship. She licked her lips. "I don't know."

His eyes swept her, lingered on the jacket she was still wearing and the hands fisted near her sternum. "Marshmallows," he decided. "This'll only be a moment. Make yourself cozy."

She looked around at the couch. She settled on the cushion closest to the door, sitting on the edge with her spine straight and her hands on her knees. "Why're we here, again?"

"You were cold. Don't lie. You still are."

She was. Desiree stuffed her chilled hands in her pockets as if they'd betrayed her. "Second?"

"Second," he granted. He glanced over his shoulder to gauge her face. "You were unsettled about something." When she began to shake her head, he held up a hand. "You don't have to tell me what about it. I just thought you'd need a minute to—"

"Calm down?"

William chuckled. "Telling you to calm down won't help. I know that much about women."

"On your own—or is that something else the grand dame Olivia taught you?"

He grinned at the dig. "You needed a minute. We'll just leave it at that."

"You're not going to offer a sympathetic ear?"

"Would you take it if I did?"

She watched his steady hand as he poured boiling water into the mugs. His long, tapered fingers picked up a small spoon to stir each in turn. "How do I know you're not going to turn around and tell them everything I tell you?"

"Them being?"

She rolled her eyes. "The Brackens. The Savitts. The grand dame Olivia. The whole down-home mob squad you've got going on here."

He plopped tiny marshmallows into each drink. He picked up the mugs and started toward her. "'Mob squad.' I'll pitch that. Mum would go for it."

"Thanks," she said when he handed her the first drink.

"Too hot to drink," he warned in a warm, acoustic undertone. "But perfect for warming the hands."

"Yes," she agreed, staring down at the steamy surface, where marshmallows were quickly dissolving. The ceramic's heat sank into her palms and numbed them quickly against the lingering bite of December. Her fingers tightened on it reflexively when William sank onto the cushion next to hers, bending over his long, folded legs to blow steam across the surface of his cocoa.

Silence had many songs. It could keen like a gull. It could knell like thunder. There was another kind of silence, though—one she'd forgotten as the distance between her and her childhood yawned further in the years running. It was the compelling hum of two people—one who needed to unload the weight off her chest and another who was willing to listen.

This song of silence was so sweet to Desiree's ears, it hurt. It was authentic. That much she knew. But trusting it…that was dicey. As was remembering just how to breach it.

William spoke first. "You went to see James."

As a prompt, it was apt. She raised the hot mug to her mouth for a testing sip. The drink burned her lips but tasted so nice she swallowed. She waited a few seconds and took another. "I went to see James."

He nodded. "How'd it go?"

"Depends on your point of view."

"I'm interested in yours."

She almost met his gaze. At the last second, she decided against it. "Are you?"

"Tell me."

He didn't demand. For that reason, she did tell him. "I

brought cash—enough to buy the Trans Am and a little more to sweeten the deal."

"What did he say to that?"

She grimaced. "He said he didn't feel comfortable taking it since he's leased the vehicle to you until he can rebuild the engine in your truck. When I asked how far along he was, he said that he hadn't exactly started, since it's an '80s model and parts aren't easy to come by."

"That's the truth, as I understand it," William admitted.

"Why not buy a new truck?"

"Why travel as far as you have for a decades-old junker?" he countered. When she didn't answer, he leaned enough to touch his shoulder briefly to hers. "We're sentimental, you and I."

Her breath came short for a second. It was disconcerting, even if the strum of his low voice was enough to make her close her eyes and savor it. She pressed back against his shoulder in rebuttal. She could all but hear him smiling to himself as he went back to his cocoa.

"Anyway," she said, "I asked him to estimate how long it would take him to rebuild your truck. He said it would only take him and his team at the garage a few days but that the parts were a week or more out."

"So you're stuck here," he surmised.

"I told him I could come back, that he could call me when the repairs have been made and the Trans Am is free. He said he wasn't sure if he was ready to sell it."

"To you, or anybody?"

"I didn't ask," she said. "I'm not sure I want to know the answer."

She felt his eyes burning into the side of her face. "You did try to steal it."

"Have I not said I'm sorry?"

He thought about it. "Not to me."

Finally, she met his stare. It was greener, this close. Evergreen. "I'm sorry."

The green softened from evergreen to moss. A smile came to his eyes once more, if not to his lips. "You might've made it," he muttered, "had I not checked the cameras at the right moment."

She cleared her throat, taking another sip of cocoa to soothe the flutterings she felt there. "Y'all should really get those locks changed."

"If this was your last offense, should we be worried about anyone else?" he wondered.

Her stomach sank. She thought about a dead man. She thought about the newspaper clipping and the address written across the back in unknown handwriting.

She thought of the strange call on the bay this morning.

How could she answer that question?

"You said 'y'all.'"

She frowned. Had she?

William tapped his knuckles against his mug. "To my knowledge, only Southerners say things like *y'all.*"

She'd lingered too long. Here in Fairhope. With William on the sofa...

"Mercedes was from Florida, wasn't she?" he asked. "Are you an East Coaster, West Coaster or Panhandler?" She kept her lips buttoned, so he shrugged. "I can always ask James."

The thought of the two men discussing her any more than necessary pushed Desiree to admit, "I'm from the Atlantic side. That's more than you need to know."

"Okay," he said softly into his mug.

She didn't need to know the shape of his lips, the way they fit to the edge of the cup. Irritated with herself and her chain of wandering thoughts, she continued. "He said I should stay, instead. Until he's certain he should sell. If he thinks so well of my mother, I don't see how he has a choice. I don't know why he'd want me around...if he knew everything."

William seemed to sense the heavy burden behind the words. "Maybe you should ask him."

She scoffed. "Maybe I should join him and his family for dinner Friday night."

"He invited you out to the Farm?"

"Apparently, it was his wife's idea," Desiree said, unable to fathom it. Adrian hadn't exactly been the most enthusiastic member of the welcoming committee this morning. "I don't know what I'm supposed to do."

"Go to dinner," he suggested. "What could be the harm?"

"You're kidding, right?"

"Believe it or not, they are friendly," William said. "I've sat at their table. And this was when Kyle was home instead of overseas. You're missing the most critical member of the Bracken posse."

"Mavis could fill his shoes well enough in that department," Desiree wagered.

"Ah, Mavis. She said something to you?"

"She warned me not to put a foot wrong," Desiree admitted, "and not to intrude. I can't imagine she'll be pleased if I show my face there."

"I'll go with you," he offered.

She blanked. "You'll what?"

"I'll go to dinner with you," he said again, "at the Brackens'."

A surprised laugh hit her. "As what?"

He lifted a shoulder. "As a friend?"

"William, I tried to steal your car," she said. "We've known each other less than twenty-four hours. What about that says 'friends' to you?"

"You're talking to me, aren't you?" he asked. "My guess is you don't talk to a lot of people. You don't talk much to anybody."

She wasn't going to think how he knew that. "I haven't said I'm going yet. I haven't said whether I'm staying. There's nothing stopping me from leaving. In fact, I *should* leave. The car's not available. No one wants me here—not really. My travel funds will be drying up soon. There's not a chance I can afford more than a few nights at the inn, much less weeks…"

"Sounds like you need a job," he said, pushing up from the couch.

It wasn't until he took the mug gently from her hands that Desiree realized it was empty. Had she drunk all that cocoa herself? Her belly was warm, and there was a satisfactory toastiness spreading through her extremities. "What kind of an employer would take me on on a two-week basis with nothing to recommend me but vehicular theft?"

"Foiled vehicular theft," he said, placing the mugs in the sink of the kitchenette. "You didn't quite pull it off, remember?"

"So I'm a bad thief," she said, "and an even worse conversationalist. Is there anything else we've established?"

He turned from the sink, leaning back against it to analyze her and the situation. "What'd you do…wherever it is you come from?"

She opened her mouth to reveal herself, then stopped. "I don't see how it matters."

"It matters," he asserted. "What was it?"

She pressed the heels of her hands into the seams of the couch cushion. "I was in marketing."

"What kind of marketing?"

"I managed bookings for a large music hall in Chicago."

"Chicago."

"Yes," she said, studying the points of her booted toes. "But I haven't… It's been over a year since I…"

"Resigned? Was asked to leave?"

"Resigned," she said. "I resigned for personal reasons. I…had to move. Now I'm in the small business market. I repair stringed instruments. Guitars. Cellos. Violins."

"Fiddles," he added.

She nodded quickly. "Yes, fiddles."

"Do you play?"

"I did." Moving restlessly to her feet, she didn't know how to expand on that.

She knew that he knew there was a story there. One she wasn't willing to tell. Instead of asking any of the questions she dreaded, he said, "I might know of something—a job you can do for a week or two. However long you need."

"You do?"

"One of my best waitresses just went on maternity," he explained. "She'll be on hiatus for a while. She worked tables, mostly, Monday through Fridays, opening to close. The position's yours if you want it."

"You want to hire me," she said slowly, not quite able to believe it.

"I can't offer you her salary," he went on. "Aside from

any tips you earn, I'd ask you to work by the hour. But there's something else I can offer."

"What's that?"

"A room." When her eyes widened, he reached back to scratch his neck. "Not like that, Dez. Come on."

"Okay." It took her a second to recover from what she'd been sure was an offer she'd have to refuse. She felt a touch overwarm at the mistake. "Okay. A room, *not* with you."

"No. It's here. Or, upstairs. It's furnished. We use it occasionally. You won't be here long, as you say. It'll keep the commute to work short since you don't have transportation."

"I can't accept this."

"Why not?" he asked, almost to the point of exasperation. "You don't seem to know what it is you want. I'm offering you time and opportunity to think it through. Even if it is just until the weekend."

"And if it's not? I've never been a bartender. Don't you have to go to some type of school for that?"

"Not always."

"I've never even been a waitress."

"You're not slow. You can learn."

"And if I'm no good at it?"

"We'll see how it goes."

"If I'm no good at it…you won't keep me on payroll out of pity, will you, William?"

"Look, if it makes you feel better, I promise not to keep you on staff if you slow everybody else down. But I don't think that'll be the case."

"Why not?"

"Because it's snowbird season. Snowbirds are messy

as hell, but they tip like kings. Money's the biggest motivator, right?"

Desiree thought of her instruments at home. She thought of the salary she'd given up to spend more time nursing them back to health. "For some people."

"Look," William said, moving toward her in a slow gait that showed how well he knew her and her caginess. "You don't have to decide right now. And my offer to join you for dinner at the Brackens' still stands."

"I can handle James," she told him, "and his family. As to the room… I will think about it."

"Good," he said. "Friends?"

His dimple was back. It teased her. "If you say so."

"Ah," he said, his eyes touching on her mouth. "I wouldn't have thought that possible."

"What?"

He beamed. "A smile."

Desiree felt herself go very still. Then her insides, those parts of herself she'd thought she'd fortified with steel years ago, started to soften. *Never mind cocoa. Beignets. Think about the beignets, girl!* "Relax, Dimples," she chided. "If you repeat anything I said here today, you and I will never have cocoa again."

He dipped his chin. "This was off the record."

He meant that. Desiree suspected William Leighton meant everything he'd said to her since the moment they met. Wasn't that a kick in the head?

"What do you really make of it?" William asked. The bass speakers were pumping on the other side of the wall as he stood outside the tavern with James, Cole and Cole's son and James's soon-to-be son-in-law, Gavin Savitt. William and his team had a full house tonight.

He should be inside working the taps. With Zaira on leave, he was already understaffed. However, the men gathered none the less out of hearing. No one needed to overhear what they had to say about the curious case of Desiree Gardet and the Trans Am.

They especially wanted none of their wives or mothers to know they were discussing it outside their purview.

"What do we make of what?" Cole repeated. He'd been thirty years or more outside the line of duty, but with his hands braced on his hips, he still looked every bit the plainclothes officer. "The crime she almost committed or the odd bit of circumstances that brought her here?"

"Or the fact you offered this piece of work a job," Gavin drawled. He was heavily shadowed from his position behind Cole, but as a former Navy SEAL, his presence was massive. It was sometimes difficult to match him with Mavis, whose stature could be described as diminutive even if her impact was long.

"She needs something to tie her here," William replied. "And I need a waitress. I threw her a bone."

"Didn't you think to do some background on her first?" Gavin asked. He turned his attention to James. "You, too. Who says she is who she says she is?"

"Oh, she's Mercy's daughter," James said. "No mistaking that. It's the car's history that confounds me more than hers."

"Have either of you figured out how the newspaper clipping came to be in her possession?" William asked.

James shifted slightly, reaching back for his wallet. He pulled it out of the back pocket of his jeans. He pulled the worn clipping out of the trifold. Smoothing it open, he offered it to Cole. "I talked to Kyle. He says he had nothing to do with it. And that's not his handwriting on the back."

Cole took eyeglasses from the chest pocket of his sweater-vest. Tilting the clipping to the light, he looked down the edge of his nose and put his detective eyes to use. After several moments, he muttered, "She claims not to know whose possession the car was in all these years. Though, from the sounds of it, she knows it hasn't been in yours."

"She knows," James said with a nod.

"And we know that it somehow wound up in the Kennards' hands, if only for a short while before it was placed in the garage with explosives. Did you tell her that?"

"No."

William reached back to scratch the curls on the back of his head. They were cold. The wind whistled through the empty piazza at his back. He wondered whether to speak his mind or keep what he'd learned of Desiree's origins to himself. "She's not a liar." The others looked up from the clipping, and William continued, cautious. "She dodges questions she doesn't want to answer, and she's defensive. But if she were lying, I wouldn't have offered her the job."

Gavin pushed off the wall to pace in a slow, restless gait that spoke of who he was even in the dark. "It's not a wonder to me you're related to Briar. To the two of you, everybody's virtuous. You've just got to give them the benefit of the doubt."

William didn't argue. He had only to think of Desiree and what he'd gleaned of her. "Sometimes all a person needs is the benefit of someone's doubt. If she's lying about anything, it's why she didn't go to James to begin with."

"I agree," James muttered, contemplative. "That's why I invited her to dinner. I think there's more I should know."

"You mean *we*," Gavin said. "Harmony and I'll stand in for Kyle."

"She won't respond to bullying," William warned him. He was careful to keep the words clear and even. "She's been through enough of it, I think, to know better."

"There won't be bullying at Adrian's table," Cole asserted. "She won't stand for it. I'd bank on that."

"The family's invited," James stated. He looked to Gavin. "All of you, as what happened this past summer involved everyone, and it stands to reason that this business with Desiree will affect all of us as well. But anybody who sits down at our table will act civilly."

Gavin crossed his arms. "I seem to remember being choked out by your son over dinner a few months ago. And I'm skeptical. We should all be skeptical."

James grunted. "You don't want to incur Adrian's disapproval, seeing as you just earned yourself a permanent chair."

"She's got a stare," Gavin admitted. "I can't handle both of 'em shaving my liver with their eyes."

James shifted from one foot to the other and groaned in empathy, as if he knew exactly what Gavin was talking about.

"There's got to be somewhere else she can stay other than above the tavern unsupervised," Cole pointed out. "I'm sure I can talk to Briar about discounting the cost of the suite."

"She doesn't need supervision," William replied. "The only way she's going to let down walls is if we give her a bit of space. She could barely talk to me this afternoon without looking over my shoulder for the rest of ya."

"On that note, what'd you find out from her?" Cole asked.

"If I told you, she'd have no reason to talk to me again, would she?" When Gavin scoffed, William added, "If she'd given me the answers we needed, that'd be different. At this point, you should know that this one's been through the wringer and we should all tread lightly where she's concerned."

James's phone went off. He snapped it off the holder on his belt and took a look at the screen. "I'm due at the Farm." Glancing around at Gavin, he said, "So're you."

"Right," Gavin said with satisfaction. "Spaghetti night. What're you grinning at, Leighton?"

William cleared his throat, tilting his face out of the light. "Domesticity isn't something the rest of us thought we'd see on you."

"Well, I'm wearin' it," Gavin reminded him. "You got anything else to say about it?"

William raised his hands. "I think it looks nice."

Cole laughed, clapping a hand to his son's hard shoulder. "Go on. Enjoy your night. You can stop in and see Briar before you start work tomorrow."

"Tell her Mavis and I say hi," Gavin said. He lingered, however, when his father moved off and James apologized and stepped aside, too, to call Adrian and tell her they'd be late.

William waited until both father figures were outside hearing bounds. "How're wedding plans?"

"I have no idea," Gavin said. "I was told to stay out of it. For once, I don't mind obeying."

"Obedience." William raised his brows. When Gavin's head canted, he said, "Another new look for you."

"Eat me," Gavin replied. "Look, I've got something to say and I'm not comfortable saying it, so listen so I've only got to say it once."

"Listening," William granted.

"Mavis is worried about you."

Ah. William found his hands sliding into his pockets. He let them sink all the way in as Gavin's scowl grew pronounced.

"I don't like it," the man said.

"I sense that." William ran his tongue over his teeth. "What's she got to worry about where I'm concerned? She's got enough on her hands."

"You got conned once by this Gardet chick," Gavin pointed out. "She's worried you're going to let her do it again."

"Is that why you're here?" William asked. "Because she sent you?"

"I said she was worried, didn't I?"

It wasn't really a question. "Well, you can tell her she's got nothing to fret about."

"You see, that's where I think you're wrong." Gavin came closer. The light struck his face, throwing the ridges of scar tissue, his battle wounds, into distinction. "Based on what I heard tonight, I'm starting to think she's got a right."

"Just tell her her mother-hen tendencies are showing," William suggested. "She'll back off."

"It's more than that," Gavin argued, heated now. "You *know* it's more than that."

William worked his jaw, considering his history with Mavis and how close he might come to earning himself a sock from her fiancé's hamlike fist. Still, he couldn't help asking, "Are you agitated because she's worried or because the person she's worried about is me?"

"I'm *ticked off* because the only thing my woman should be worried about at this point is what dress she's going to walk down the aisle in," Gavin said. "She's been through tough times, too, you recall. She's earned herself enough peace to worry about the little things. *Just* the little things. Instead, she's got her ex-lover on the brain. You're damned right I'm agitated."

"She doesn't have anything to be agitated about," William stated, firmly.

"You'll tell her that."

William nodded. "Yes. Yes, I'll tell her."

James returned, sliding his phone into his pocket. To Gavin, he said, "Done?"

Gavin frowned at William. When William didn't break under the pressure, he shifted away. "You'll tell her."

"I said I'd tell her," William said, near exasperation.

James lifted a hand in goodbye when Gavin moved off toward the parked cars. "Good luck, William."

When they had left, William took several deep breaths, drinking cold sea air. He could use a lap along the shore with the wind slapping him in the face.

Instead, he turned toward the warm lights and boisterous noise of the tavern and went back to what he knew.

Chapter 5

"Is this where you're supposed to be?"

The Uber driver couldn't be reading Desiree's mind, but neither could he have echoed her thoughts better than that. The turn for Carlton Nurseries was marked by a broad sign, visible even in the darkening blue twilight. Beyond it, somewhere, was the residence of James and Adrian Bracken. They owned the plant nursery, a farmhouse and the sprawling acreage surrounding it as well as the airfield beyond.

Desiree had visited the airfield days ago. She knew she was in the right place. Still, she had questions.

Is this really the place I'm supposed to be?

"Ma'am?"

Desiree wriggled from her thoughts and reached for her bag. She took out a tip and passed it from the back seat to the front where the driver waited. "Here. I can take it from here."

"Looks like quite the walk up the lane there," he commented. "You don't want me to drop you off directly?"

"I'm fine," Desiree said, slipping the cross-body strap of her bag over her head. She adjusted it at her hip before opening the door and getting out of the car. "Thanks for the lift," she said before closing the door. She stepped back and watched the sedan roll away.

A walk would do her some good. Or at least that was what she told herself as she faced the empty graveled lane. She read the nursery hours on the sign. It had closed a while ago. There were no lights other than those illuminating the sign. The lane to the farmhouse was unlighted and encroached heavily by trees, some unseasonably dense with foliage.

Desiree shook off her unease and began to walk, wrapping her long wool scarf more closely around her neck. There wasn't much of a breeze, but the air was chilled just the same. The scarf was one of the rare pieces that didn't follow her neutral color palette. It was a patchwork of colors. A kaleidoscope. She'd bought it because it reminded her of the quilts Mercedes had loved to fold everywhere for those rare winter nights the heater couldn't take the sting out of.

Desiree wore flat soles and wide-leg slacks paired with a silk blouse under her overcoat. It was ridiculous how much time she'd spent staring at the limited items in her suitcase, wondering which pieces would be appropriate for an impromptu dinner with her mother's ex-paramour and his family. All things considered, business casual had felt the way to go. It helped that it was the part of her wardrobe she felt most comfortable sporting.

With the breeze, she'd decided it would be best not to try to tame her hair. This weather, so close to that of the Florida marshes, encouraged it to be its willful self. It rode high, a bouncy plume. She'd tied a silk handkerchief around the base of it and hoped for the best.

The trees were thick and held the worst of the breeze at bay. It tossed in the limbs overhead. They swayed and creaked. She quickened her steps down the shoulder of the road, pulling the strap of her satchel tighter across her chest. She couldn't see beyond the bend in the road a hundred meters away where she assumed the Bracken house would be.

She hated this time of year when dark came fast and early. She liked the wide-open summer hours when light stretched into the evening, awakening the dream of a midnight sun.

Desiree didn't like to admit the truth plain, having chosen to live alone for as long as she had. But she'd never been a fan of the dark.

Keep moving, she thought as unrest pricked at her heels. The breeze tossed the long arm of her scarf over her shoulder. It waved like a flag as the gale picked up, bringing the smell of salt to the woods. It took nearly everything she had not to break into a half jog.

There was something in the woods. She saw it slinking through the shadows of the pines. *An animal*, she told herself. A bobcat. Or a dog.

A big, silent dog. Inadvertently, she shuddered. She found her steps slowing as curiosity took hold of her better sense. A dog that didn't seem to want to venture beyond the shelter of the trees? A chill raced along her spine, bringing her to a halt.

Whatever it was, it stilled. As she probed the darkness,

trying to pick apart shades of gray and silhouettes, her lungs went cold. Okay, dogs normally ventured closer, and every other animal she knew tended to skitter off when confronted with something bigger than itself. Possums played dead, she recalled, but this was no possum.

Her breath came fast and shallow. "Hello?" Her voice carried, but it wasn't rife with bravado. It lifted, disjointed. Telling herself she was brave, she tilted her head, trying to get a bead on the hidden figure, and took a step toward the woods. She didn't expect an animal to answer. In her mind, she knew better.

Shadows didn't so much shift as coalesce around a tall, thin figure. A very unanimallike figure.

She stopped breathing altogether, realizing she was staring at a man. "James?"

No answer.

"Who are you?" she demanded, this time stronger. "Are you Gavin?" She hadn't yet run into James's son-in-law-to-be. He'd been a sailor from what she'd gathered from others.

What kind of a soldier stares out of the woods and doesn't answer?

She squinted, trying to read the guy. Something about the set of his shoulders...

Her stomach knotted. Under her blouse, she broke into an unwarranted sweat. *Mary, Mother of God...* Her fear grew talons and teeth, and it tore through her. *It can't be...*

The last shred of daylight joined the gloaming blue, or her eyes finally adjusted to the dark. She was suddenly looking at a face. Thin, craggy and very, very familiar...

She took several steps back in winding retreat. Her heel caught on a root, and she toppled over into the road.

The fall jarred her, but she scrambled away from the woods... Away from the face that came at her in nightmares...

The gravel underneath her seamed the nightmare around her with memories. It bit into the heels of her hands, and she remembered. Being on hands and knees, vision going in and out, watching her own blood drip-drip-drip onto the stones of her driveway outside of Chicago not so very long ago...

Light overwhelmed her. For a second, Desiree wondered if she was about to pass out. Then the single blast of a horn severed the scene. She shielded her eyes from the spotlight of headlights and righted herself on legs that shook like matchsticks under her weight. Blinded, she froze, unable to discern whoever was behind the wheel of the large vehicle. Breathing raggedly, she managed to keep herself right side up as both the driver and the passenger doors opened.

"Dez?"

Her chin wobbled as she opened her mouth. "William."

"Dez. What're you doing?" He came around the hood of the truck, his familiar shape coming together in the piercing glare of the vehicle's low beams. "You okay?"

He touched her arm. She jerked back, riding high on defense. Her lungs were still shredding from the cold air. It came out on a wheeze. "I'm fine," she said automatically. She repeated it, as much for herself as for him. "I'm fine."

His eyes, concerned and narrow, passed over her. "Looks like you've had yourself the fright of a lifetime."

He had no idea. She didn't want to, but her eyes ventured over his shoulder, to the tree line. She couldn't see if the face was still there. Not with the lights.

William caught on to her. He scanned the woods, too, wary. "You see something?"

"No," she said quickly. She shook her head, locking her legs. *It's in your head, Dez. It's all in your head. No matter how real it looks...*

William's questioning gaze swept her again. He took a step toward the woods.

"No!" she said, grabbing onto him. *Don't go over there!* her mind screamed. Her fingers flexed into the sleeve of his flannel jacket. "No, it's...it's nothing. Nothing."

He expelled air on a small white cloud. "If you saw something, you should say."

"Why?" she wondered. Damn it, her jaw was quivering like a deer.

"Because..." He lowered his voice and took a half step closer. It was enough for the warmth of his form to reach across the space between them and take hold. "...these woods...they've been known to host secrets."

"What, like ghosts?" The words hardened in her throat, making it difficult to swallow.

"Something like that," William replied. "So, did you see anyone, Desiree?"

Only a dead man. He'd think she was crazy. And... after that, she couldn't dissuade herself entirely that she wasn't. She felt cold, so cold. Out here in the cutting breeze. Inside her bones. Wrapping her arms close around herself, she tried for casual tones. "I caught a root or something with the heel of my shoe. I fell, and it happened fast, so I..." She shrugged away the rest.

"You're not hurt, are you?" he asked, eyeing her up-

swept hair, which now looked, she was sure, as much a
fright as she thought she'd seen.

Her hand went to the handkerchief she'd bound there,
patting springy curls back into place. "My ego."

His eyes softened, a hint of a smile around the outer
rim where the light touch of crow's-feet appeared when
he was in good spirits. She'd noticed that before. She
held on to it now, allowing herself that luxury to bring
herself further back to present.

"Hey!" someone called out of the dark, chasing fear
through her again. "Are you gonna let the woman shiver
till her bones rattle apart, or are we giving her a ride?"

William let out an exasperated breath, raising his hand
to the head of the driver hanging from the open window
of the truck. "All right, Mum." He tilted his head at Desiree in silent invitation.

Any other time, she might refuse. Tonight, she
could've jogged to the shelter of the warm cab. "Thanks."

He led her back around the passenger side. The truck
was an extended cab pickup, a large four-by. "This is
your mother's?"

"She likes a Ford."

"She's so small…"

"Yeah. Don't get me started on *her* ego," he commented and opened the back door for her. He held out
a hand.

There was no running board, it was a long step up
and damned if her legs were steady. She took his hand
and let him boost her into the cab.

The heat was a welcome reprieve. William closed her
door quickly, and the warmth enveloped her. She tried
releasing the rest of her tension. It refused to drain until

William's door opened, too, and he climbed in. "Mum. You remember Desiree?"

"Sure," Olivia Leighton said with a half smile over her shoulder. "Trouble?"

Desiree stopped herself from biting her lip. "Just a fall. I'm fine."

"I'm glad to hear it," Olivia said. When William eyed her, she clarified, "That you're fine. Not that you fell."

"Thank you," Desiree said, feeling adrift. As Olivia eased off the brake and hit the gas, she couldn't help but let her eyes gravitate back to the woods.

Nothing, she saw at a glance. Not that there was anything there before. She hadn't seen a man. She knew that, because the face she'd seen belonged to someone she knew to be incontrovertibly deceased. And even if she believed in ghosts, she *hadn't* seen his.

It made no sense for her stepfather to haunt Bracken land. Not when he'd died in Illinois.

So, that left her sanity in question. She scrubbed her face with her hands. *Well, it wouldn't be the first time, would it?*

The face had been *so real.* The shape. The worn quality of it that displayed all the self-abuse and bad habits that had eaten away at the man, his appearance, his core…

She found herself shuddering again. Quickly, she turned her mind elsewhere. To the silence—what she imagined to be the suspicion—from the front seat. She couldn't go down this road again. Especially not with dinner with James and his family moments away.

The steel-enforced rods she'd built for herself that she'd always relied on snapped into place. They were as automatic as any of the defense mechanisms that had buoyed her through a life on the run. She wouldn't let her demons come back to haunt her. Not now when she was finally free of them—physically, at least.

She'd stood outside the white clapboard farmhouse for several minutes staring at the door trimmed in a poinsettia wreath and twinkly lights. Framed in the window, she could see a Christmas tree, neatly appointed, and the star at its crest.

The Bracken abode was like *Better Homes & Gardens*. Only…better, she discovered. After the scare from the forest, it shined like an impossible refuge she wished she could afford to seek.

She'd stood on the doorstep scrupling until William's hand settled on the curve between her neck and shoulder. She gave a rabbit jerk at the touch but didn't move out from under it. She was so on edge her teeth were rubbing together.

He was so warm compared to the chill that was still buried in her like a hatchet. "It's just a house," he murmured. He tuned his voice low so Olivia, who was rapping loudly on the door frame, wouldn't overhear. "Inside, there's just dinner and a family."

A family of lions, she thought grimly. And she the solitary wildebeest loping into their midst.

Wildebeests had horns, right? She felt hers lower as she followed William's urging and trailed Olivia over the threshold.

Adrian was on the other side. "Desiree," she greeted. "We're happy you made it. Here, let's take your coat."

"Oh," Desiree said. Ducking underneath the strap of her purse, she shimmied until she had one arm out of a coat sleeve. Adrian took her bag. Desiree felt the coat hovering in midair and realized that William had a hold of the collar. Quickly, she shrugged out of the other sleeve. Smoothing her blouse with both hands, she muttered thanks to both of them.

"Something smells delicious," William said, freeing himself from the plaid jacket. It had tan suede patches on the elbows. Underneath, he wore a denim-colored shirt he might've taken the trouble to iron for the occasion.

"I'm afraid dinner's running a bit behind," Adrian said, pulling a face as she hung their coats and Olivia's inside the entry closet. "I thought we'd do chickens on the grill, but the men had ideas of their own."

Desiree followed close on their heels, taking in the decor. There was a fire cindering in the hearth. Rugs everywhere. Even flowers and greenery were in profusion—naturally; Adrian *was* the local florist. There were wood floors and brown leather couches that were worn in a few places but functional and nicely in tune with the aesthetic. Framed photos were in abundance. Desiree eyed the one above the mantel. A bride and groom were the focus, the one in white being Harmony. That made the groom in navy dress blues James and Adrian's son, Kyle. James and Adrian stood to the left of the couple, beaming, with Mavis and who Desiree could only assume was her fiancé, Gavin, to their right. There was a small girl in the center of the frame, too, and several canines sprawled at their feet.

What the hell am I doing here? Desiree wondered. Just a family? Never mind the men's Dwayne Johnson–like physiques and their beards. This was the frigging Deep South edition of *The Brady Bunch*!

"Do you like fish, Desiree?"

She blinked at Adrian for several seconds before the words seemed to sink. *Fish?* "Um, yes, but it's winter."

"There's plenty to be caught in cold water if you can stand it," William noted. He was still at her side.

"And James and Gavin were out most of the night doing just that," Adrian acknowledged. "Kitchen's this way. Come on back."

Desiree hung back, letting Adrian and Olivia go forward. Then she turned to her escort. "I told you I didn't need your help tonight."

William sighed. "And her claws are back," he muttered.

"What?"

"Nothing," he said. "I just thought the suit of armor was gone."

"The only one wearing a suit of armor around here is you. It's so shiny, it's burning my eyes."

That startled a laugh out of him. The little birds'-feet appeared at the corners of his eyes. It wasn't enough having to deal with him being the perfect gentleman or the way his voice twanged like a Fender. He had to laugh at her sarcastic jokes and charm the mess out of her, too. "If the Brackens are just a family, then why're you hovering?"

"I heard you before," he claimed, lowering his head so they could talk out of earshot of those in the kitchen. "You don't need me. I respect that. I'm here because Mum was hell-bent on joining the fray. The grand dame does overstep. I didn't want her to say anything that'd make anybody feel any more awkward about the situation."

"You're mommysitting?"

"You wouldn't need to ask if you knew her," William muttered, raising his brows.

"I don't think she likes me," Desiree guessed. "Not that I blame her."

"I blame her," William stated.

It was so plain, the way he saw it. "Why *do* you like me?" she wondered out loud.

His gaze seized on her. Evergreen. It reminded her of spring. Natural warmth. It scaled her features. For a brief moment, it passed over the line of her mouth. Desiree felt herself go very still. "You're real."

"Real." She parroted the word, trying to make it gleam the way he did.

"Yeah," he said. "You're realer than a storm or the foghorns you hear rolling off the bay in the dead of night. You're realer than most anybody else. You're real to me. That's it."

No, she thought as her lips parted. That was everything. When was the last time someone had come up against her sharp points and thought, *Let's do that again*? He was either as out of his head as she feared she was…

…or he was the last good man in the world.

"I don't mean to interrupt…"

It was Mavis. Desiree couldn't seem to move.

William answered. "Sure you don't."

Mavis observed them both with knowledgeable eyes. "They're forming assembly lines. One for fish, the other for shrimp." She zeroed in on Desiree. "You don't mind getting your hands dirty. Right?"

Hadn't Desiree done that already? "No," she replied. She glanced up once more at William. *Bad idea*, she decided when his soulful look shot straight through her. She turned away and followed Mavis into the kitchen.

Chapter 6

"You've done this before."

Desiree glanced up to meet William's observation. Her fingers didn't stop. They were wet and likely numb from the ice in the bowl before her, but they kept peeling the shrimp with a precision only the experienced could muster. "Yes," she replied, handing him a naked crustacean.

Quickly, he passed the fork over the back of the shrimp to devein it before extending it to Harmony, who was in charge of rolling them in the batter to be fried. "Don't elaborate or anything," he told Desiree.

He thought he saw the muscles around her mouth work. As usual, the slight smile didn't meet her eyes. It was something to see them quirk. She started to reach for her hair then stopped.

He liked her hair high. It threw her regal profile further

into distinction. Her chin was level with the counter, her brow high, jaw firm, lips soft…

William made an effort to look away before Harmony had to rib him. *Make it a little more obvious, won't you?* he chided himself. Desiree was still on trial here for some, and he couldn't escape the fact that he was being watched by Mavis, Gavin and even, perhaps, his own mother for signs of attachment.

He'd never been great at playing it cool, and they all knew it.

Desiree looked around to see if anyone was listening. Seeing that everyone was content in their own chatter, she leaned toward him and said, "I *am* from Florida."

"But you've never had flounder," he said. "Else you would've known you catch them in cold waters."

"I have had flounder," she clarified. "I've just never fished for it."

"What *have* you fished for?" He liked the idea of regal Desiree—or a younger version of her—casting a net over the surface of a bay or wading into surf with a rod. He imagined she hadn't looked as straitlaced as she did tonight in her pressed trousers and silk threads.

"Oh…" she contemplated, "bass. Shrimp. Mullet. Catfish. Crab. Snapper…"

Impressed, he missed the shrimp she tossed him. Picking it up off the counter, he made quick work of it before passing it on. "Why, Miss Gardet. If I didn't know any better, I'd say you were a regular outdoorswoman."

"Maybe I was. Once." She sent him a sideways glance, measuring. "Does that intimidate you?"

"Did you bait your own hook?"

"Can't bait, can't catch," she recited. Then she frowned

over what seemed to be an old saying and reached for the next critter in the bowl.

He wondered over the hitch. "I caught a lemon shark once."

"You? How long?"

"About yea big," he said, judging the width of the counter.

She laughed in a short burst. "You're a liar."

"Oh yeah?" he countered.

"Any fisherman who's ever caught anything as noteworthy as a shark would have had it weighed and measured at the dock and could rattle off the exact numbers on a dime." She wagged a finger at him. "And here I thought you were the last good man."

"I'm not lying." He held up two fingers. "Scout's honor." At her narrow stare, he admitted, "It might've been more of an assist. We all took turns in the captain's chair bringing her in, and it was technically out of season so, no, we didn't stop at the dock. And we were so hungry by the time we got it home, there was no time for a photo op. Just eatin'."

"Uh-huh. And who's 'we'? Anybody in this room?"

"It was my brother, my dad and me," he explained.

"No clear and present witnesses. You are a dirty, rotten liar, William Leighton."

"I can still prove it." Raising his voice, he called, "'Ey, Mum!"

Olivia turned from the wide breakfast bar where she was busy multitasking with a Budweiser and a lemon juicer. "Yeah, Shooks?"

"Do you remember eating that lemon shark Dad, Finnian and I caught off the coast in high school?" he asked.

She scowled. "That was a shark? Finny told me it was swordfish."

James spoke up. "I heard it was yellowfin."

Mavis made a face. A rigid vegetarian, she was handling leftover squash from the fall crop. "Jesus. At this rate, it was dolphin or porpoise."

"It was a shark!" William argued. "I swear!"

Every other person in the room voiced their qualms on the subject.

A naughty laugh juddered underneath the noise of the ill-fated inquest. It took William a second to realize it belonged to Desiree.

In the space of a moment, he noticed many things. The way her whole face changed when she was taken with laughter. The two infinitesimal capillaries under her eyes, not like wrinkles but just as fine. The ones at her temples, a mite thicker. The way her eyes crinkled almost to slits and her teeth gleamed white as a beached sand dollar.

Christ, she was beautiful. He'd known it before she'd laughed. Now he was completely taken by her.

She caught him staring, and the laughter died off quickly, leaving barren traces behind. "What?"

He couldn't help it. He beamed at her. "You laugh like a pirate. You do," he insisted when she looked away. He nudged her. "Don't think I'll be forgetting it."

Nope. That laugh would hang with him far longer than Desiree Gardet planned to stay.

"How're we doing on shrimp?" James asked, coming over to them.

"About done, I think," Adrian said, scooping the latest batch from the fryer.

"I only have a dozen more to peel," Desiree agreed.

"You're doing a fine job," James said. Approval washed over the man's face as he watched the quick, clean work of her hands. "I wish we'd had you over the summer when Kyle was home. He and Gavin hauled in sacks from the Pass. Adrian swore she'd never head another shrimp again."

Desiree sobered all too quickly.

A curly-haired girl raced into the room. "Is it time to eat?"

James scooped the child up in one swoop. "Not yet, but it sure smells good, doesn't it, Bea Sting?"

"My tummy's rumbling," Bea said, eyeing Adrian and Harmony, her mother, around a basket of shrimp. "Can't we eat now?"

James glanced at the women. "Do we have an early-bird plate for this wildling?"

Adrian reached up to open a cupboard. "Have a seat next to your cousin Olivia at the bar, Bea. You can be our guinea pig."

William noticed the way Desiree watched James with Kyle's stepdaughter. A stillness came over her, something not unlike disquiet. Her curiosity wasn't ambivalent. "That's Harmony's daughter," William explained. "James and Adrian have always treated her like their own."

"Why?" she wanted to know.

"I don't know," he said. "Because we're all family, in a way, even if we aren't all blood relatives."

"Who here are you related to?" she asked.

He thought about it. "Mum, obviously. She and Briar are first cousins, so Harmony and I, too. And Bea. Gavin, but only by marriage, since he's Briar's stepson." He glanced around at the others as Bea settled in with her dinner and Adrian and Olivia doted on her. "Harmony's lived here on the Farm since she and James opened a side business together. They've been in operation as long as Bea's been alive. And Adrian and James don't have any grandchildren of their own…and aren't likely to, if talk's true and Kyle's sterile. I don't see Mavis having children, either. She's had some health problems."

Desiree turned away as James began painstakingly mixing horseradish and ketchup to make the girl her own cocktail sauce. She went back to peeling shrimp, remote.

It took William several seconds to ask the question on his mind. "Was it just you and your mom? Or were there others?"

She peeled the last shrimp slowly, using her thumbnail to separate the shell from the meat. "She married, once. Never took the guy's name. Not that she should've. He wasn't exactly faithful."

"Was he good to you at least?" William wanted to know.

She reached up without looking, scratching the space above her eyebrow with her pinkie finger. "For a time."

These were deep waters, he sensed. "I'm sorry."

"For what?" she asked.

"For whatever you had to go through to get here," he said plainly. "I'm sorry."

"How do you know it wasn't what I deserved?"

"Dez." He shook his head, trying to draw her back to him. "How old were you? A kid?"

"I was a full-grown adult when Eric Kennard came after me in a bad way," she answered.

His mouth parted. "What?"

"My stepfather. He was a lowlife who used her and then used me. One too many times."

"No," he said, backtracking. "What was his last name?"

"Kennard."

William felt the blood drain from his face. He looked around at the others. He and Desiree had been speaking in near whispers, and no one had caught on to the name except him.

Kennard.

Desiree looked at him for a long moment. "William, what's wrong?" Fear struck her. The same fear he'd seen earlier on the road. "You didn't know him, too. Did you?"

The words were spotty, strung together uneasily. He shook his head. "No." He'd never heard the name Eric Kennard. But damned if he hadn't heard of the Kennards and the troubles James, Adrian and the rest of the Brackens had had with them.

It couldn't be coincidence. Desiree had spoken the name here, at the Farm. There was a connection between her and James and a deeper one between James and Desiree's mother that went back decades. Kyle had been an infant when Adrian had married Radley Kennard and divorced him shortly thereafter on grounds of domestic abuse, before she and James had reunited and built all they had together. Radley had had five brothers—every single one of them a bad egg like him.

What were the odds one of them had wound up in Florida—romancing the very same woman James had?

"What's wrong?" Desiree asked. "Is there something I should know?"

"No." Before he brought the specter of the Kennard-Bracken feud into this house or raised questions about the man who had hurt the woman in front of him, he had to be sure. He had some digging to do, on the Brackens' behalf. On Desiree's. Everybody's.

The degrees of separation between all of them might be closer than anyone had anticipated.

"I wanted to pull you aside," James said as he and Desiree walked from the farmhouse to the barn. "I figured we should talk in private."

Desiree kept her hands in the pockets of her coat. She put some space between herself and him. "Thank you for inviting me to dinner. It was—"

"Not as terrible as you imagined, I hope," he said with a glimmer of mirth.

"No," she agreed. "It wasn't."

"You pulled your weight. I wish you would've eaten your weight, too. You earned it."

She wasn't as easy with him as he was with her. "I know you've got questions. About my mom. But I've got some for you, too."

"Okay. Shoot."

"Why did you leave her?" Desiree questioned. "I understand you both needed each other in some way. It didn't end bitterly. Otherwise, you wouldn't have left the car. So…what was it that made you leave?" Her lips fumbled, but she went forward and said everything she needed to. "Because she might've needed you. She might've been better off—had you not."

James's tread had slowed. "It didn't end bitterly. The trouble was, we didn't know how it started to begin with. I wasn't in a good place. I was—I still am—an alcoholic. I met her in the ER. She was there when I was brought low…lower than I thought I could go. She was there when I had the wake-up call. She got me in touch with AA, pushed me to go to meetings. I lost my job in all this, my apartment. She invited me to sleep at her place until I could get on my feet."

"That's how it happened," Desiree gleaned. She wasn't comfortable learning this, but she felt she had to.

"Yes," he said. "You're not really supposed to date when you're getting sober. But…your mom. She had a way about her. You're right—I might not know why she needed a wreck like me, but I certainly needed her. She was a ballast when I had no footing. I moved on because I thought she needed better. Someone as steady and constant as she was for me."

"Seems you found that again," she said, looking around the barnyard. There were horses. She heard chickens roosting nearby. There were a couple of dogs milling about. "This looks steady to me."

"I landed on my feet," he said. "By the time I did, I knew I had to come back to Fairhope, to sort things out. My mother died not long after. Cancer."

"I'm sorry," she said and meant it.

"We named Mavis after her."

"Adrian was here, too," she guessed. "When you came back."

"Yes," he said. "She'd been raising Kyle without me. It became clear pretty quickly I never should've left to begin with."

"So it was all just a big mistake," she surmised. "Leaving Fairhope. Whatever you had with my mother."

"No," he argued. He came to a standstill, turning to face her fully. "I was sick before I ever left Fairhope. I came back only when I'd become the man I should've been to start with. It's taken a long time for me to come to terms with it. That boy who left couldn't have been a father. Mercy helped put me on the right path to becoming a responsible adult. If it weren't for her, I might not have any of this."

"She never talked about you," she told him. "I don't remember her once speaking your name. But she liked weak men." When his lips firmed together, she went on, unabated. "She thought she could fix them. And when they were fixed, they normally left—until they fell back into a bad pattern and came crawling back for more fixin'." Desiree tried not to resent the fact that the one who hadn't come crawling back might have been the one to save them both.

James stopped. His hands were in his pockets, and Desiree judged by the way his breath clouded the night that he was just as cold as she was. However, he looked long at her. "It's none of my business...but were any of these men your father?"

Her heart hitched so quickly it felt like a stab. She started to turn away.

"Desiree," he said, touching her elbow. "I need to know."

"What would it matter at this point?" She shrugged, out of answers. "She never told me, anyway. Not for certain."

"What *did* she tell you?"

She tried to recover her breath. She shouldn't be out of air, but she was close to panting. "He left before I was born. I never met him. Even when she knew she didn't have much time...she wouldn't tell me."

James's gaze circled her features. "How old are you?"

She didn't want to do this. For as long as she could remember, a part of her had wanted to know the truth. Had suspected, from the moment the Trans Am went to the mysterious man in Alabama. Now, facing James, curiosity dried into a husk. "It's not important."

"It *is* important," James argued. "I didn't get to watch my son grow up. I couldn't stand to think that there might've been another life I wasn't there for."

"So stop thinking about it," she suggested. "Whoever my father is or was… I'm an adult. I look after myself."

"Everybody needs somebody in this world," he told her. "Take it from someone who had to find that out the hard way."

"You've got a good situation here," Desiree said, looking around to encompass everything James had gained. "You've got a nice home, a good business and a family who loves you. What would Adrian think if it were true…if you did have a child with another woman?"

"Adrian was the one who brought the possibility to my attention," he revealed.

"She what?" Desiree asked, bemused.

He nodded. "It's why she wanted you here, as much as I do. To explore the possibility that you might be my daughter."

An unsteady breath wracked her. Those words. It hurt to hear. "What'd you have in mind? A hair sample?"

"Nothing as drastic as that." James lowered to the stump of an old tree, planting his feet in the grass. The barn light that had been behind him now shone freely on her face. He could study her, unhindered. "For now… it'd be best to start with your birth year."

Desiree frowned. "If she'd wanted me to know who my father is, she'd have told me. I asked her to tell me. She chose not to. She chose not to tell you, either. Otherwise, she wouldn't have just sent a car. There'd have been message. A letter."

"There was."

She froze. His head was down now, his hands braced on his knees. "Excuse me?"

"There was a letter," he revealed. "I found it once we started working on the car. It was between the glove compartment and the body. Must've slipped back there, at some point...through the years it took to get to me."

Desiree fought. She fought with all her might to close her mind to the question that grew thick in her mouth. Finally, she had to spit it out. "What...what did it say?"

"I haven't read it. It's still sealed in the top drawer of my dresser upstairs."

"Does the wife know about this, too?" Desiree asked, sardonic. His nonanswer was enough. "What are you waiting for?"

He loosened a pent-up sigh. "For a while, I thought I'd turn it in to the police. It could've been a plant—part of the scam that brought the car here to begin it. I had nothing to compare the handwriting on the envelope to your mother's. And the lawyer she hired... I couldn't contact him. He's no longer in practice."

"You want me to verify it," she said, understanding.

"Or you could open it." When she only stared at him, James raised both brows. "You said you wanted answers long ago, at least."

Desiree cursed. "Why would she give you a letter and not me?" She pressed her hands to her face and turned away, emotions raw. "Screw the letter. Why wouldn't she have told me, face-to-face? She had time. We had years together. If she wanted me to know, she'd have given me the truth."

"Like she should've given you the car," James finished. She heard him come to his feet. "Desiree, what if for some reason she couldn't tell you? What if she sent the car to me as a way of bringing us together?" She faced him once more, but before she could argue, he spread his arms. "We're here, aren't we, and it's the car that's done it. Can you honestly say it would've been different, years ago had the Trans Am come to me then?"

"This is why you're keeping me here," she realized. "This is why you won't let me go." She looked to the farmhouse where his wife, his children, his adopted grandchild, his friends and his tidy lifestyle waited. "I don't belong here. If it's true, you can't expect me to drop everything...my whole life...to be a part of this."

"You did drop everything," he said quietly. His eyes were wise. "For a car, of all things. Something tells me you're looking for something bigger."

Even as Desiree shook her head in refusal, something nagged at her. *He's right. Dear God in heaven—he's right.*

James cleared his throat. "This isn't easy, I know, but...won't you stay? For a little while, please. I feel like we owe it to her...to ourselves to figure all this out. I understand that William's offered you a job and a place to stay for the time being."

Of course, William had told James. He'd probably told everybody everything she'd told him, just as she'd feared he would. "I don't know."

"I can sign the title of the car over to you," James said. "I'd like for William to use it, for however long it takes to fix his truck. But I can go ahead and give you the title. And when he no longer needs it, it's yours."

Desiree weighed the pledge carefully. "Even if I leave? You'll let me go, like that?"

"If that's your decision," he granted. "Yes."

I'm scared. The urge to tell him—this man she knew so little of—about her fears and her insecurities made her want to sink farther away from it all.

I'm scared I might want this. I'm afraid I can't have it, even if I do.

I'm scared of wanting at all.

William convinced his mother to drive Desiree back to Hanna's Inn. It took less effort than it did to convince Desiree that she didn't need to call another Uber.

The drive was mostly silent. William took the back seat. His mother had watched her words at dinner for the most part. She went so far as to compliment Desiree on her scarf on the road back to the bay. "Do you knit?" Olivia asked.

"No," Desiree said, running her hands over the brightly patterned accessory. She paused then said haltingly, "My mom thought I should learn. She always wanted to do it herself. With her workload, she could never find the time. Neither did I."

"I love knits," Olivia murmured. "Roxie Strong knits beautifully. She owns the wedding boutique above Adrian's flower shop. I don't know where she finds the time between family and business. I'm like your mother that way. Roxie says she does it to relax."

"Must be nice," Desiree said. "My mom used to say if you've got a skill, make use of it. I never thought about using it as a hobby."

"Me neither, unless you count shootin' cheap whiskey and chasin' it with something spicy," Olivia drawled.

If William wasn't mistaken, Desiree gave a quiet chuckle. "I played."

"What?"

"The violin," Desiree revealed. "Once Mercy figured out I was musically inclined, she set me up with the best music teacher she could find. Before I knew it, I could play three instruments. They told me to pick a focus. I liked violin."

"Why?"

Desiree thought about it so long William thought she wouldn't answer. "I liked the feel of it," she said finally. "The shape of it. I loved sawing at it, making it weep."

"You don't play anymore."

Desiree's head turned fast in Olivia's direction. "How do you know?"

"You *liked* the feel of it. You *loved* making it weep. What made you give it up if you had the heart and the hands for it?"

Silence fell heavily over the cab. William shifted, trying to catch his mother's eye in the rearview mirror.

Desiree's voice was small. "I fell out of love with it."

"Shame, that." Olivia raised her eyes to her son's reflection. She raised her brows.

William sighed, trying to settle against the back seat. Desiree had said she could take care of himself. And he was just as curious as everybody else about her past. But that didn't mean he wanted Olivia to commence with round two. *Stop wheedling her. She's not my date,* he wanted to tell her.

Thankfully, no one spoke again until Olivia pulled into the inn parking lot. "Thanks for the drop-off," Desiree said. "You must've gone out of your way…"

"Hon, you can owe me," Olivia said with her Cheshire cat grin. When William moved to disembark, too, she turned around. "You going, too?"

"I'll take her in, then walk to my place." He rolled his

eyes when his mother made a thoughtful noise. Desiree was already outside, so he leaned over the seat. "Thanks."

"For what?"

"For being yourself," he said then popped the latch.

"I got word from your father," Olivia pointed out. "His book tour's winding down. He'll be home for Christmas."

William nodded. "You won't be alone at the orchard much longer."

"You don't have to worry about me, Shooks, even if you do it so well. Here." She rummaged around in the console before passing something over the back seat to him. "For the girl who doesn't do anything to relax."

"Mum…"

She wheeshed at him. "I can't stand to think of her sitting up past midnight thinking about whatever scared her out of the woods."

"You like her," William realized.

Olivia grinned softly. "You're tuckered. Sleep tonight."

"I love you, too," he replied and shut the door. He rounded the front of the vehicle and threw up a brief wave as it backed out, tires spitting gravel on takeoff.

"Why does she call you that?"

William glanced around. Desiree waited on the front steps of the inn, hands gripping the railing. "What?"

"Shooks. I've never heard it as an endearment."

He moved to the steps, tucking the book against his side as he walked her the rest of the way to the porch. "My dad's British. He's also a writer. She took to calling him Shakespeare when they met. They named me William. To her, Finnian's Finny and I'm Shooks."

"What kind of writer is your dad?"

"Fiction. Fantasy. Historical." He lifted his shoulder. "The man lives to bend genres."

"Would I have heard of him?"

"Are you a big reader?"

She wavered, then admitted, "I used to be."

Used to be, he fathomed. Just like she *used* to be a musician. She *used* to be a music-hall booking person. She *used* to live in Florida. Chicago. With all this *used to be*, he was getting a clearer picture of the past Desiree, while the present Desiree remained a mystery. *Don't push*, he recalled. "Gerald Leighton."

"Oh." Her eyes rounded. "I have heard of him."

"You've read him."

"No. My mom did. She loved those books. The ones about the time traveler?"

The book under his arm grew heavy. He reached for it. "Rex Flynn."

Desiree stared at the cover of the hardback with his father's name stacked in taller type than the title. "Oh my God." Her eyes came back to his. "You're pimping him."

William laughed out loud. "Call it what you will..." He offered the book to her. When she began to shake her head, he said, "Dez. It's a book. You can't make me believe you can fall out of love with reading like you fell out of love with playing the violin." Her gaze dropped away from his. They strayed to the shadows, evasive. He went on, determined. "Just give it a try. What's the harm, really, in spending a few minutes between the pages?"

Desiree licked her lips. "I haven't read... Not since..."

"Your mom passed?" He nodded. "Books take you back to her."

"Yes." It was a whisper. Still, she didn't look away from the cover. Her hands twitched. Then they rose. She cradled the hardback. "What the hell?" She tried to make the words light, but he heard the tremble behind them.

"Might help you sleep better," he said and shrugged when she looked to him. "Always works for me."

After a second, she gave a silent nod.

He watched her fold the book against her middle.

There was no way he could kiss her. He thought about it. Like a lynx, he thought about it. He thought about her. Her strength, her vulnerability, wrapped up as one in a tight coil. There was no unraveling one without the other. They were a part of her flesh. A part of her spine. They were everything he'd come to admire about her. They were the reason he respected her.

He wanted her, and he respected her. Maybe one day she'd look at him less guardedly. Maybe one day she'd trust him. There was more to this wariness, this unease she had with the personal. With the simple offering of friendship. Not today, he knew. He swallowed and accepted it. "Good night, Dez," he said simply. He started down the steps.

"Hey, Dimples."

Surprised, he looked back over his shoulder. He started to smile at the nickname. "Yeah?"

"You're right," she told him. "I didn't need you tonight." The muscles around her mouth worked. It took a minute for them to part and expel a heavy breath. "But I'm glad you were there. With me. For me." She groaned. "Wow. I am really bad at this."

He didn't say anything. Neither could he make himself move away.

She gathered herself. "I do think you might be it—the last good man in the world…"

"Ah, now. You're making me blush."

"No, I'm not." She stopped, seeing him better under the lights of the porch. "I am."

"Ruddy English complexion gives everything away." He did his best to tamp down the rise in his cheeks for both their sakes.

"He blushes." She almost looked disconcerted. He thought he heard her say "damn" under her breath. Her feet shifted. "Well... I'm going to go. Before I embarrass either one of us further."

"Right. Okay. No, wait," he decided. "You haven't said whether you've given my offer of a job any more thought." When she turned from the door, he asked, "Have you?"

She measured herself, as she always did. Breathing carefully, she twisted the door latch and said, "I'll see you tomorrow."

Even as she went in, taking the book with her, William smiled. He stayed there, smiling, for some time.

"William."

He jumped out of his skin at the sound of Cole's voice. "Christ on a cracker," he muttered, finding the man in the parking lot behind him. "You're a frickin' ghost."

"How's our guest?"

William's eyes tracked to the windows, debating what to say. "She's...okay." He thought beyond what had happened on the porch and at dinner. He thought to the look of her in the headlights of his mother's Ford. And again when she'd evoked her stepfather's name. Was it a betrayal of her trust to share what she'd revealed to him? She didn't know of the connection, how close it came to the Brackens, to everyone who'd been involved in the fallout of the Kennards' setup this past summer. Clearing his throat, William asked, "You got a minute? I might have something to run by you."

Cole gave a slow nod. "It's a nice night for a walk."

Any less nice and it'd be sleeting, William considered. And he'd have to walk a ways from Desiree's doorstep to say out loud what he thought had happened to her and how they were all tangled up in it.

Chapter 7

Desiree didn't see the Wet Floor sign until it was too late. As soon as she stepped through the unlocked door of the tavern, she opened her mouth to call out. The bottom of her foot hit a slippery patch of floor, and her leg went out from under her.

The table saved her. The chairs stacked on top of it tumbled to the clean floor.

She'd barely gained her footing when she noticed something stirring on the other side of the tavern near the pool tables. Bracing her arms on the table, she saw a familiar figure sacked out on top of one. As he sat up and looked at her sleepily, she frowned. "I'm not even going to ask," she said, noting the rumpled locks on his head. They were floppy and golden—a ramshackle halo.

William eyed her dryly. Drawing one knee up, he scratched his midsection over the gray buttons of his oxford shirt. "That floor there's wet."

"You don't say." Straightening from the table ledge, she tiptoed her way to what looked like a drier piece of flooring. He gave an impressive yawn. "Rough night?"

"Not sure." He sounded genuinely perplexed. "If so, the morning wasn't much better."

Desiree opened her mouth to ask then stopped. He might be her new boss. He might even be her landlord. But that was all she needed to know.

He slung his long legs over the side of the pool table. He scrubbed his eyes with the heels of his hands like a boy waking from a long night's rest. When he was done, he blinked at her again. "Not injured, are ya?"

"Don't worry," she said half-heartedly. She checked the elbow of her overcoat, making sure the seam was still intact. "I won't sue."

"That's something." He busied himself righting the chairs she'd scattered, setting the legs on the floor. "I didn't think you'd show."

"It's not like I've got a lot of options."

William leaned against the back rail of one chair. "You up for a crash course in waitressing tonight?"

"That soon, huh?" she asked, trying not to betray her nerves.

"I need the hand, and you said you wanted work."

She had decided to stay on in Fairhope. The inactivity had done it. She wasn't accustomed to being inactive. Whether she'd been hopping as a booking agent or stringing instruments in her living room to make rent, she'd never not been active.

"Did you bring any bags?" he asked, looking around.

She turned to show him the small duffel hanging from her shoulder.

"You pack light."

"I wasn't expecting a month's vacation."

"It won't feel much like vacay after eight o'clock tonight," he noted. "Just as a warning."

"You promised you'd fire me if I stink at it," she reminded him. "I'm holding you to that."

"Wouldn't expect anything less." He walked to her. "Here."

When he touched the strap of her bag, she gripped it. "It's all that I have."

He managed to slide it off her shoulder in one easy motion and hook it over his. "I'm just going to carry it upstairs."

"It's not even heavy." His morning eyes were killer. Greenest leaves in a winter-coated glade.

"Good, I won't strain myself."

She was fighting a smile, she realized with a start. His faded jeans were thin at the inner corners of both back pockets, she saw as she followed him. Didn't he own something that wasn't worn out or wrinkled?

The wardrobe went well with this morning's rumpled demeanor.

That still didn't explain why he'd been sleeping. After lunch. *Inside* the bar, this time. "Do you suffer from narcolepsy?" she asked as they ventured past the hatch and into the hallway past the tavern.

"Huh?"

"This is twice I've found you sleeping in odd places."

"Oh, that." He bypassed the office, though he paused to switch on the light. He dug in his front right pocket, and she heard the jangle of keys. "No. I log late nights here, as you'd expect. Lately, I've been getting up early for classes."

As he stopped at the last door in the narrow hall and

found the right key on the ring, she noted that there was an exterior door at the end, likely leading out to the inn gardens. *Good to know.* "Classes?"

"Business school," he explained. "I've been trying to get enough credits to finish my bachelor's." The key jammed into place in the lock, and he cranked it sideways with his fist, gaining entry. "Better late than never. Right?"

"Right," she found herself agreeing. When the door opened and he gestured her in, she didn't question the move. She took the lead and found a winding set of steps leading up to the second floor. "This way?"

"Straight up." Methodically, he wiggled the key off the ring as he trailed her. "I was supposed to finish my degree before I took over for Mum. But life has a way of happening."

"No kidding," she said, thinking about her own education. By eleventh grade, she'd been accepted to Juilliard. Then life had taken its first cruel turn. "So you spend all afternoon and evening here…then you spend all morning at school."

"And here you were thinking I was a party animal." The stairs creaked loudly as they made their way to the small landing. He had to pitch his voice over them, even with the slight echo the chamber offered.

There was a large barn door. It was locked, too, with a padlock that fit nicely into a hook on the wall. As he unlocked it, too, she studied his shaggy head. His long spine under the textured gray shirt. His shoulders, sturdy and nonchalant as they bent over the keyhole. There were muscles, nicely toned, in his forearms, she saw, as he turned the lock. He might be lean, but he was packing a little somethin' under all his disheveledness.

He shoved the door open. "Welcome home."

When he offered a slight bow, she grabbed her bag off his shoulder. It was heavy enough that it fell willfully into her grasp. "Stop that."

He chuckled slightly. As she circled the room, taking it in, he watched from the door. "We call it Lookout. Mostly 'cause my grandparents could look out that big window there and see my mother coming and going after hours."

Again, *not* what she was expecting. It was a small space with a big bay window opposite the big door. As Desiree crossed the room, the vista of the Eastern Shore opened up before her. She'd taken the scenic route between Hanna's Inn and Tavern of the Graces. How had she not noticed then how blue and crisp everything looked? She dropped one knee to the window seat at its base and sank down to gawk.

"There's one bathroom," William was saying as he roamed around switching lights on between the living room and kitchen area, "the size of a linen closet. The hot and cold in the shower are reversed. But there's a stackable washer and dryer unit in the bedroom closet, so you won't have to outsource your laundry. And the original stove's still operational, believe it or not."

Desiree glanced around at the space. There were deep-textured rugs. A small couch. The fireplace was filled with neat rows of hardback books. Odd touch. Yet it added to the charm. There was a teeny chandelier to crown the space, giving the austere flooring and the exposed brick wall between the living and bedroom a touch of the sophisticated. Large sand-bleached seashells lined shelves. Small ones filled basins.

"The best thing is, it's heated," William revealed, giving her a knowing look. "It's harder to get cool air to rise, so it's not a great place to stay in the summer. Winter's another story."

She liked how he was looking at her. It was easy, lazy look of someone who was familiar with her in all the ways that mattered. The look of someone who had the potential to be more. She found herself answering that look, wanting to be familiar with him…in all the ways she couldn't afford.

Why did he have to be so effortlessly charming? So obliviously sexy. Her face heated fast as she heard the words echo through her mind. He was *sexy*, damn it, whether he dressed well or combed his hair or not.

She rather liked unkempt. It was windswept like a winter's bay. Those curls looked glossy in the light. Thick enough for her to sink her fingers into…

She turned away from him and her thoughts. To anchor herself, she traced the corner of an old-fashioned writing desk. Lifting the lid of the ornate box on top of it, she didn't find the vintage typewriter she imagined, but a record player. "The grand dame Olivia lived *here*?"

He stopped the restless movement of his feet by spreading them apart. Lifting his chin at an angle, he scratched the stubble on his jaw. "When she was little. And for all the 'wild single years,' as she calls them. When she brought my father home to Fairhope, it was here. After they married, they moved out to my great-grandparents' pecan orchard off Highway 181, where there was more elbow room for a family."

More family history. The man had reams of it. "Why is it empty now?"

"Nobody's claimed it in years."

"Isn't it an obvious choice of living for you?" she asked. "For convenience's sake."

"A little too convenient," he said wisely. "I wanted to be near the water. But the tavern takes a long bite of hours out of my week. Some separation between work and home is necessary. I moved into a duplex a few blocks away. The view's not near as good, but it stays quiet. Mum wanted the noise. She liked being able to pop in on her staff if she took a night off, to keep them on their toes."

"Is she really as formidable as she seems?" Desiree wondered vaguely.

"When she wants to be." He crossed his arms. "When potential investors suggested converting this space into a party room or open deck, she went for her shotgun. Never did see them again."

Desiree had no trouble imagining Olivia Leighton with a gun. "What about your brother... Finnian?"

"Yes."

"He never stays here?"

"Finnian never stays anywhere. He's a rebel with a cause. He won't rest until he at least solves the issue of global corruption." His eyes came to rest on hers. He scanned her, to the point that she felt naked. His voice shifted, gentling. "Nobody's going to run you out before you're ready. I promise."

Desiree tried to look away. But...*green*. And *I promise*. That had a nice ring. And he strummed it so good from the base of his throat. Her eyes touched on the knot of his Adam's apple. "Is he anything like you—your brother?"

"Some people say we look alike," he said with a twist of irony. "The likeness ends there. He was never satisfied with small-town vibes. While he was in a hurry to jump ship, I was past the point of settling in."

She licked her lips. "And…no one minds? That *I* stay here, of all people?"

He moved, hands going into his front pockets when she might have tensed at the slim divide between them. "Wouldn't matter if they did," he said, finite. "Consider this your safe zone. For as long as you need."

"You're not worried about me breaking into the till after hours?"

"Dez." He let out a small breath. Frustration riddled his features before he tucked it back. His jaw muscles flared. Lowering his chin, he said, "I trust you. Why can't that be enough?"

"Because you have no reason to trust me," she said, bemused by the man all over again. She shook her head. "Not one."

"You need a reason?" he asked, his expression cooling for the first time in her memory. "All right, here it is." He placed his hand on her arm and held her through the automatic flinch. Even in his ardency, he paused to let her relax. She felt the small brush of his thumb over the surface of her sleeve before his voice and his eyes seized her attention once more. "That first night, at the inn—"

"I was *horrible* to you," she finished.

"You were scared," he said, "and for none of the obvious reasons. You're a good person who's scared to make connections, who's been in one too many bad situations in life." Dipping his face from his height, his eyes widened with sincerity. "You haven't heard that enough, have you? That you're every bit as good as you say I am."

Close with him, she shouldn't say what she felt she needed to say next. There should be distance…plenty of it...just to be safe. But she couldn't bring herself to shrug away his touch this time. "Look." She licked her lips, stared at the buttons on his shirt. "You're not saying all this or...doing all this because..."

He waited as she strung the words together, pushed them out.

Her pulse wasn't right. It just wasn't. "...because you have some kind of feelings for me. Are you?"

He didn't answer right away. Then, almost down to a whisper, he said, "You know what I wish?"

She began to shake her head, then stopped. She did want to know.

"I wish you could've belonged here," he said, "instead of wherever it was you come from. I wish you'd have run here...whoever it is you ran from."

She closed her eyes. *God. Who* says *things like that?*

Him, she answered. *He does.* She blinked rapidly, because her eyes were starting to sting. "Bad things happen to people everywhere, whether they deserve it or not. It doesn't matter how nice the setting, or not. Bad things happen, William. A lot of the time, for no good reason."

"How did he hurt you?"

She lost her breath. She saw his concern. Worry. Anger. All for her sake. "Who?"

"The Kennard guy."

"My stepfather."

His brow creased. "Was there someone else?"

Yes. Two men had ruined her. *Two* men had stripped her of everything. Her future. Her dreams. Her chance for normal. "He wasn't the first." When he cursed, her lips gaped in surprise. "You don't want to know, William, so please...*please* don't ask."

He looked down, as if he needed to settle himself.

When he brought his gaze back to hers, she was shocked to see he'd channeled whatever anger he had into softness. "Can I ask instead when the last time anybody held you was?"

"Held me," she repeated numbly.

"*Held* you."

She opened her mouth. "I... I don't know..." Trying to recover some of her fleeting defenses, she asked, "Why? Is this your moment? Is this why you brought me here?"

He shook his head slowly, eyes caressing. She could feel him—his good glow. It felt good to share it, even as the parts of her that hurt shrank away from the light. His fingertips skimmed off her shoulders. His touch fell away. "If you trusted me. If you trusted yourself. But no. Not now."

Their verbal tussling—they'd done plenty of it over the last few days, going back and forth. Pushing, pulling, coaxing, deflecting. It was enough to make her dizzy. Yet it didn't make him angry or irritated. He didn't distance himself from her for it—not like other men. He kept coming back to this with her, and a lot of the time he smiled doing it.

What's wrong with him?

Nothing. There's not a thing wrong with him, other than his crazy faith in me.

...consider this your safe zone, he'd said.

Safe. She was safe in these rooms. In this space between her and him.

"You didn't answer," she reinforced. "Where're your feelings at? I need to know."

"I won't force them on you," he said. "I won't force myself on you at all, if that's what you're waiting for."

"I'm not." And there, at last, she found she could place

her trust in something. He *could* hold her, even if only in that understanding. "I'm *not* waiting. Not with you."

His head lowered. "Well." She watched the muscles of his face contour. He was smiling again, if only a little. "That's something, too, isn't it?"

She didn't expect the emotions. They charged her, filled her, depleted her. If she brought her head to rest on his shoulder…she'd be safe. "Don't," she said, half to herself. "Don't get excited. I only give in inches."

"Not every man takes a mile."

His dimples had disappeared again. She had to stop trying to wipe them away. "You…you smell nice."

He raised his gaze back to hers, brow arched. "I smell nice?" he echoed.

"Not at all like I expected a bartender to smell."

"What *should* a bartender smell like, Miss Gardet?"

The dimples were back. *Yes.* "I don't know. Jim Beam. Grilled cheese."

"Grilled cheese," he mused, bewildered. He laughed. Then he touched her shoulder again.

She didn't flinch this time. Not even a little. She was sure he noticed the shift as much as she did. Putting a stop to the forward motion before she started to lean in, she reached up. His hand dropped away at her urging. "Four o'clock?"

"Four," he stated, smile still hanging from his mouth. He moved back, respectful as ever. After digging in his pocket, he extended his fist. When she held out her hand, he dropped the keys to the apartment onto her palm. "All yours."

"What do you know about beer?"

Desiree took a glance down the line of gold-and-marble-handled taps that gleamed in the lights of the tavern. She lifted a shoulder. "It has calories?"

The bar hand, Ines, blinked at her new protégée and puffed out her cheeks. "Oh, boy."

"I told you," Desiree said. "Untrained and unqualified."

"All right, so you're a virgin," Ines said, nodding. "That's okay." She was in her early twenties. Her hair was pixie cut and magenta. Her nose boasted a silver ring, accessorizing nicely with her silver-tinged lip color. The details nearly made Desiree squint.

As a teacher so far, Ines was patient where patience was warranted. Popping her bright purple gum with her front teeth, she swapped it to the other side of her mouth and picked up a glass with the bar insignia on it. "We serve beer in bottles and on tap. These glasses are draft. Have you ever heard the expression 'build a Guinness'? No? Well, there's a proper way to pour—or build—a draft. You tilt the glass like this, pull the nozzle, let it pour against the side of the glass to prevent the head from building..." At Desiree's frown, Ines elaborated. "The head is the foamy stuff on top." She passed the drink off to Godfrey, the only other person assigned to waiting tables other than Desiree, and propped a hand on her hip. "Haven't you been to college?"

"Is this what they're teaching kids nowadays?" Desiree waved a hand when the stud above Ines's brow hiked. "Kidding. Yes, I went to college. Keg parties weren't really my bag."

"Bag of what?" Ines asked.

It took Desiree a moment to realize that Ines genuinely didn't understand her retro slang. "Doritos?" she guessed, trying to place the expression.

"Huh." Ines shook her head. She grabbed the first tap on the row. "This is the house special. The Leightons brew it themselves. So if anybody asks for the special, or Leighton Lodge, as it's called, this is what you want."

"Thanks," Desiree said, trying to shuffle all the new job information into neat columns in her mind. The noise from the jukebox wasn't helpful, even if it did fit the scene. There were fifteen to twenty patrons lined up along at the bar top and scattered around the high tables. From what she understood, there was a pool tournament between two groups of city workers kicking off within the hour. "I'll try to keep up." A tap on her shoulder brought her head around.

William, whom she hadn't seen since her arrival, held up a black garment. "This is your apron. Sorry I didn't have it sooner. Briar was kind enough to have it cleaned."

"You'll need this, too." Ines handed Desiree a booklet. "Zaira could log orders without it. It might come in handy for you your first night. Give her your pencil, boss."

William reached up to where he'd tucked a carpenter's pencil behind his auricle. As he handed it to Desiree, he gauged her readiness. "Godfrey's going to work the tourney side so you can concentrate on the quieter tables. I'm going to ask you to keep an eye on the windows, as well, to see whether any of the tables are filling up outside. That's unlikely with the weather the way it's been but still a possibility."

"Got it," she said with a nod, mapping her side of the bar and the view of the courtyard.

"Dez."

She glanced up to meet his smiling eyes. His expression deepened into dimples and laugh lines as he held her attention. "Relax," he said. "Waiting tables is nothing compared to stealing cars."

A small taste of mirth spilled fresh on her tongue. Glancing around the see that Ines was busy, she set about tying the three-pocket waist apron securely around her middle and murmured as low as she could and still reach his ears, "Don't expect me to call you 'boss' like she does."

William glanced at Ines over Desiree's head and pressed his lips together, having the decency to look sheepish. "There aren't many who do."

Lifting her chin, she took the order booklet and stuffed it in the first pocket with the pencil, which was still warm from his ear. "You're not going to clear your throat? Shift your weight around? Smirk at the conquest?"

"Conquest?" He nearly choked on the word. "I never—"

"No?" she challenged, tightening the knot at the small of her back.

"No!" he protested. "She's Roxie and Byron Strong's girl. The younger one. She's almost ten years my junior."

He looked appropriately horrified. Desiree couldn't contain a small well of relief. "She's into you."

"You're starting to sound like my mother." He shook his head. "I *never* would have thought that possible."

"What about Mavis?" Desiree asked. She had the satisfaction of watching him blanch. "You know her family, too, and I picked up enough talk from dinner the other night to know you two…you know."

"It was years ago. She's engaged, if you didn't notice." He tilted his head. "Your turn."

"My turn?" Desiree blurted. "I don't have any. Conquests, I mean."

"None?"

"She's a virgin," Ines hissed helpfully, leaning around Desiree to grab a fresh dishrag.

Desiree jumped at the intrusion. "Wait. No. That's not what I—"

Ines peered at William. "Is this a professional line of questioning? I thought you had rules. The customer's always right. Don't loiter around the jukebox. Don't flirt with the drummer from the Styx River Band…"

"That one applies specifically to you," William added.

"Buzzkill," she griped. "And number four, don't sleep with the underlings." She snapped her gum at him. "I believe that one applies specifically to you. Boss." In one lithe movement, she lifted a tray loaded with bottles to her shoulder. "Order up," she called to Godfrey as she sauntered off.

William scrubbed the plane of his forehead with two fingers. Desiree thought back to what had happened in the apartment earlier. "How long has the fourth rule been in place?"

"Forever."

"You hired me," she said cautiously. "With feelings, as you say."

"I hired you because you need work," he put it simply. "Not for selfish reasons. Though I'll admit being near you isn't a chore."

When several seconds had passed between them, Ines leaned in again. "Menu," she muttered, handing Desiree a small laminated card. "Memorize the house wines. All food is stored on the dry side of the bar. Chips go in baskets on wax paper. Salsa goes in the little dip bowls. If anyone asks for oyster shooters, run it by William. That's his specialty. I'll drop the crab claws if anyone wants them. Just stick the orders here…" She pointed to a small clothesline above the bar top strung high enough so patrons couldn't see. "When they're finished, I'll ring the bell." She hit the call bell next to the blenders.

William nodded in agreement. "Table orders are rung up on the left register, nearest the hatch. Your tips are yours. If you pick a tip up off another table, place it in Godfrey's jar. He'll do the same for you. Ines and I split bar tips, but your and Godfrey's are your own. Unless the tables are full, you'll get a break every half hour or so. Flag Godfrey if you're planning to step out so he knows to cover you. Any questions?"

Looking around, Desiree calculated how long it had been since she'd worked with others. She'd been out of the booking game for a year, and her instrument-repair costumers normally reached her by email through her website. For a split second, she wondered if she could handle not the workload itself but the interaction with so many strangers. She was no longer great at communicating with people she came into contact with on the daily. She smoothed the front of her apron and lied. "I'm ready."

Ines and William exchanged a glance. "She's all yours," he said and watched as Ines linked arms with Desiree and led her away.

The proud glint in his eyes stayed with her. Determined not to let her performance dim it, she let Ines lead her to her first table. "I'll walk you through your first run. Return costumers. Snowbirds. By the way, a little smile? It goes a long way."

"I'm smiling," Desiree informed her.

"Let your eyes feel it."

"Haven't you people heard of wrinkles?" Desiree asked out of the corner of her mouth.

Ines laughed as they came to the couple sitting hip to hip. "Welcome back to the tavern. Did you enjoy our three-dollar special last week?"

The woman brightened. "Yes. Though this time we were thinking margaritas and chips."

"Ooh, you're in luck," Ines said. "I just watched the boss put together a fresh batch of the Lewis mix. It's his third-generation margarita recipe."

"Sounds like what we need," the man said.

"We'll have that right out for you." Ines tipped her head to Desiree. "This is Desiree, our new server for this evening. She's going to take good care of you. Right, Dez?" She raised her brows in an infectious smile.

Desiree tried to mirror it. Her face was going to hurt by the end of the evening, but what the hell? "Of course."

"We'll go easy on you," the woman promised.

"I appreciate it," Desiree said. The smile came a little more naturally. Maybe she *did* have this.

The night wasn't terribly hectic. The jukebox was turned down—a rare occurrence, Desiree learned—so the tournament players could concentrate. Desiree's tables were light of traffic, so light William decided to give her a margarita-mixing tutorial since it was the hottest item on the menu.

Before the tourney was over, she thought she might have the mix down. Ines passed sample cups to William and Godfrey. Godfrey raised his cup to her. William's eyes shined over the rim of his. "Not bad," he said.

She'd watched him all night. She'd been so subtle about it, she had herself halfway convinced she wasn't watching him. But by now she'd memorized how the sleeves of his worn button-down were rolled to his elbows, how the first three buttons were undone. The hem was untucked from his faded jeans, which, she'd noticed when he bent to grab a liquor bottle from under the bar, had substantial tears in the knees.

She'd watched his ease with customers, regulars and newcomers alike. He could talk to anyone, no matter where they came from or what they were doing there. He could encourage them to speak whether they wanted to or not. He had a way, she knew from experience. He was a twinkly eyed empath. With dimples.

People weren't like that. People didn't get to thirty twinkly eyed. He might not be a clotheshorse. And he might have one of the worst fishing stories she'd ever heard. But he had something other thirty-year-old men didn't—the willing capacity for sheer, unselfish attentiveness. How could anyone not trust him?

How could I not trust him?

His hands were busy again, passing bottles over the bar in exchange for flimsy greenbacks. Desiree saw Ines nudge him as she stepped around him to fill a pint with the house draft. It didn't faze him. Despite its wear, he looked fresh in the forest green shirt. He'd combed his hair tonight, it looked like. His eyes laughed.

The jukebox was playing some smoky, reminiscent number. Desiree closed her eyes and took a breath. She *couldn't* fall. He could be the safest, most trustworthy man in the universe, and she still couldn't fall for him.

She wasn't here for him. She wasn't going to stay for this. No matter how curious…how much she yenned for that place inside her chest area opening up into a distinctly William-esque shape.

It hadn't admitted anyone...*anyone* since she found herself alone at her mother's graveside. No father. No stepfather. No family. No friends. From that point, it had been Desiree Gardet—or Desiree Lawry, or Desiree McCullough, or whatever alter ego she'd crafted for herself—against the world.

She straightened her shoulders as the blender finished churning. She poured the margarita mix into a hurricane glass for a customer at table eight. She turned to the bar to place it in the center of her tray when she saw the flash of the window on the entry door. She glanced up briefly to assess which direction the newcomer was going...and came to a stop.

"No." The whispered word was out of her mouth before she'd known it had left. Numb, she watched the male figure in a ball cap shrink to the back of the tournament crowd.

He'd looked up for a split second after entering. He'd looked up enough for her to see the shape of his jaw, the length of his neck. He'd looked at her and she'd lost the will to breathe.

Her stomach fisted. *Not again.* It cramped. She had to fight the impulse to retch. Pressing a fist to her belly, she held the edge of the bar to keep from bending over double. The blood was draining from her head too fast...

She had to be crazy. She *had* to be. Because she'd *seen* him this time. She knew. The man who'd made her life a living hell...the monster she'd thought she'd vanquished...had just walked into Tavern of the Graces.

Chapter 8

William saw, in an instant, Desiree's posture cave. He saw the glassy veil of fear over her dark eyes. He saw her complexion turn to wax. He moved quickly past Ines, past Godfrey, taking large steps to meet her. "Dez."

"No." The word hung limp on her lips. "No. No, no, no."

He bent low to her ear. "Office."

"I don't think I can make it," she said faintly.

"You can make it. I got you." He took the first step, guiding her along. "Come on."

She staggered after him. By the time they reached the swinging doors, her lips had gone as white as her face. Dread slammed like a mallet into his sternum. "Wait," he said as the doors parted to close them in the hallway. "We're almost there."

"Uh-uh," she said and nearly slid out of his grip completely as she shrank toward the floor like a noodle.

William cursed a stream. He bent underneath her shoulder, catching her over his. Lifting, he walked her the rest of the way into the office and slapped the door shut.

He didn't make it to the couch before he slid her off his shoulders. "Dez?" Her feet missed the floor, sliding. When he saw her eyes in the back of her head, his sweat turned cold. "Goddammit. Dez." Holding her fast, he slid to the floor with her, cradling her close so she wouldn't get hurt. "Come back, Dez. Come on back now."

She blinked. Then again, more decidedly. Her eyes passed over him, rolled back once before they locked on him again and registered. Her breath feathered across his features. "What…"

"It's all right," he said, nodding in reassurance. "You're all right."

Her gaze wheeled around their surroundings. "Why… why're we on the floor?"

"You had a little spell," he told her, keeping his tone even. How it wasn't as tachy as his pulse, he had no idea.

Alarm flashed across her face, and her color waned again.

"I caught you," he said in a hurry.

She closed her eyes. "'Course you did."

She'd nearly hit the deck…and she was still giving him a hard time. He might've smiled. "Do you need anything? Water? Whiskey? Oxygen? Don't ever do that again." The last sprang from him, rife with anxiety. He shook his head. "Never mind." He shifted to his knees, then his feet. After teetering for a split second, he took lengthy strides to the couch, where he'd meant to put her in the first place.

"Ooh," she said, head lolling. "Black spots…"

"Put your feet up," he said, stacking pillows beneath her. "Don't argue with me," he said before her mouth could open more than part of the way. "I want your feet up."

"This impromptu showing of *Sleeping Beauty* is closed for rewrites," she said vaguely.

He lifted his hand to touch her again, then paused in the act. He propped it on the wall over the couch instead. He scanned the length of her, wondering what else to do…if she could be hurt in some way, physically… "What brought it about? Do you need something to eat?"

"I eat, okay?" she groaned.

"All right… Did you have a—a seizure? Or a panic attack, or…"

"I don't know."

She sounded small. Hanging shadows were visible on her face.

"I must be going crazy," she muttered, half the sentiment getting lost in her throat. "Don't ask…don't ask me why. But I'm pretty sure I'm losing my mind. I don't want to do that again."

"You're not," he told her, willing it to be true. He hung his head.

Her gaze flickered to his. "Are *you* okay?"

"My heart's rolling around on the floor somewhere," he admitted. He could admit that. Right? "I'll find it later."

"William."

He watched her blink away her fear, constructing the Desiree he'd come to know. It nearly pulled him apart, the need to touch her. "Ah, babe. You don't have to be so strong."

Desiree turned her face away from his, toward the back cushion. "You don't get to tell me what I need to be."

"I told you. It's safe. You're safe."

She closed her eyes. "I can't. I'm sorry. I can't."

He'd never wanted to hear an apology less.

The door opened behind him. Godfrey pushed his way in. "Hey, man. Dawes Whitaker just took the cup, and the reporter from the *Courier* wants a snapshot for the paper—"

William sent a look over his shoulder, not moving from his stance as a buffer over her. Godfrey stopped talking. He jerked a thumb over his shoulder silently and disappeared, closing the door.

Desiree sat up, tilting her face away from him completely.

William moved back into a crouch as she scrubbed her hands over her face.

She lowered them to her knees. "This is affecting my job performance."

"I'm *not* going to fire you." He said it with vehemence.

"Damn it, William."

"I'm not." He reached for her despite the steel plate in her jaw. His knuckles grazed her cheek, and he watched her lips part in surprise. Leaning forward, he pressed his brow to hers.

He stayed until his heart had gone back to a natural rhythm. Until he heard her breath hitch again. Then he shifted away and came to his feet. "Go upstairs. Take a rest. You can come back if you want. Or call down if you're done for the night. Do you need me to take you?"

"I'm fine," she said, pressing up from the couch cushions. She stood, proving herself right.

He judged her constitution. Hearing the noise level rising in the next room, he moved to the door.

He watched her walk to the stairs. He watched her go

through the door. He would've watched her go up had Godfrey not hailed him from the swinging doors. Biting back another curse, William answered the summons.

She came back down. It was after closing. Ines was counting the till. Godfrey was washing dishes. The tables had been stacked, and William was mopping the floor. The jukebox played something soft and '90s by Collective Soul.

Ines was the first to notice her. "You came back!"

Desiree saw William look up from the mopping. He stopped. She cleared her throat. "I came to help. Is there something that needs to be done?"

Godfrey looked to William. Ines, too, watched as William gave him a nod.

Godfrey shut off the water, dried his hand on a spare towel and walked to the line of tip jars. "We've all collected our share for the night," he said. There was a little Cajun in his words. Something about it had made Desiree comfortable from the off. He handed a roll of bills to her. "Here's yours."

Desiree folded her arms. "I don't think—"

"Take the money, Dez."

William's demand wasn't harsh. But it wasn't arguable, either. Lifting her hand to the offered cash roll, she took it between her fingers and lowered it to her side without counting it.

Ines was smiling, still. Did Ines ever stop smiling? "Are you feeling better?"

Nobody else had seen her pass out, had they? She nearly looked to William in question. "I'm fine. What can I do?"

"I'll take this for you," Ines told her, taking the apron

Desiree had brought back. "You can fold the napkins, if you like."

Desiree noticed the pile of unfolded linens in front of the till. "All right."

"By the way," Ines said as Desiree skirted the bar to the open hatch, "you earned your take. You might be a natural."

Desiree released a doubting breath. "You're sweet." She reached the stool in front of the linens. Glancing around at William, she saw him busy at his work again. His shoulders were high, she noted, masking any impression she could have gained from his face. Boosting herself onto the high seat, she started folding the napkins.

Godfrey finished washing and drying and was the first to leave. Ines announced the final tally on the night's sales and the dent in inventory before writing the next night's specials on the board and saying a cheerful good-night, leaving William and Desiree alone. He'd moved on from mopping the floors to checking to make sure the blenders were clean and the taps were polished. She'd finished folding napkins and had stacked them neatly behind the bar near the baskets and cutlery. Collective Soul had moved on to Stevie Nicks, and Desiree's hands were officially empty. "What happens now?" she asked as William straightened from replacing the rubber rugs over the clean work area.

He faced her fully for the first time since she'd come back downstairs. He pulled a cleaning cloth out of his back pocket and reached back to wipe his neck. The skin around his open collar was misty with perspiration.

When he didn't answer right away, she lifted her shoulders. "You fire me. Right?"

"No."

Stubborn as an ox. Desiree set her jaw, ready to debate. "Look—"

"You performed your job well. You don't get fired for that."

"I had to leave."

"I told you to go."

"That doesn't mean—"

"Would you have left?" he asked. "If I hadn't told you to go, would have come back to the taps?"

She might have, she thought. She might have had to slap herself around a bit in the employees' bathroom. The face hadn't been real, she'd chided herself over and over again. No matter that she kept seeing it in the waking world, on top of nightmares. It wasn't *real.* "I'm not worth this, you know," she said without answering. "I'm not worth this kind of faith."

He turned away from her. Her mouth fumbled in surprise as he walked away. Reaching over the swinging door, he took his coat off the peg. He started to put it on.

Desiree couldn't watch him do the same with his scarf. "You don't need this. Me or my mess."

He turned at that, the green of his eyes sulfur. "You let me be the judge of what I need, all right?"

How could he speak to her so evenly when he was clearly so angry? Finally. She'd brought anger out of him. "You want the whole story?"

"I wouldn't argue," he informed her.

He'd stopped winding his scarf. There was a small stool, a resting place, behind the till. Bracing her hands on her thighs, she folded to the seat. Lifting her finger in the air, she made an unwinding motion. "You might as well undo what you just did. This is going to take a minute."

William stood, unchanged. Then he did as she suggested, reaching up to unravel the scarf and take off the jacket. He set them on the bar then reached over it and hefted one of the stools from the other side to theirs.

When he'd settled on it and given his attention back to her, she swallowed. Holy crap. She was going to do this. Her stomach felt slippery. Ignoring the clutch it gave, she did her best to begin. "I'll start from what you do know—that I played violin. I played it well. So well, my teachers started whispering Juilliard to my mother before I knew what that was. She made me practice for hours at night. I wanted to do things that other girls did—run around, look at boys, get invited to sleepovers… Foolishness, she called it. 'You got a gift,' she'd say. 'Best hone it, let it take you places. Then you decide what and who you want in life and take it.' We lived humbly. I don't think she thought it was enough for me. I should've told her it was.

"When I got to high school, she hired a tutor to work with me after school. He'd been to Juilliard. Was the best violinist in the state, all told. He came to our house. He never asked questions about the drive into the marsh. About our circumstances. About my stepfather coming and going…about my mother spending more and more time in bed… Every weeknight, he came. And he stayed. We trained. Sometimes he ate dinner. He wasn't so much older. Or at least I didn't see him as older. I found out he was in his early thirties. But that was after.

"Had I known…" Desiree took a bracing breath, gripping her knees. "I don't know if things would've been different. Mom didn't know—that he started being more than my tutor. That I started to see him as more. She trusted me. She trusted him. *I* trusted him. So much was changing. I knew she was getting sicker. She wasn't able to be there for me as much as she had before. My stepfather was gone again, and she didn't think he was coming back. He…my tutor…felt like the only person in the world who was constant when I needed constancy."

She ran her hand over her nose. There were no tears. There would be no tears in the retelling. "It's amazing how quickly constancy can fade, even when you need it most. Eric came back—my stepfather. He saw what my mother couldn't. He told me how wrong it was. How ugly it was. He said that I was ruining the man's life, that he could have him tossed in jail for statutory rape. He threatened him. I thought the guy would fight back. Fight for me. Instead, he left without a word. I never saw him again."

Desiree was no longer able to look at William. "I never got to Juilliard. I hardly finished school when Mom's health turned. I took some classes at the local college. I stopped playing. She couldn't see what Eric was doing. He was using again, in the house, under my nose. I didn't have the heart to tell her. He hung around until she was gone—for the house. The land. Whatever money she had stashed in cubbyholes. I couldn't count on him to care for her when I wasn't there. I lived in fear that I could come home and she'd be gone, that she'd have been alone when she…" She shook her head vigorously, closing herself off from the emotions. She bit the inside of her lip, almost to the point of bleeding.

Warmth draped over the back of her hand. She opened her eyes and saw that it was his. Long, tapered fingers. Rough around the edges but smooth. He didn't say anything to interrupt the well of the past, but he was there and he wanted her to know it.

"She was in so much pain," she went on. "She never complained. Before she fell asleep one night, she said, 'Why don't you play?' 'Would that make you happy?' I asked. She said yes, I should play again. So I played. She fell asleep to the sound of me playing, and I cried because it made me feel dead. What kind of gift makes you feel dead inside? I slept in the chair next to her bed. By the time I woke up, she had passed. I should've played at the funeral, but I couldn't. There was no one there to hear, anyway. All those people she'd healed. All the men she'd cared for, even the lowlife she'd married...not one of them showed up. I was so angry. She left the house to me and the land...everything except the Trans Am. It was the one thing I needed to escape. And it was gone."

"Your stepfather was the one who took it?" William asked quietly.

Desiree nodded. "Bastard drove off with it one day while I was working. He took the car and all the cash he could find, our jewelry...everything portable of value. He came back when it was all gone. I assumed he sold it all, even the car, for drug money. He came back to take more. He threatened me, then took off again. I knew he'd come back like a bad penny. I knew I'd never be rid of him. I wasn't going to be like my mother. I wasn't going to depend on somebody who used me. So I sold the house and the land. I changed my name and my hair, and I took the bus to Atlanta."

"Did he find you again?" William asked.

"Eventually," she said. "Apparently, I'm no better at life on the run than I am at stealing cars. He got violent that time when I tried to refuse. I gave him what I had and changed my name again and moved to Charlotte. Then Philly. Finally, I went west to Chicago. I helped get the West Fifty-Eighth Theater back on its feet by booking fresh talent. I thought I found a home there. I went so far as to move outside the city limits. I bought a house on the water. I realized, after all that time, that I missed the water. I started sitting out on the back deck at night, listening to it. I stopped looking over my shoulder. I started dating. I didn't have much luck. I don't know if you've noticed, but I'm rusty when it comes to social interaction…"

"Nah, you?"

She took the good-natured ribbing. "It hit me. How much I never let myself feel it. How I never let myself feel anything. It wasn't until after Chicago… I needed time to myself. I moved again, one last time, giving up my house, my job… I went back to what I knew—music. I didn't play, but before I left Florida, while I was in school, I worked at a place that made and sold stringed instruments. They took me on for a little while as an apprentice. I felt like I had a knack for it. So I opened up an online repair business. My stepfather couldn't find me anymore. He was dead. For the first time, I was free to go where I wanted, do what I wanted…live the life I wanted, like Mom said. All I could think about was getting what little piece of her I had left. There was no going back to Florida. There was nobody there…"

"But there was her car," he mused.

She nodded. "I put out some feelers. Nothing came of them until I received the clipping in the mail with the address."

Neither of them spoke for several minutes. Then she took a bracing breath. *Finish.* She had to finish. "Once my stepfather died…once the storm broke, I started to feel…everything. Her death. What happened before it.

The betrayal. All that time alone. It was a good thing I'd decided to work from home, because I wasn't fit for any workplace. I was a head case. And now I feel like I'm going down that road again."

"You've been through hell," he said. "It's okay to be a head case."

"The kind of head case that goes into a dead faint after working a few hours in a bar?" She scoffed.

"I don't think it was the work that did you in," he said. "There are psychological triggers. You can understand them, anticipate them—it doesn't make them any less powerful."

"That doesn't make me mentally fit," she pointed out.

"Nothing you do is wrong."

"Stealing a car?"

"You did that because you didn't want to come face-to-face with someone your mother knew."

"You're not going to blame her for any of this."

"Everyone she told you to trust let you down," he asserted. "Every one. I'm not saying that was her fault, but it's no wonder the thought of James scared you so badly. To you, the idea of taking off with the Trans Am was safer than confronting him."

She felt ill. "It's *not* her fault."

"Okay," he said, easing off. "I'll acknowledge that, if you acknowledge you haven't been at fault for any of it—for your music tutor coming on to you then abandoning you, for your stepfather's behavior, for not getting to Juilliard, for being alone your whole adult life…even for not loving to play violin anymore. Not one bit of that is your fault. You have been a victim of circumstance since before you understood what it was to be an adult, and I'm not going to let you put yourself down for it."

"How do you see people the way you do?" she wondered. "How do you see me?"

The space between his eyes lined. His hand was wrapped around hers. It tightened. "I'm lookin'."

Keep looking at me. She wanted to be seen in that light, the improbable one he saw around her.

Was this what intimacy...*true* intimacy felt like?

She wanted to know. "Can I?" At the quirk of his brow, she asked, "Look at you the way you look at me?"

The line of his mouth softened. His eyes made their tracks, the ones good humor had engraved through the years. "Sure."

She held herself, clutching both her arms to keep herself in place. "First person to blink?"

His smile came fully now. So did the dimples. "Deal."

It was playful and childish. He brought that out of her. Her naughty laugh and the fun-loving streak she'd thought she'd kissed goodbye alongside innocence. It was impossible for her to be guarded around him anymore.

It had been so long since she'd stared into a man's eyes. She locked onto William's. Green, as she'd expected. Smiling. Her palms were slick, she was so nervous. She smiled, too, unsteadily. She had to work at the pattern of her breathing, smoothing it so it sounded as normal as his.

Thirty seconds ticked by. Her smile faded. He was seeing her, she realized, as much as she was seeing him. She was no longer a closed book. *Focus*, she told herself as panic started to stir and the urge to blink tried to take hold.

She found that she could be bold. She could be brave. And eyes could be hypnotic. She found that the iris had many facets. His were evergreen, yes, but she saw the seasons change in the space of minutes. New spring tones, deep summer hues…whatever green that was that made leaves in the undergrowth light up in a stray beam of sunlight from the canopy. She saw the first yellow of autumn peering through…microscopic snowflakes…

Her lungs were full, she realized. She sighed. His gaze passed from her left eye to her right, shifting slowly. Did he see how soft she felt? Could he see how open? Could he see her heart growing despite the fact that it was warped?

Her eyes began to sting. She was the first to blink. She blinked several times, reaching up to dab them on the sleeve of her sweater. "Okay, you win."

He didn't reply. Her hand was in his again. Somewhere along the way, her fingers had clutched his back.

They'd crossed over…into that space she'd felt when he'd shown her the apartment and made promises she'd never heard before. They'd crossed onto that plane that he'd carved for him and her alone. A place where she couldn't be touched by anything but him.

There was proximity there, and intimacy. It was a raw place. Yet he was right—she was safe.

She wet her lips. "I'm still not sure—if I'm ready for this," she whispered. "I'm worse than damaged goods. I'm no good at all."

"Who says you can't make a fresh start?"

"Now?"

"You decide."

"You're like a saint or something," she muttered.

"No." Pressing his lips together, he came to his feet slowly. He leaned over the distance between them.

She closed her eyes as his mouth came to rest at her temple, touching his shirt over his sternum.

He was everything she'd convinced herself people couldn't be.

"I want it to be right," he murmured, "so you'll never have to wonder whether it's wrong."

"Huh," she breathed. "Do you…practice this stuff?"

He didn't move away from her.

It took her a few seconds to realize that she was being held. William was holding her, and it was wonderful. Not at all like the intrusion she'd felt when testing the waters with men in Chicago.

"Do you want me to walk you up?"

He meant to her door—because he was chivalrous and stuff. She let him pull her to her feet. "I found the way before. I can…maybe do that again." Though her legs weren't going to be any less jellified this time. When he relinquished her hand to grab his coat, his scarf slid to the floor. She bent to pick it up. She waited until his jacket was in place. Instead of handing him the scarf, she told herself to be assertive.

He bent his head so she could hook the scarf around the back of his head. Instead of wrapping it, she tucked it into the front of his jacket, making sure it was snug against his throat. "You won't be walking? It's colder tonight."

"I won't be walking," he assured her. "Is there anything you need?"

"I'll let you know," she said.

He nodded. "Switch off the lights?"

"Okay." She waited until he reached the doors. "Good night."

He threw a smile over his shoulder. "'Night, Dez."

She heard the sound of him locking up from the outside. She looked around the bar. It felt big again with everyone gone. She tried to see it again, what had made her feel so afraid before. Then she stopped, focusing on the newfound warmth, the toasty goodness intimacy had brought. Hanging on, she switched off the light.

Chapter 9

"If what you're telling me is true, one of Radley Kennard's kin might have been Desiree's stepfather."

As far as bombshells went, it was a big one. William saw it come down on James. He watched the man take it. Next to him, Gavin drew himself up like a bulwark. James rubbed his fingers over his mouth, scrubbing until William wondered how his titanium wedding ring didn't fall off. "I thought you should know," William said, wishing he had brought better news to Bracken Mechanics after his morning classes.

"You talked to Kyle," Gavin noted.

"I did," William said. He'd messaged the man overseas. "He talked to some friends of his in Washington. There's no record of an Eric Kennard, not in relation to Osias or Radley Kennard. And there's no record of Mercedes Gardet's marriage to anyone."

"So how do we know your girl ain't lying?" Gavin asked.

William had prepared for this. Still, his protective instincts flared. "She's not lying," he said simply.

James held up a hand. "You're sure you heard right—that her stepfather was named Eric Kennard? Not something else?"

"Yes," William replied.

Gavin cursed. "Effin' Kennards. They're the gift that keeps on giving."

"I don't want Adrian to know this," James said instantly.

"Mavis, either," Gavin said. "Which means Harmony can't know."

"Nobody can know," James agreed.

William knew the men were circling the wagons around their women, just as he wanted to do with Desiree. He knew that Adrian had seen the worst side of the Kennards and that Mavis's walk down the aisle was only a handful of weeks away. However, he couldn't stem the thought that the Bracken men had tried hiding details from the women in their lives over the summer and it had blown up in their faces. "What about Desiree? What should I tell her?" Was it his place to tell her? Or did James want to be the one?

"Since Kyle couldn't confirm it," James pondered slowly, "and I'm not about to let Gavin here walk up into Osias's swamp house and force-choke answers out of those who're still there, I'd say the best way to move forward is to get Desiree to positively ID the man."

"Cole was able to get copies of mug shots of all the men arrested over the summer," William pointed out. "He also has one of Osias."

"What about the police sketch?" Gavin wondered. "The one of the guy who was stalking the woods around Harmony and Bea's place."

"She has it," James said. "I think I can get it."

"They're going to know you're lying," William warned. "Harmony. Adrian. Mavis. When they find out you're doing this without their knowing, it's not going to be any more pretty than it has been before."

"They're our women," Gavin said, arms laced over his chest. "You let us worry about them."

"I don't like lying," James said. "But I can tell you the look on Adrian's face every time she hears the name Kennard. She can't sleep, still—after all this time. Best we sort this out among us. It might not be anything to alarm anyone, in the end."

William shifted from one foot to the other. "There's one other thing. Cole used his guy in the county office to speak one-on-one with Osias. He showed him the handwriting on the back of the clipping, asked him if he recognized it."

Both men had gone rigid. A muscle moved restlessly along James's jawline. "And?"

"He wouldn't say one way or the other," William said. "But Cole thinks he knew. 'The bastard grinned like a fiend,' he said."

Gavin looked to James, who scratched his bearded chin thoughtfully. "Even in jail the dirty codger's got a longer arm than the law."

"Isn't one of his sons out?" Gavin asked.

"Liddell. He rolled on Osias during the arrests. Got out a month ago."

"Should we talk to him?"

"No." James gave Gavin a single look. *Back off*, it said.

"How're we going to know for sure—"

"You think Liddell's going to admit to any more than Osias has? He was bred by the biggest dirtbag in the county."

"So what do you want to do?" Gavin asked. "Sit and hope William's wrong about everything?"

James met William's even stare. "She should look at the mug shots. We'll see if she recognizes any of them. We'll go from there."

Would Desiree be speaking to William by that point? He'd withheld information from her. She was just beginning to get comfortable...with her position at the tavern and the living arrangements abovestairs. William had a feeling if she knew what the men were discussing, she'd rabbit at the first opportunity.

"One of us should be there, don't you think?" Gavin asked.

"No," James said again, decidedly. "She doesn't trust me as much as she trusts William. And you... You know I love you like a son, but you're intimidatin' as hell."

"Why is this a bad thing?"

"It's a bad thing," William confirmed. Gavin grumbled but subsided.

James pulled something out of the pocket of his coveralls. "Give Desiree this while you're at it. It's something I promised her."

A decorative hand looped James's first and last name over the front of the envelope. The writing was worn and smudged. At some point the envelope had been folded in half, though it remained sealed. Whatever was inside had come a long way.

"She'll know what it is," James said, "but tell her she knows where to find me—if she needs me."

"I will," William agreed.

* * *

Desiree couldn't decide what was longer—nighttime or morning time. She slept well in the apartment. She could pull the blackout curtains together and camp out in bed until she'd slept off the late-night shift. She'd done three in as many days. She was a wary night owl, by instinct if not by choice. However, being on her feet from five to twelve—sometimes later—made her sleep four hours solid.

Dawn woke her, curtains closed or not.

She started walking. Braving the cold, she suited up, wrapping her scarf around the lower half of her face. First, she took a turn around Briar's gardens because the fog was too thick to wander around without knowing where she was going. The second time, she followed the sidewalk north up the shore until she'd found a picturesque park with a neatly appointed courtyard complete with roses and a fountain. A long public fishing pier strutted out over the bay, a fair walk in and of itself. A public beach adjoined the park on one side with a grassy knoll on the other, complete with tall trees and benches overlooking the salty bay.

The third day…when she was sure no one was watching, she brought the book. She found a bench tucked away from the small trickle of dawn walkers like her and found herself opening Gerald Leighton's latest bestseller to page one.

The dedication caught her off guard—*To my boys, the best of men.*

She took a deep, icy breath, like she was about to dive into waters she had no business treading.

She got lost there for the better part of the morning.

As she made her way back to the tavern, a bit dazed

from the surprise foray into William's father's imagination, it took her a while to realize that the sun was warmer today than it had been. It made her think of the apartment's window seat. The view from there. The warmth that flooded the cushions when the sun hit them just right. She found her steps quickening as she unraveled her scarf, letting the cool breeze off the bay kiss her throat.

"Desiree? Is that you?"

Desiree looked around. She'd nearly wandered past the turn for Hanna's Inn. The woman standing in the leaf-strewn clearing under the magnolia tree was nearly unrecognizable in a baseball cap and windbreaker. "Oh, hello," Desiree greeted Briar.

"I'm sorry," Briar said, smiling. "It looks like I've interrupted a daydream."

"You haven't," Desiree protested. Lied. She lied. She had been daydreaming—about books and spring and what the highway that curved along the Eastern Shore would look like when March hit. Green and florid, alive and luring. "What're you doing?"

"Kudzu," Briar said, pointing to the sign. "I like nature to have its way in some areas. But this…" She gripped a vine and began to tug. The thing was half-dead from winter's bite but wrapped snugly around the base of the sign. "It's a curse."

Desiree made a noise. "Yeah. Kudzu. Mom used to call it the cockroach of Southern plant life. It just keeps creepin' back."

Briar laughed despite her efforts. "Your mama and I would've got on famously."

Desiree could see that. Briar had the same openness, the same willingness for compassion that Desiree remembered chiefly in Mercedes. What was that like? Desiree wondered. Had Briar ever let the wrong one in? "Do you need a hand?" she asked.

"No," Briar said. "That coat suits you like a dream. And there're thorns here. I wouldn't want you to get snagged."

"You're sure?"

Briar waved a hand. "I'm sure Cole will be out shortly to wheedle me into going back inside. It's a nice morning, though, isn't it? I couldn't say no to the sunshine."

"Me, either," Desiree found herself agreeing. She lifted her face to the rays.

"How are things with William?"

Desiree blinked several times at the Briar's intuition. The man had been on her mind. Books. Springtime. Morning walks. And, yes. William. His soulful eyes, his soft dimpled smile and his hand clutched in her own.

…I want it to be right—so that you'll never have to wonder whether it's wrong…

"We're fine," Desiree said. Then fumbled. "I mean, I'm fine with him. He's fine with me. We're both fine with each other."

Briar's eyes were very round. The kudzu no longer held her attention. "And the apartment? How're you liking it?"

Desiree thanked the woman for saving her. "I like it. The view's just as good there as from the suite at the inn."

"He told you about the hot and cold on the shower?"

"He did." Desiree nodded.

"Good man." Briar's smile broadened. "He is a good man, isn't he?"

Desiree found herself reaching for her hair and snatched her hand back down. "I was, um…just on my way back."

"Are you working with him tonight at the tavern?" Briar asked.

"Yes, I think so," Desiree said quickly.

"Tell him Cole will bring something over for dinner."

"Okay. I will." She made tracks through the gardens and around to the back door of the tavern. She used the key William had given her to get through the exterior door and the one in the hall to the stairs. The padlock was hanging loosely from the barn door. She'd left it that way. Unwinding her scarf, she hung it on the coatrack next to the door and paused to nudge the thermostat down. The rooms held heat well enough. No need for more since the temperature had decided to bump up a few degrees.

She was placing the book on the round corner table next to the couch when she stopped. She'd left her satchel there…hadn't she?

She glanced around quickly to the counter that separated the kitchen from the living area. Beyond it, she looked to the table where she'd eaten a small bite before venturing out. No bag.

Something stirred restlessly inside her. Her bag should be *here*.

She rounded the corner table with its small accent lamp to walk to the bedroom. She didn't make it but a few feet before she saw the mess on the floor.

Her bag had been upended. An accident, she told herself before panic could rise up her throat. But no. Her wallet was open. The cash she'd hidden carefully under the flap of the inside pocket was scattered across the rug. Her ID was out of its plastic window. She reached out to pick it up then stopped. It was here. Her identity.

Her one emergency credit card. She did a quick check and saw that, yes, all her cash was there, too. So what was missing?

She went down to all fours, sorting through the remnants of organization. She tossed aside breath mints, headache pills, hand sanitizer, an extra headscarf. She shoved her smartphone, sunglasses and feminine products aside. "Oh, God," she uttered when she realized the one thing that wasn't there.

The deed to her mother's car. James had given it to her in good faith the last time they'd made contact. He'd signed it over to her with the promise to have it returned as soon as William's truck was running.

She stopped, straightening from her crouch on the floor. Everything went into glaring focus. Her hearing sharpened. Her heart knelled in her chest. Her vision roved slowly around the room...

The face from the tavern came back. She'd told herself it was just like the vision in the woods, leftover remnants of past specters.

The car, though... Why was the only thing that was missing from her bag the deed to the vehicle that had kept her tied to the devil from the moment he took it? He'd known she wanted it. He'd dangled it over her head several times. *Give me what I came for and I'll bring it back for you...*

She stopped breathing to tune her senses further. The downstairs door had been locked, but the padlock hadn't been. Fumbling, she grabbed the nearest weapon at hand—an iron poker next to the hearth, there more for decoration than anything now that the fireplace was filled with books. Thanking whoever had left it, she peered into the bedroom and wondered if anyone could fit in the closet or under the bed. The shower. Behind the curtains. Every shadow jumped at her. Her foot hit an old board. It creaked, and she jerked. Muttering a reverent curse in silent chastisement, she moved toward the kitchen.

Halfway across the living room, she heard it. A teeny whistle. Her eyes ventured to the lookout window above the cushioned bench seat. Her lips firmed even as they trembled. She took a step closer.

The center pane was unlatched, cracked. There was an indention in the center cushion that didn't belong to the shape of her behind. More, the shape of a large boot. She nearly shrank away from the sight but stopped herself to scan the outer pane. A cat would have had the sense not to climb all this way with so little to break a fall. It was a straight drop to the bricked piazza. However…there was a smudge of garden dirt on the sill, and the mums in the window box had been trampled.

Desiree scrambled back across the floor. She dived for her phone. It took her fingers forever to press the right code, then dial the right number. Finally, she pressed it to her ear and looked wildly around again. *Answer. Please, answer!*

"Hello?" William answered on the third ring.

"Somebody broke in." The words tumbled out on top of one another, racing a dry, disconcerted sob. "S-somebody was in the ap-partment and I d-don't—"

"Whoa, whoa. Take it easy. Where are you?"

Her voice was high. It almost squeaked. "I got back from a walk and it's gone. The title to the car. He took it. He must have!"

"I need you to listen to me, Dez, okay? I need you

to run next door. Don't think about it. Just go as fast as you can. Stay at Briar's until I can get to you. All right?"

She thought about grabbing her bag. But what was the point? Whoever had intruded hadn't wanted anything of value. Just something sentimental.

"Dez?"

William sounded frantic. She nodded, then realized he couldn't see. "I'm going."

"Right now?"

"Right now," she echoed. Grabbing her keys and, for some reason, the book, she left everything spilled across the rug and raced back the way she'd come.

William stared at the bay window. Desiree had left it open. There was the indention in the cushion. The dirt on the sill. The broken flowers in the box. But worst of all was what she hadn't seen.

Burn. The word had been written in the light layer of dust on the inside of the pane. The letters shrank and the word listed from left to right.

Cole stood next to William. He was holding the news-paper clipping. "Look at the *U*."

William hadn't had to look. He'd seen the way the stem of the uppercase vowel skewed more sideways than down. Like a kindergartener learning to write. It was the same on the back of the clipping. "The title's the only thing missing."

"She hasn't had a chance to check the rest of the place."

"She doesn't have to," William said. "It's what he was after."

"Where's the car?"

"I drove it to class this morning, then to the garage to

meet James and back here when I got her call," he told her. "It hasn't left my sight."

"Did you change those locks?"

"Haven't got around to it yet." Though it seemed Desiree was right; they did need to be changed. Had that been a guess? How had she known someone was still on the hunt for it besides her?

Cole scowled. "If the Kennards are behind this like we suspect they've been behind everything up to this point, how did they know she was living here?" He glanced sideways at William. "Have you seen them or any of their associates inside the tavern since she moved in?"

"No." William thought about it more keenly then shook his head. "No," he said again. "None of them have been here. Not since July."

"Are you sure about that, William?" Cole leveled with him. "You need to be sure."

William rubbed the underside of his chin. "I don't see everybody who walks in, but if they'd been there, they'd have been brought to my attention."

Cole braced his hands on his hips. "Everything I've got's telling me to call the Fairhope PD and have them sweep the place. We have a partial boot print. He was ballsy, climbing this high up in broad daylight. There's got to be at least one witness if they do a canvass of those at the inn and neighbors' homes. I guarantee we can get some fingerprints, too, off this sill. Most of the Kennards have been in the system."

"Will you give them the clipping?" William asked.

"I can't withhold evidence."

William eyed the telling *U*, first on the page then on the glass in front of him. *Burn.* "She's not going to want the police."

Cole jerked a shoulder. "It's your building, your apartment. If you give the go-ahead, she doesn't have a choice."

She'd be interviewed. They'd dig into her past. So on top of learning he'd withheld info, her private bubble, or what was left of it, was about to be punctured.

William had only to look at the suggestion on the window. There was no way he was going to let Desiree burn. Not when he might be holding the cards to save her. "Make the call," he said weightily before turning away from the intruder's message.

Chapter 10

The detective, Slatter, grilled Desiree for the better part of an hour. Not in the confines of a police station. Not this time. He chose the private office space tucked behind the inn's entry hall. The only blessing was that William wasn't in the room. Instead, Briar's husband, Cole, stood against the wall near the door. She watched the afternoon light begin to slant through the blinds and climb gradually up his torso. The way he held himself, she realized...

He had the air of a cop. How had she not seen it before? No wonder she'd never been at ease in his presence.

"It says here you were a person of interest sixteen months ago in a case of suspicious death," Slatter mused after looking over her file.

Desiree began to sweat bullets. She steadied herself. Lifting a drinking glass from the desk, she tried to think of the water inside as cleansing. It did nothing. "Yes," she admitted.

"Let's talk about that," Slatter said.

Desiree could feel Cole's eyes boring into her and avoided looking at him directly. "How is that relevant to what happened this morning? Am I a suspect? Do you think I scaled a twenty-foot section of wall and broke into my own place of residence?"

The detective held up his hands in a mild sign of acquiescence. "There's no reason to be upset, Miss Gardet. We've established that the title of this 1976 Pontiac Trans Am is the only thing missing from the rooms you are staying in. You say this vehicle has been an item of interest to you, Mr. Bracken and your stepfather. It disappeared for a number of years until it became embroiled in a would-be homegrown terrorist plot not even a year ago now." Slatter leaned forward. The chair squeaked beneath him. "I do not believe you are a suspect in today's break-in. However, since what was written on your window is what we believe to be a personal message, I'd like to follow through with some questions from your file."

Her blood was buzzing in her ears. She looked into her glass. A cleansing wasn't going to come close to what she'd need after this.

"On August sixteenth of last year, you claimed that an intoxicated white male broke into your home in Illinois and demanded something of you."

"Cash," she said. Her hands wanted to wring. Instead of letting both the men watch the ripples on top of the water, she set the glass on the table with a clack. "He wanted my cash."

"The file says although it was never reported prior to

that night, this was not the first time this man had done this."

"No," she said.

"In fact," the detective went on, as if she hadn't spoken, "you say this had happened half a dozen times before the night in question."

"It had," she acknowledged.

"And what did he offer you in exchange for these funds?"

Desiree closed her eyes. *Smart cop.* "My mother's car."

"Which you'd claimed he had stolen when you were nineteen."

"Yes."

"This man was your stepfather."

After a beat, she nodded.

"There's no record of this, either."

She shook her head. "He and my mother never filed the paperwork. I never knew why…"

"Because this man wasn't who he said he was."

Desiree frowned at him. "What?"

Slatter picked up the sheet of paper in front of him and handed it over the desk. "This was the man."

She blinked at the photocopy. The face was younger, leaner. But it was the same. Her hand hung suspended in the air, not quite touching the paper. "Y-yes."

Cole moved for the first time since they had entered the room. Desiree watched him come to attention, pushing off the wall to get a better angle on the photo.

Disbelief crossed his face. And recognition.

Just like that, Desiree felt cold again. "Why're you showing me this? I've already been over this already with the Chicago PD."

"Yes," the detective granted. "But the report on the events of August of last year has been updated since. Chicago Police confirmed that this man, Eric Kennard, was originally a resident of these parts thirty-one years ago. Only then, he went by the name Radley Kennard."

"Christ," Cole hissed. "Jesus H. *Christ!*"

Desiree didn't know what was more perturbing—that her stepfather had known Fairhope...*lived* here, or the complete disintegration of Cole's stoic demeanor.

"It's a hell of a lot more than coincidence," Slatter noted. He offered her the photo once more. When she waved it away, he put it back on the desk with his files. He read from the page, "'Radley Kennard of Fairhope, Alabama, was thought deceased after his release from Baldwin County Prison, where he served a sentence for breaking and entering and assault against former spouse Adrian Carlton—now Bracken. Fingerprinting on Eric Kennard, the deceased in Illinois, has been found to match Radley Kennard of Alabama.'"

It wasn't a surprise the bastard had lied about his name. Neither was it a mystery why he'd never been able to formally marry Desiree's mother. What *shook* her were other pieces of the puzzle... *Fairhope. Baldwin County Prison. Attempted murder. Former spouse—Adrian...*

Her stepfather had been married to James's wife. More, he'd acted violently against her... The connections didn't just exist. They screamed like bottle rockets.

"This doesn't make sense," she heard herself say.

"But it does," Cole said. He was beside her now. For a split second, she felt he'd aligned himself with her and she felt a flash of reprieve. "It lines up perfectly. The only missing part of this is who's acting in his place now. Radley's dead."

Desiree thought about the specter in the Brackens' woods. The stranger in the tavern that had sent her into a tailspin. "Is he?" she asked, scarcely audible.

"We've got positive ID on a body at the Chicago morgue," Cole stated. "He must've retraced James's footsteps to Florida. That's the only way he would've found you and Mercedes."

"How do you know he followed James there?" she wanted to know.

"James put Radley behind. He would've done a great deal more harm to Adrian and potentially Kyle, too, who was just a kid, had James not stopped him."

"I remember when Radley was picked up from the Carlton place," Slatter said thoughtfully. "James didn't just stop him. He did some damage of his own."

"I pulled him off the guy," Cole said. "I think if I hadn't, there wouldn't have been a man to lock up at all."

The path of violence between the two men was something Desiree didn't want to contemplate. "So…you think Eric…or *Radley* couldn't get what he wanted here so he decided to punish James some other way by…taking up with my mother?"

"Only Radley knows his motives," Cole muttered, "and he's over a year in the ground."

"It would explain why the car was of such interest to him," the detective riddled.

Desiree shook her head. "In that case, wouldn't he have wanted to hurt my mom? Why would he marry her in all but name and stick around for all those years?"

Cole tracked her features. "Did it ever occur to you that you might be the answer to that?"

"Me? How?" she asked, impatient.

He paused. "I'll tell you if you tell me whether you think there's a possibility you might be James Bracken's daughter."

Slatter's eyebrows beetled in interest. "That would be something."

When Cole spoke again, it was more gently than Desiree would have thought possible. "His target might've initially been Mercedes. But what if he found another—a blood relative—and decided to play the long game instead?"

Desiree was wiped back nearly a decade to the house in the marsh where her mother's absence still throbbed like an abscess. The night before her funeral…

"You should come with me now," Eric insisted.

Desiree wrinkled her nose. He was soaked in his own sweat. He reeked of BO. Of the sickly-sweet substance he'd gotten lit off of. He roved restlessly from one end of the room to the other. His facial muscles were jumping in unnatural rhythm. "I don't want to go with you."

"You can't talk to me that way!" he sneered. "You're a baby. A girl. You need a man to look after ya."

"I'm not going anywhere with you," she said, trying to keep her cool.

He upended a table with a deafening clatter. Mercedes's trinkets were smashed underneath it. The little porcelain shepherd, his sheep, the dairy maid… They were flea-market finds Mercedes had adored. "Goddamn it!" he roared. "I did not waste all this time to be mouthed off to by a half-grown female!"

"I'm an adult," she told him, clear and loud. "I took care of my mother and myself much more than you ever did. All you've ever given us is shame."

He jerked a finger at her. "It's a shame I can't bring her back so I can tell her all the nasty things you did with that tutor!"

Desiree had to bite down on an upsurge of rage. "Get out," she said, gritting the words Mercedes should've said long ago. "Get the hell out of my mother's house."

Eric moved toward her over broken shards of porcelain. "I didn't tell her. It would've killed her sooner. I spared her. I did you that favor. Now you'll come with me where I'm goin' and you'll be good about it. The good little mama's girl you always have been."

The urge to take the hanging mirror down off the wall behind her and smash it over his big, ugly head was almost too much for her.

"I'm all you got now, child," he warned. The muscles around his mouth twitched into a half-mad grin. "That teacher ain't comin' back for ya. Even he knows better than that."

"I don't care!" she screamed, shattering over the heat of her ire. "I don't care what you say! I'm not going with you!"

He charged. He would've run her down if he weren't drugged. As she ducked out of the way, he tripped over his own feet. Reflexes slow, his face went crashing into the same mirror she'd fantasized about smashing over his head...

She was so shocked by what happened, she stared stupidly at his prone form for several minutes.

The shaking snapped her out of it. He was bleeding, but she saw the rise and fall of his back.

He was still alive. And if she didn't run now...he'd have his way. He would take her where he wanted to go with her.

Run!, a voice in her head screamed.

She looked around at her mother's house, at her mother's things. If she left, she'd never return. She knew it... like she knew she couldn't go with her stepfather. She wouldn't survive his control.

Run, Dez! the voice insisted. Run now – even if it means you never stop running!

She packed what mattered in ten minutes flat and left the monster lying on the floor...

In the office, Cole was talking. Pointing to other things on the neat chain link that bound her to people she'd only just met... James. Adrian. Radley and somebody named Osias Kennard. Radley's father, she learned, dazed.

"He chased you from state to state," Cole explained. "You say he never stopped looking for you, even after you repeatedly changed your identity. If he was smart enough to trace James to Mercedes, he'd be able to find a way to get what he needed, which you thought was drug money. Instead, what he needed was you."

"Could be why he sent the Trans Am back here to his family," the detective guessed. "He couldn't catch you. What if he chose to bait you?"

"Whoever's behind this now," Cole said as he went to the window to look out, "they're out to finish it for him."

"Finish what, exactly?" Desiree asked.

Did she really want to know?

No.

Cole and Slatter exchanged a glance. The man behind the desk cleared his throat, stacking papers together. "I think we'd better get you a protective detail, Miss Gardet."

"Especially if you plan on staying at the tavern," Cole agreed.

Stay? How could she stay? She'd thought she had come here for herself. For Mercedes. For the car. Instead, she'd been playing into a skillful hand laid by a dead man.

The detective didn't wait for her answer. "I'll take this back to the station. We'll see what evidence the team gathered from the apartment. We'll analyze the handwriting on this newspaper clipping. All we've got now's speculation. I can't get a warrant until we get some undisputed evidence."

"We'll get it," Cole said, confident.

"Let me know if you think of anything else to add," Slatter said to Desiree. "I'll arrange for that detail immediately."

She opened her mouth to protest, but Cole's hand came to rest on her shoulder. He waited until the officer left the room, calling to others scattered throughout Hanna's.

"You can't run now," Cole said.

"You can't keep me here," she responded. "None of you have that right."

"It's not safe out there with the guy working on Radley's behalf free. Leaving won't make him go away."

Getting up from the chair, she walked the small space of the office. Suddenly, she felt claustrophobic, trapped by the room—the half-closed blinds and nightmares—all over again. "I don't know what to do." She scowled at her own weakness when her voice cracked.

"Slatter didn't ask you a key question," Cole noted. For the first time, Desiree saw him choose his words with care. "Did you kill Radley Kennard?"

Desiree managed to keep her feet. Just. "I'm not a killer."

Cole's eyes wavered from hers. He leaned against the jamb of the door, folding his arms, as if trying to set her at ease with his posture. "When Radley broke into Adrian's place, back when she was living alone with Kyle, nobody'd called her a killer, either. But I have no doubt she would've ended it there had she been able to. The man came after you for years. He threatened you, stalked you, just like he did her. A life on the run isn't easy. Maybe he pushed you enough. Maybe things got out of hand, and you took a life in self-defense."

She felt her shoulders caving. She didn't have the energy to snap her spine back in line. "You'll tell William."

"It's not about William. It's about motive. If you killed Osias Kennard's son and he knows it, he's got arms outside his cell. They might not just want you as a bargaining chip. They might want you here because you took one of their own. A blood vendetta."

Blood. Desiree was afraid to close her eyes for fear she might see blood again...

She'd thought it was over. She'd thought she could make a new start, a *fresh* start and, for the first time, a healthy one.

To know it'd all been an elaborate trap set by the very man she'd thought was no longer a threat to her...it was too much to deal with.

A voice in the hall alerted them to another's presence. "Here he comes," Cole warned.

William. She passed a hand over her face. It was dry, at least. She felt she'd aged ten years in this room.

"Go easy on him," Cole told her. "His intentions were good."

Desiree heard the unspoken and took another knockout punch. "How much of this did he know?"

A knock clattered against the door. William peered around it. "I saw them leave." His gaze snagged on Desiree. "You okay?"

Desiree regarded him—the one person she'd thought she could rely on after a life of little faith. *How much, William?* she wanted to know. *And how long?*

She grabbed her long coat off the back of the chair. She carried it with her as she bypassed both men to get away as fast as possible.

The air tasted like rain. The mist was thick. It had pressed itself against the windows of the bay houses. William almost lost sight of Desiree as the low clouds hemmed together, moving in a slinky, silent front off the bay. "Dez," he called, sprinting to catch up. "Stop, Dez."

He thought she would keep going. She took several more long-legged strides. Then she slowed.

He ran to catch up. His class schedule and late nights left little time for exercise. When he was finally even with her, he was panting. "I'm sorry," he said in a burst. "I'm sorry you had to find out this way."

"Find out what? That you're a liar?"

William knew excuses wouldn't solve this. He'd cut her too deep. "I wanted to be sure. Especially after your first shift at the tavern. I didn't want to put you through any more than you've already been through."

"You weren't wrong." Pivoting so the bay was in front of her, she held the coat she'd never put on. She'd balled it over her stomach. Her hands were buried in it. "You were right. There's other stuff, too. I'm sure Cole will tell you."

"I don't want to hear it from him." Enveloped by cloud

bank, he stood with her on the shore and wished she would look at him. "I'd like to hear it from you."

She gave a low, sour chuckle. "I'd have liked to hear it from you, too. Not them. And *not* during an interrogation, of all things."

"They don't think you did anything wrong, do they?"

"I don't know what they think," she said shortly. "I hardly know what to think myself. I thought I was starting to understand what it is about this place. This town. This weird family dynamic you've got going on. How all of you—your family, the Brackens, Cole and Briar— are all tangled up in each other's lives… But now…" She loosened a breath laden in grief and self-reproach. "Now I see how much an outsider I am. I'll never know what it's like to be part of what you've got, and I was stupid to think for a second I could even be on the margins."

"Don't." He touched her. She was unresponsive. "You can be a part of us. There's a place for you here if you want it."

"What, because I'm most likely James Bracken's love child?"

He blanked. "What?"

Desiree saw the shock reverberating through him. The lines of her brow dug deeper. "Why couldn't you have just been honest with me?"

It was a plea, and it nearly broke him. "I thought I went about it right. I was wrong."

"It's typical. *So* typical."

"What's typical?"

"That yet another man could be *so* disappointing."

He breathed into the silence, watching with her as the fog drifted across the water's surface. Neither reached for the other. The white cloud wisps never dropped beneath their hovering line to test the water's surface. They were together and yet, inexorably, apart.

William dropped his chin. "Please," he said in a near whisper. "Please, Dez. Don't leave over this."

"There's someone coming after me. He took the thing that I stayed here for—the title. Tell me what I'm supposed to do, William, because I'm out of answers."

He placed his hand on the small of her back. Standing close to her, he thought about nosing into the springy curls on the back of her head. She smelled sweet where the air was salty. "Come back to the inn. You don't have to go back to the apartment. I'll get your things myself. Briar and Cole will have a room—"

She flinched. "I can't go back there."

"Why not?"

"I should've gone home like my instincts told me to. Living my kind of life…it hones gut feeling. Survival instincts. This is the first time I didn't listen, and now I'm paying the price."

"Why did you stay?" William asked.

"Because you smiled at me, damn it!" she snapped. "Because you fixed me hot cocoa when I was cold. Because you were there for me at the Bracken farm…and every day since. I'm good at goodbyes. Only two times in my life I couldn't say goodbye. I didn't say it to my mom. Not really. I've been numb for ten years where she's concerned. And I couldn't say goodbye to you." She pressed her hands over her face. "Stupid. I'm so *stupid*. And you were stupid, too. I tried to warn you, but you wouldn't leave me, either."

He tilted his head to hers. Her hair teased his brow. He smelled the bay on her now. His bay. His home. "How could I?" he wondered out loud.

"A smart man would have." Her dark gaze was hollow when it swung to his. She stepped back, marking space between them. "A smart man would've known I was bad news from the moment I walked in the door. Like Cole."

"You're not bad news," he said. "You've been treated badly. I'm here to break the cycle. You can trust me. You can trust James and the Brackens. You can trust Cole and Briar. You've got people in your corner. Stay, Dez. Stay so we can help you end this thing with your step-father's family. So you can be free."

"There's not one thing I haven't lost in this fight."

"You haven't lost me," he insisted. "I'm here, aren't I?"

She pressed her lips together. "I don't know…"

When she began walking away again, he worked against his emotions to keep them from ricocheting.

Changing direction, she walked to the inn. There was relief. He joined her. "If there's anything I've learned over the past year, it's that there's strength in numbers. I've seen you. I've seen what you can take and you've told me more. But everybody needs to lean every now and then."

She didn't say anything until she'd reached the gazebo that belonged to the inn. She turned to him in the shadow of its roofline. "That's what they make signposts for."

William knew her signposts were pointing her out of town. Back up the interstate. She'd follow them until she was clear of Alabama and the Southern states. She'd follow them until she disappeared again and made a new name for herself. He thought about her starting over. His gut wrenched. How did she do that over and over? How did she do that alone and survive?

Pieces of her, the tidbits he'd managed to grasp during her stay—the naughty laugh, the wry sense of humor, the young woman she'd been whom he'd gleaned through what she'd shared of her history, the pieces of her mother that lived on with her—had barely latest this long, he suspected. The music was gone. How much longer before the other parts of her were, too?

The exhale that plumed into the already-cloudy air fell raggedly from his mouth. "I'm sorry I didn't tell you. I knew what you needed from me, and I failed."

Her eyes raced over him, and her chest rose and fell. "You've only prolonged the inevitable. I was never meant to stay."

Things changed. Circumstances changed. People changed. Neither one of them was the person they'd been when Desiree arrived. She had ties here. She had people. Had she been without those things so long she'd forgotten how to reach for them?

"I can't make you stay," he muttered. "Your choices are yours. You said that the first night, and you're right. Just remember you're free to choose, because you have choices. Your gut's telling you to leave. But you can't live your entire life off your gut."

"I can't live a life in the crosshairs, either," she argued.

"No," he agreed. "Sometimes, though, you've got to consider your heart. What's it telling you?"

"It's hard to tell," she said. "Maybe I don't have one anymore."

He sighed. Reaching into the pocket of his jacket, he pulled out the envelope he'd received. He held it for a moment. Would it have the answers she needed?

He offered it to her. "James wanted me to give you this."

She looked at the envelope. He saw her throat work

around a swallow. She took it, hesitantly. She folded it in two, pressed it against the coat still balled to her stomach.

"You're wrong," he muttered.

She looked at him incredulously. "About what?"

"Your heart," he said knowingly.

She frowned at him deeply, then shifted onto her heels.

William didn't follow this time. He let her go alone, her curls a dark halo around her head.

Chapter 11

Desiree took one piece of William's advice—she asked Briar for a room. The innkeeper was gracious enough to divert an incoming guest to one of the suites in the new wing so Desiree could have the comfort of the Bayview Suite.

She didn't settle. Even after William brought over her things, as promised, she sat for a time on the edge of the blue quilted duvet with her overnight bag packed on the floor and her satchel beside her. Her jacket sat beside her, too, and underneath it, the book where she'd pressed the envelope.

She'd seen James's name written across the front of it before she'd folded it. She knew the handwriting was her mother's.

She couldn't bring herself to open it. If the sight of Mercedes's penmanship hadn't made her heart swell, she might've discarded it altogether.

Desiree turned her mind elsewhere.

William was right about one thing; she did have a choice to make. There was no one to stop her from going. She could leave right now. She could go someplace she'd never gone before. The West Coast. It was warm in some places there. She could go to Canada. There were warm spots there, too, right? The Kennards were wrongdoers, most of them with jail time. They wouldn't be able to get over the border. Would they?

The smell of the lavender sachets that lined the drawers of the antique boudoir seeped through the tirade of mixed emotions. She realized that her eyelids were drooping. She felt how much her joints ached. What was it about grief and rain that made everything ache? She leaned her shoulder against the lace-trimmed sham at the head of the bed. The bedsprings creaked as she tucked her legs onto the covers. She left her shoes on and stared at the ray of light creeping through the window next to the bed. It was a fragile thing. She reached out to touch it. The light spread across the back of her hand. It didn't warm it.

Faith was just like that. A fragile thing you couldn't feel or touch. If you held it over your head, it wouldn't stop you from getting wet—or crushed by the falling scaffolding of what you'd thought was a readjusted life.

She felt cold and crushed and so exhausted, it took her back to the days after her mother's death. The days after Eric's—or Radley's—last break-in. She curled in on herself farther and watched the light move across the bed table as it started to change…

A knock startled her out of sleep some time later. It felt like minutes. Desiree was shocked to see the room in near dark. She pulled the cord on the lamp. Throwing her legs over the side of the bed, she twitched the curtains closed over the window, then went to the door. She hesitated before she could touch the knob. "W-who is it?"

"It's James."

Jesus and Mary. Desiree's hands balled. She pressed them to her eyes. She was still fuzzy from the long doze on the bedcovers. She was dazed from all she had learned in the last six hours. Now she had to face James.

Rubbing the sleep out of her eyes, or attempting to, she then scrubbed her hands back over her hair. It had gone wily from weather and neglect. She shook herself, hoping to snap the steel rods in place.

They didn't work. She panicked for a split second, wondering if they would ever work again. A person could only fall so many times before they broke.

She unlocked the door and snatched it open.

James filled the space of the jamb. Desiree considered herself tall for a woman. Even so, her head rocked back to meet his gaze.

It looked like she wasn't the only one who had aged in a day. That was something.

"Did Cole call you?" she asked when his lips parted. He would've asked if she were okay. She didn't want to answer that.

"Briar called," he said. "Cole and I spoke just now."

"Oh." Every ounce of dread she was feeling imbibed the syllable.

Concern wove through the deep furrows around his temples. "Can I come in?" he asked quietly.

Was there room enough in the small suite for the two of them and their combined issues? She stepped back in answer, opening the door wider.

"Thank you." James strode to the center of the room.

He pivoted to face her as she closed the door. "You haven't unpacked."

Her state of indecisiveness was obvious. *Great.*

"Did William give you the letter?"

"Yes," she said. "It's her handwriting. I haven't opened it."

"Oh." A muscle in James's cheek ticced. At a loss, he studied the wallpaper behind her. "I know this is uncomfortable…"

"That's an understatement," she groaned.

"However," he said carefully, "I'd like to know what you're planning to do. Whether you're staying…or going. Either way, I can help."

"Wait. You aren't going to try and stop me?"

"I would prefer you didn't leave," he told her. "Whatever the letter says, we'd like you to stay."

"Who's we?" she wanted to know.

"I want you to stay," he stated. "Adrian does, too."

Desiree studied him closely. "How much have you told her?"

"She was in the briefing with Cole just now."

Looking around, she saw that the wall was close enough to catch her. She leaned against it to gather her thoughts and what was left of her strength.

He waited. His emotions strengthened on the outer shell of his face, too much to conceal. "Goddamn, Dez. It's a goddamn mess I've put you and your mother through, and I'm sorry. I'm so sorry."

She was tired of men apologizing. She didn't know how to console anyone. Not when she felt like a mouse trapped inside a closed Tupperware container. "Can I ask you a question?"

"Anything."

"In the woods near your house," she said slowly, "I saw a man. Or I thought I saw one the night I came to dinner. William mentioned that if there was someone there, I needed to say. It looked so much like my stepfather, I thought I was having a delusion..."

He nodded away the rest. "In light of everything now, you think you really saw someone. William was right. You should have said something." He removed the baseball cap from his head. Cradling it in his hands, his fingers fiddled over the brim briefly before he began to explain. "You've heard of our troubles over the summer, but you might not have heard that there was someone sneaking around the Farm—specifically over at Harmony's place, closer to the airfield. Random things started to occur—a tree fell on her house, some hoses in the engine of her plane looked like they'd been cut and her daughter, Bea, started talking about a man she'd made contact with in the woods. She called him the Caterpillar Man, because he gave her a mason jar full of caterpillars. Poisonous caterpillars."

Desiree fought off a shudder. "Who was he?"

"We never could get Bea to identify him positively. He covered his face well with a hat and sunglasses each time they met. But police did arrange for her to sit with a sketch artist."

"You want me to look at the sketch," Desiree supposed.

"If you can," he said. "I've arranged for Harmony to drive it over. She'll be staying here with Bea upstairs with her parents. Hopefully, I can convince her not to come back to our woods until this is over, or until Kyle comes home again."

Desiree's pulse ticked up several notches. If she recognized the man in the sketch, it meant there really was someone there that night, watching her from the trees.

If Olivia and William hadn't come along in their truck, what would have happened?

"There's something else."

"Of course there is," she said ironically. Her mouth twisted into an unfelt smile.

"Our woods border on the airfield, and there's a vacant parcel of land between ours and the swamp on the other side. The swamp belongs to Osias Kennard. It's where he raised Radley and his other sons. We believe that the man from Bea's sketch is one of them."

"Cole said they were in jail," Desiree said quickly. Too close. If James was right, she'd come too close… "Aren't they?"

"Osias is likely serving a life sentence," James revealed. "His son Cecil and several of his nephews are behind bars as well. But there's one—Liddell—who was released just a while ago."

"Do you have a photo of him?" Desiree asked.

"We will."

Desiree looked to the window. She thought of the apartment window, the missing title. Had he waited for her to leave before breaking in? Or had he expected her? He'd missed his chance in the woods. The message Slatter had mentioned from the windowpane, the one she'd missed, pierced her mind.

Burn.

Just like the phone call she received at the beginning of her stay.

"I'm scared." It shot out of her, an unbidden confession. "I don't know why I said that." She hadn't been able to tell William. She had hardly been able to admit it to herself. She'd carried the weight of a heavy life. She'd been blinded by fear. She'd been forced to act against it, to commit one damning act of survival.

Was she coming to all that again? If she came up against the intruder, the stranger in the woods, was she going to have to relive everything she'd struggled to put behind her?

She was scared—of the stalker. Of Osias Kennard. Of a dead man's reach. She was scared of the place all these factors might push her to visit again. That dark, dark place she hadn't thought she'd be able to claw her way out of the first time.

James took a step toward her.

She straightened against the wall. "You're not going to try and hug me, are you?"

"Not unless you tell me you need it."

She thought about it. Her gaze tracked past him to where the envelope was buried inside Gerald Leighton's book. "If I recognize Liddell in the sketch or the mug shot or both...will it be enough?"

"I think so," he determined. "Though, as Cole reminded me downstairs, fingerprints from your apartment would clinch things with a certainty."

"What if there are others?" she wondered. "You said there were more of Radley's family. Could they be involved, too? Could his father send more after me if Liddell fails?"

"We can't know for sure," James admitted. "But Liddell did roll over on his old man so he didn't have to serve more than a few months' time. There's a possibility he could do so again, if caught."

Desiree scrubbed the place between her eyes. The jetlag feeling she'd woken up with was turning out to be the beginnings of a mountainous headache.

"I could have ended this a long time ago."

"Ended what?"

"Radley. I could've saved you the trouble of this pattern of abuse he clearly never fell out of even after being released on good behavior."

She saw the truth of that in him and the guilt and shame behind it. "It doesn't matter."

"It does matter," James gritted out. "It matters a great deal, Desiree. This never should've happened to you. *He* never should've happened to you. There hasn't been a week since that night he hurt Adrian that I don't regret not finishing it."

Desiree swallowed. She gleaned something of herself in him then for the first time. Gripping her arms, she held herself. "Okay."

"Did he ever treat you right?" James asked. "Over the years, was he ever good to you at all?"

Desiree thought it over. "He didn't treat me badly until Mom passed away. Then the threats started. Then the break-ins and…"

"Did he hurt you," he asked, sounding as if he might dread the answer, "like he hurt my wife?"

Several images slashed across her conscience. The bones in her fingers bent awkwardly. The shape of a bruise on her chin in the mirror. Blood sticky on her blouse, metallic in her mouth, wet on her fingers and the rocks of the gravel drive she'd gripped to bring herself back to focus…

She caught herself reaching for the space beneath her collarbone and shut down any thoughts from the final night Radley attacked her. The night he lost his life. "Only when I refused to give him what he wanted."

"How often did you refuse?"

Every time. Every time she'd argued—bruises. Every time she'd tried to call the police—broken fingers. Every time she'd fought back—blood in her mouth. "I never wanted to be the victim. I know I ran after, every time. But I tried…"

"I'm sure you did, baby," he said and stepped to her as she dropped her head against the back of her folded hand. "Hey," he said when she had to take several breaths.

Too many. Too many feelings today.

She felt his hands come to her shoulders. They passed from her elbows and back up. "You did right. You did right by yourself all those times you told him he couldn't take from you. There's power in that. You need to re-member." His grip tightened. It was certain. "By the time this is all over, you'll have your power back, and you'll never have to know what life is like without it again."

Desiree kept her head down. She hoped he was right. There was magic in that vision of herself. Not a victim. Still, it didn't take her away from the crumbly edge or the crappy situation they had all fallen into.

"I'm going to help you," he assured her. "Everybody downstairs, we're here to help. It's about time somebody had your back."

A sound escaped her. She let him squeeze her once more in that reassuring way of his. He even rocked her a bit by the arms.

"You all right?" he asked quietly after she lifted her head.

She jerked her chin.

"Wanna come downstairs? If you're ready, we can get started."

She thought about the people there. She thought about facing them.

Then she thought of herself marching in with somebody like James Bracken at her back, and she gave a sure, single nod.

"Ms. Gardet."

"Officer Rolls," Desiree greeted. She liked to think that she spoke to her shadow of the last two nights without hitch. He was a plainclothes officer who looked relaxed in a sprawl against the wall next to the kitchen door of Hanna's Inn. "I thought your shift ended at eight."

Rolls grinned. He took a strip of foil-wrapped gum out of a coat pocket and began to unravel it. "I'm with you through midnight." He offered her the gum. When she shook her head, he folded a stick into his mouth. The muscles of his cheeks churned as he began to chew. "Why? I thought you liked me better than Officer Picks."

She wasn't accustomed to speaking casually to officers of the law. The duo assigned to her protection detail, though, had almost made her uneasiness drain from the point of introduction. Both were kind and fresh-faced and, she feared, younger than she was. If inclined, she might be able to forget why they were there in the first place.

If.

She didn't mind either Rolls or Picks, she found. However, she still found it hard to sleep more than a few hours in the Bayview Suite. The message, *Burn,* was singed into her mind like the result of a flash-bang. She hadn't ventured out walking again.

With Picks near, she *had* spent the morning on the inn dock, gathering the lull of waves and the pace of boats. Trying to anchor herself to this place. The present. She'd even hunkered down in the bricked-off piazza at the tavern to bury herself in a world that didn't involve the Kennards or her stepfather. She'd nearly gotten lost once more in Gerald's Leighton far-reaching world and had sworn Picks to secrecy on the subject of her hour's study.

"I won't choose sides," Desiree decided. "Though… I will say you have a better singing voice."

Rolls's cheeks puffed with pride. "You think?"

"Officer Picks warbled through Briar's club sandwich luncheon." With a slight smile, she chose one of Mercedes's old sayings. "I'm sure I've heard better from a cat on a hot tin roof."

Rolls guffawed. "Stay away from the man at the karaoke Christmas party. His Mariah Carey sounds more like Fred Durst."

"There may be some talent in that," she mused.

"You've business at the tavern, I hear."

She sobered. "Presently."

He nodded once at the door. "Right this way."

Desiree thought about whom she would be meeting. There weren't likely to be any pleasantries in store for her.

She'd done her best not to think about William. It had taken some effort. The tavern was always in view. She'd felt it at her back while standing on the dock, watching clouds furl and unfurl over the bay. She'd felt it even closer on the piazza. She might've mistaken the near heat of the brick wall for the telltale warmth of William's presence.

She hadn't spoken to him. She'd hardly seen him over

the last twenty-four hours, not with his bar and school hours. There was some trepidation, walking into the tavern after everything.

She didn't like the dark as her and Rolls's feet crunched over the gravel-lined parking lot once they'd rounded the tavern. She was glad for the noise she heard within, glad for the heat from the press of bodies and activity she found as she followed Rolls into the establishment. He pulled off his hat, and she did the same.

Friday night bounced even in the off-season, she found. The tables were stacked with customers, small parties with heads leaned close to one another. Larger parties hemmed around the pool tables. At the bar, only a few stools were lonely. Desiree couldn't help the direction her eyes trekked—straight to the side of the bar where William, Ines and Godfrey buzzed back and forth to fill the needs of customers. She was surprised to see Olivia pop in from the swinging doors carting a large case of beer. "Who's buyin'?" she hollered. Her cackle rang through the crash of '80s rock as several patrons hailed the summons.

William relieved his mother of the case and set it on the bar, where he restocked the fridge underneath the counter. Desiree saw him waver when his eyes collided with hers.

There was a room's width between them, but she swore she felt the glide of that look. He sized her up slowly. Checking that she was whole.

He'd chipped away at the steel plating she'd worn. He'd made her confront parts of herself she'd buried or forgotten.

Did that make her more or less?

"Desiree, over here!"

Desiree glanced sideways to a high table where Harmony Savitt, undisguisable with her long, flaming-red braid, waved her arms. She was sitting shoulder to shoulder with Mavis on one side and James on the other. Gavin held the last chair. He stood at her approach.

"Thanks," Desiree said awkwardly. She gripped the edge of the table and reached back to scoot the stool closer.

Someone beat her to it. She looked around to find William and quickly turned back. "Oh."

"What can I get you?" he asked after she'd taken her seat. He reached around her to grab the empty chip platter. With his arm pressed to hers, his torso against her back, she closed her eyes for a split second. Remembering what it was like to be held.

She did miss the warmth, she found. Safe, safe heat. She missed *him.*

"Dez?"

She didn't know who said it. Blinking, she adjusted her weight on the stool. "I'll have a glass of red, please."

When she looked around again at him, there was a hint of a smile hanging around his mouth. His eyes didn't meet it. "Glass of red, on the house."

"That's not—"

"Anything else?" he interrupted, addressing the others.

"Another water for me," Mavis said.

"Me, too," James chimed.

"Ines'll have it out in a jiff," William said. He grunted when a customer bumped into him, shifting his front against Desiree's back more firmly. His hand cupped her under the elbow, steady. "Sorry," he murmured.

The low baritone resonated against her eardrum. She

nearly shivered. "It's okay," she whispered. He probably didn't hear it. When he moved off, she felt awash in something else.

Regret.

It wasn't until James said her name again that she realized she'd tracked William's progress back to the bar. The others' faces were blurry for a second. Her fingers bit into the ledge of the table, and she attempted to refocus.

"Are you sure you're ready for this?" James asked quietly.

Concern was etched in his brow again. It was in his eyes. "I'm ready," she said. As if it were true.

Harmony lifted a manila folder from her lap and set it carefully in the center of the table. "Here's the composite sketch made of Bea's Caterpillar Man over the summer."

"A point, before we take a look," Gavin inserted. "Adrian and Harmony have looked Osias Kennard and two of his three living sons, Cecil and Liddell, in the face in the past six months. Neither one of them has been able to positively ID the person in the sketch."

"There's some resemblance to Osias and Liddell, I think," Harmony added. "But that might be because I'm seeing what I want to see."

"It's good that you're seeing this," James pointed out to Desiree, "as you've only ever seen mug shots of the men in question."

Desiree nodded slowly. "Let's see it, then."

Mavis lifted the corner of the folder. She spread it wide and rotated it until the sketch stared Desiree in the face.

Desiree made herself bring it closer. She could see why identification would be hard. The subject was wearing a billed cap and large sunglasses over the upper half of his face. He was smiling. The sight of bared teeth made the fine hairs on the back of her neck shift.

Harmony folded her arms on the tabletop. "Anything?"

"Give her a minute," Gavin ordered.

"Take your time," James told her. "Then tell us whether you have any impressions."

Her stomach was in knots. They grew tighter the longer she stared at the drawing. The trouble was she didn't know whether it was that toothy pencil-etched grin or the way the others were staring holes into her.

A breath shuddered out of her. She gave in and pushed away the folder. "I don't know." Harmony cursed, and Desiree fumbled. "I'm sorry."

A glass of red wine landed between Desiree and the sketch. She'd never been so grateful for alcohol in her life. She looked up at Ines, who smiled grandly at her. "It's good to see you, girl," Ines said.

"Oh," Desiree said in surprise. "It's good to see you, too." She meant it. Enough to give something of a smile in return.

Ines patted her shoulder. Someone called her name two tables over. She nodded at them before saying, "Please stay. I want to catch up."

"Okay," Desiree found herself agreeing. She bit her lip as Ines went ahead to take the next order. Godfrey was nearby, as well. He lifted a friendly hand to Desiree before moving off to be bar.

Her smile crumpled. Now she had a knot in her throat to match the ones in the stomach. Lifting the glass, she took a long sip.

Harmony was closing the folder. "I'm really sorry," Desiree told them. "I wish there was *something* I could do to help."

"Is there anything we can do for you?" James wanted to know.

Hadn't they done enough for her? She'd thought having to stay on a few extra weeks in Fairhope had been a curse. Somewhere in the last few days, things had changed enough for her to see it more as perhaps a blessing in disguise. When the knot in her throat grew, she simply shook her head.

James squeezed her wrist. "I'd stay, but I don't like leaving Adrian alone at the cottage. Your officer will get you home?"

Home. A funny word. "Back to the inn," she confirmed.

James sent a pointed look across the table. "Gavin, I trust you to get our young ladies home safely to their beds."

"Oh, he'll be tucking one of us in, and it ain't me," Harmony said suggestively.

"I'll escort them," Gavin answered for himself.

"Good." James picked up the folder as he rose. Pulling out his billfold, he dropped enough cash on the table to pay off their tab. To Desiree, he offered, "Call if you need or think of anything."

Desiree waited until James left before pressing her hands to her face. She'd been tired for too long. The emotional twists and forays over the last few days had been enough to turn her inside out.

The others were quiet for a while, long enough for the jukebox to kick into the first chorus of Guns N' Roses' "Knockin' on Heaven's Door." Finally, Mavis leaned toward her. "Look, I know, all right?"

Desiree peered at her. "Know what?" she asked bracingly.

"That you might be…" Mavis stopped, paused and said again, "That you and I might be related."

Harmony stared beadily between the two women. "No shit!" she exclaimed when the speculation hit home. Her jaw dropped, and she swatted her brother. "Did you know about this?"

"Pillow talk," Gavin replied.

Well, that took care of the chain of uncertainty. Desiree didn't so much sip as chug her wine now.

"I never would've put that together," Harmony mused, staring back and forth between the other women.

"They've got the same scowl."

All three women turned their heads to Gavin. Harmony pursed her lips. "You're still blind, right?"

"Not in the ways that matter," Gavin pointed out. "It's the stewing kind of scowl. You don't have to see it to feel it."

"Huh," Harmony said as if that made total sense. Her eyes rounded. "Does *Kyle* know about this, too?"

"No," Mavis and Gavin said as one.

"That ain't right."

"It isn't exactly something you say over the phone," Mavis defended. She mimed talking into a receiver. "'Hey, bro. Drop the grenades, 'cause there's a strong chance we've got a secret sibling. Oh, and there's also a good chance the Kennards are out for her blood, too. Don't rush back, commando. We got this!'"

Desiree wasn't enjoying listening to them talk about her like she wasn't there. Cradling the glass, she looked around the room. There was a large group knitted together near the bar. The noise of the room had shifted in their direction. In fact, shouting from the center of the pileup had started to clash with the music.

"*I'll take any one of you boys!*" came a lone reedy voice. "*Come at me! One atta time!*"

There was some laughing, jeering, a bit of encouragement. Desiree saw William come swiftly out of the hatch. He veered toward the jukebox. She watched him yank the plug, shutting off the speakers in the middle of "Barracuda."

The full bar fell into an odd, ready sort of silence. Gavin had grown taut next to her. Desiree's fingers bit into the tabletop once more as William directed himself into the group. He tapped the shoulders of onlookers. They parted for him quickly, revealing the man at their center. An older gentleman, stocky and bald. His face was red, from drink or rage—it was difficult to tell. He saw William approach and stopped jawing long enough to lift a shot glass from the bar and swig it back.

"All right, Potter," William drawled. "That's enough for you."

"What's it to you, boy?" The words tumbled over one other. Potter pointed a finger. It was off aim, but the sentiment was there. "Ain't I a good-payin' customer?"

"Listen to him, Eugene," Olivia said from the far side of the bar.

Potter snorted in her direction. "I's sure do miss when you was in charge, Liv. You didn' begrudge a man his libations. Neither'd your ma. God rest her soul."

"I'm sorry you feel that way," William said. "I call the shots now, though, and I say you've had one too many."

Ines nudged in close to him. "Sorry, boss. I should've kept count—"

"He knows his limit," William stated. "He's been warned before. Haven't you, Potter?"

"Have your way then," Potter challenged. "What're you waitin' on, sonny? Afraid to throw an old man out?"

"No," William said evenly. He didn't look angry at all. Just mildly annoyed. Not once had he raised his voice to the man. "I just know we can handle this peace-like, without making a scene. Now come on." He took a step forward. "Let's get you home to Retta."

William misjudged him. Heck, Desiree misjudged him. One moment Potter was swaying on his stool, and the next he moved like a cobra, throwing a mean right fist into William's face.

William staggered into the men at his back. They managed to catch him by the shirt before he could crash into the floor. Gavin pushed away from the table, and both Harmony and Mavis came to their feet.

Desiree felt herself moving, too. Not toward those muscling Potter toward the exit. Gavin took care of that. She shouldered her way through those ringed around William. "He hit you," she mumbled stupidly.

He was staring into the floor, hands braced on his knees. "Ah, yeah. Geezer did it real well."

He sounded amused. She touched his back. "William? Are you all right? Should we call someone? Do you know a doctor?"

"I'm fine." He sniffed, rubbing the bridge of his nose. He straightened slowly, arm spanning her waist for support.

She let him hang. "Your nose is bleeding."

"Hellfire." He angled his face toward the rafters. A thick stream of dark red crept closer to his lip.

She looked around. Snatching a napkin off the nearest table, she said, "Here…" She balled it up and raised it to his nose.

"Thank you." His hand cupped the back of her fist. He closed his eyes, his tawny lashes thick.

"He needs ice," Olivia said, approaching. "Trade."

Desiree took the offered baggie. Ice swam inside. Quickly, she swapped the two so the ice was pressed to his nostrils.

"Are you okay?" Olivia asked William, thumping his shoulder.

"I'm great," he muttered, deep.

"Hate to say you asked for it…"

When William only groaned, Desiree shook her head. "He *asked* to get hit in the face? I thought he was just asking the man to leave."

"Potter's belligerent when he's in his cups," Ines explained, joining them. She stroked William's sleeve. "Sorry again, boss."

"It's all right," he murmured, tipping his chin down again. His eyes remained closed, and he took the baggie from Desiree so she could lower her hand. "It should've fallen to me to count his shots. He likely took advantage of the fact that I wasn't." Taking a step toward the door, he added, "I should make sure somebody gets him home."

"No," Desiree said, tightening her hold around the back of his hips. "He should be arrested."

"He's got a grandkid," William told her. "His wife's on disability. They depend on his paycheck. Besides, he'll be back tomorrow, hat in hand with an apology."

Desiree's lips parted. "This has happened before."

"His accuracy's usually off," William puzzled. "Usually." When she scoffed in disbelief, he shrugged. "I should've been faster on my feet."

"You need to lie down," Desiree insisted. She wasn't nagging, she told herself.

She'd smelled it—his blood. The warm copper tang had wrenched her gut. She knew what it felt like—to take a hit to the face. She knew what it smelled like—blood in her nose. She knew what it would look like and feel like tomorrow—purple-rose around the inside corners of his eyes and a soreness wound tightly with intermittent throbbing. She swallowed the bile at the back of her throat. "I'll check on him if you go with Ines to the office."

"I said I was all right. Didn't I take it well?"

She saw color in his face. Embarrassed color. She looked to Olivia, uncertain.

Olivia pulled a face. "No offense, Shooks, but I've seen trees fall more gracefully."

"Thank you, Mum," he drawled. He sniffed and took another step for the exit.

Desiree scrubbed her hands over her hair as he kept walking. "I'll take over for you. Godfrey or Ines can work the bar while I take a section of tables. You won't have to worry about taking a breather." Despite the hubbub, it seemed no one had decided to take their leave of the place except the men who'd escorted Potter out.

The corner of his mouth twisted into a short smile. "I like that you worry 'bout me. But I'm still going to make sure he's all right. I'll need to call Retta to let her know what to expect when he gets home."

"I'll call her," Olivia offered.

He waved a hand before pushing through the door.

When Desiree only frowned after him, Olivia linked an arm through hers. "His moral compass is as tightly wound as his wristwatch."

"You say it like it's a bad thing," Desiree noted.

"Aren't you annoyed?" Olivia wondered.

Yes, Desire found. She refused to say as much.

"You're questioning if he ever thinks of himself," Olivia said. "And, secretly, you're impressed because if selflessness is his chief flaw, it makes you wonder why you've been fightin' him so long."

Desiree pivoted slowly to face her. "How do you know that?"

"Because I'm you," Olivia mused. "Or I *was* you some thirty-odd years ago when Gerald Leighton walked through those doors. I fought the man like a wet cat."

Desiree heard a surprised laugh bubble from her throat and quickly closed her mouth.

"He waited," Olivia went on. "Like a saint. It terrified me, because I started to see that he was everything he said he was. No tricks, no gimmicks. And it terrified me because he looked at me like the greatest prize on Earth. Like I was the kind of woman who deserved a life with a man like him. It scared me so much, I hurt him, badly enough I didn't expect him to come back."

Desiree gnawed her lower lip. She hadn't expected this much candor from Olivia.

Someone came through the doors. Desiree found herself going up to her toes in anticipation. It wasn't William. She came back down to rest on her heels and felt Olivia's close survey. "But he did," she surmised.

"Hell, yes, he did," Olivia said, sounding astonished by the fact to this day.

"And?" Desiree prompted when Olivia didn't continue.

Olivia raised a brow. "And I never let him leave again.

Unless he was on a book tour. Like now." She let it sink in, then tipped her head to the side. "How's the book?"

"What book?" Desiree asked.

"The one you've been reading." Olivia winked. "On the sly."

"I... It's..." Desiree pictured the book in her room at the inn and how it had helped her cope with the nights much better than staring at the ceiling. She'd read more than half of it. Truthfully, she might've finished it...if she didn't dread being without the promise of those final chapters. "I love it," she found herself saying. "I haven't felt this way about a book since..."

Olivia smiled when Desiree trailed off. "He'll be home for Christmas. Gerald will. Do you have plans?"

"For Christmas?" Desiree thought about all the Christmases she'd spent on her own. Running. Anonymous. "No."

"Well." Methodical, Olivia took off her Santa hat and handed it over. "If you can handle men in kilts and eggnog, we'll be more than happy to fix that."

Chapter 12

The numbers on the computer screen ran together. William lifted two fingers to his nose to pinch the skin above his reading glasses. He hissed at himself for setting off a chain reaction of pissed-off nerve endings. Impatient, he took off the glasses altogether and dropped them on the keyboard.

"The numbers will be there tomorrow."

William wanted to growl at his mother. He held off. She didn't deserve to be sniped at no matter what level of pain he was in. "So will the shiner."

Olivia leaned back against the desk, facing him. She took another look at the damage. "It's ugly."

He began to roll his eyes, then reevaluated, closing them instead and pressing his fingers over his lids.

"Did you take some meds?"

"A couple."

"You sleep on your face."

"What's your point?"

"You won't be getting much shut-eye tonight."

"Sleep's not an option, whether I sleep on my face or not."

She tutted, running her thumb across his stubbled chin. "If you hadn't moved my granddaddy's shotgun out of here, I'd drop it over Eugene Potter's head. This is too pretty a face to be hitting."

"Say more nice things."

She chuckled. "I'd have hit him back. But you're not like me."

"No."

"You're a lover, not a fighter. A glorified pacifist."

"I prefer diplomatist," he intoned.

"You can't win every war with words, Shooks. How many hits are you going to take before you learn?"

"I don't fight with fists, Mum," he answered wearily. "Not all men do."

"No." She sighed. "Should I send the girl in—to lick your wounds?"

"Leave her alone."

"Hard to do when I've invited her to Christmas." Olivia's smile stretched when William looked at her in surprise. Thoughtfully, she pulled on her gloves, one finger at a time. "Finny's coming home, too, so she'll have to sleep in your room. Hope you don't mind."

"No," he said, trying to keep up. Christmas, with Desiree. Desiree, in his room.

"She helped with closing."

William raised his brows and instantly regretted it. "Did she?"

"Mmm-hmm. She scrubbed tables, stacked chairs,

mopped floors. A couple of newlyweds tried to come in after hours. I thought she was going to chew them up and spit them back out."

"You invited her." It was slowly dawning.

"See to it she doesn't talk herself out of it. I'd like to observe you two at a closer range."

"Or…" he calculated as she backtracked to the office door, "deep down, you're a kind old soul who doesn't like the idea of anyone on their own for the holidays."

"'Tis the season," Olivia said with a wink before disappearing into the hallway.

William studied the desktop. He pondered the urgency behind the continued knell between his eyes. His mother was right. All this would be here tomorrow morning. It'd be good to get to the business of things with more clarity.

He pushed back from the desk as footsteps announced the arrival of someone else. "All finished out front?"

He expected Ines. Desiree answered. "It seems so. Olivia dismissed the others. Godfrey's taking out the trash, and Ines said she would lock the front and court-yard doors."

William wanted to pivot to her. He resisted, flipping off the power strip behind the computer. He reached for the lamp. "Good."

Her hand came to rest on his arm. "Are you all right?"

"I will be," he said, lowering his voice to the level of hers. When silence met his reply, he added, "You don't have to worry about me, Dez."

He expected her to back off as always. To demur from close contact. Instead, she gripped his sleeve. "Are you not looking at me for a reason?"

He frowned. His habit of looking people straight in the eye was coming back to bite him. She knew him well enough. Evasion had never been what she needed. He rearranged his feet, turning his toes until they pointed to hers. His raised his eyes.

She assessed the early bruising. Her lips parted. They fumbled closed before she firmed them into whispered words. "Most men wouldn't have taken a lick like that. Not without a fight."

"I'm not most men," he stated. "I thought we'd established this."

"You're not like any man," she murmured. Her hand slid down his biceps and came to rest palm to palm against his. Slowly, their fingers laced together, one by one until the link was as intimate and sound as it could be. "Any man I've ever seen."

He'd glanced down at their entwined hands, wondering if the link really existed. When she didn't let go, he shook his head, unsure how to proceed.

He knew what he wanted. He wanted to lay his slouched mouth over the firm line of hers and linger there for a while. And though she might've been standing toe to toe with him, though her dark eyes might've been softly tracing the shape of his face, he knew he could no more take what he wanted than he could wish for a snowy Christmas.

William cleared his throat, dropping his gaze to the shoulder of her gray knit sweater. He gave her hand a squeeze. "Will you let me walk you home?"

She shook her head slightly. "I've got a detail."

"Right," he said with a nod. Unable to help himself, he looked at her some more. He ran his gaze up the length of her regal neck, over the sharp point of her chin. He looked at her mouth and felt tangled up in need. Finally, he met her ink-dark eyes and did his active best not to fall in. "I'd still like to see you home. I won't feel right unless I know you're there."

She heaved a sigh in what he thought must be exasperation.

Then she stepped in farther, fitting her front to his front. She gripped his upper arms, gathering him to her. He heard her inhale before she rose to her toes.

It was no less a shock when her lips met his. The mental gears ground to a halt. For a split second, he thought he imagined it as much as the handhold. Then her hand cupped the back of his neck. She pushed up farther from her toes, anchoring herself to him, and he lost himself completely.

It was impulse. Terrifying impulse. She'd thought about the challenge of staring the man in the eye for minutes and how she hadn't looked away. She'd remembered how the intimacy hadn't hurt. In fact, after, she'd felt courageous and bold and free in ways she'd forgotten.

She grabbed the feeling again. She kissed the man.

She meant it to be quick. It didn't go beyond simple contact. He didn't press or take. He let her lead.

Desiree waited for the tension that normally came with a man's touch. A man's mouth. Proximity to a man.

She found other things. Impossible things like hope. Intimacy, again. Those tender rays of trust.

She broke away. His head came down after hers, not in possession—as if he didn't want to be snatched from the moment any more than she did. Their mouths parted as her heels touched down on the floor. She bit her lip. No excuses came. Her head was featherlight. Her heart was winging through her chest, and she couldn't speak through it.

He didn't need her to speak, she found. He didn't need her to break a lull that should've felt clumsy. Instead, William stroked the curls that had fallen in disarray over her temple.

She felt raw. She was still broken. But for the first time in a very long time, she understood that she wasn't irreparable.

"I should go," she whispered, unable to bring her voice up further.

He nodded mutely. The pad of his thumb caressed the center point of her forehead. A forehead she'd always thought too wide. She gave in to the impulse again and laid it on the center of his chest.

His arms brought her in, as she'd known they would. She closed her eyes and breathed. She could love. Maybe—just maybe—she could do something even more crazy. She could let go and accept love in return.

"Come to Christmas, Dez," he murmured against her hair. "I'd like to spend Christmas with you."

He was rocking her in some slow, infinitesimal dance. She gripped the back of his shirt. She was consciously moving forward now with him, and they were both going to need to hold on from this point.

Something shattered. In the next room? Far away? The sound of tinkling glass hitting the ground with force jolted them both to attention.

She looked around for the door. "What was that?"

He held her by the shoulders. "Everyone should've gone by now." Giving her a squeeze, he willed her to stay in place. "I'll check it out."

Someone beat him to the door. Desiree saw the man's face and the baseball bat in his hands and cried out. "William! No!"

The man gave them a grim smile before he slammed the office door. The walls rattled from the impact. William pounded on it with one hand and cranked the handle. "Shit!"

Desiree was at his back. "Can't we get through?"

"Nah," he ground from his back teeth as he tried forcing his way. "It's stuck again."

Desiree felt the creeping sensation of panic. She breathed carefully to clear her head. It was impossible. That face. That smile. "It's him," she said. "He's—"

"I saw."

William couldn't have said anything she needed to hear more. Up until now, she'd been the lone witness to every sighting of the man. A small part of her had still been under the impression that she'd imagined it—that she might be coming unhinged…

William threw his shoulder into the door.

"The phone," Desiree said, shutting down any thought for the man on the other side. *First, get us out of this room.* Then *deal with the psychopath.* "We can use the phone to call out."

He dashed across the room, knocking the receiver out of its docking station. He put it to his ear and punched the call button. He hit it again. "I think he's cut the line." He replaced the receiver in its cradle. Looking around at her, she saw the truth in his eyes.

This wasn't like the apartment. Cole and Slatter had agreed that had been reckless. This… Waiting until closing. Letting the other employees go. Cutting the phone line. *This was premeditated.* Desiree looked back at the door, swallowing oily fear. "Officer Rolls. He's out there. He'll come for us."

William was silent on that point. He went to the

door again and felt along the jamb. "There's air coming through here near the bottom. Maybe I can wedge something in. Force the door open."

"William," she said, the words wavering faintly. "Do you smell something?"

He stopped, sniffed. He looked around at her.

"Smoke." It left her on a croak. The stranger had told her, hadn't he? *Burn*. He'd told her he'd burn her world to ashes.

And William in it.

Desiree rushed the door. Cranking the knob as far as it would go, she worked to force it open on her own.

"Dez, let me get something—"

"It's got to open," she cried. Sweat popped on her temple. She felt it melting down the line of her spine.

"Don't hurt yourself. I've got this."

"Just push with me. It'll go!"

"Dez!" He shouted it, bringing her up with a hand under her shoulder.

She looked around and blinked. She wasn't hazing out. The room was starting to smoke. She closed her mouth around a whimper.

"We'll get out." His eyes were hard green. They didn't stray from hers. "Okay?"

She jerked her chin. "Help me?"

"Yeah." He nodded. "You push and I'll wedge."

She watched him pick up a broom and unscrew the brush side. He fitted the head of the broomstick into the space between the door and the jamb near the bottom. "Count of three," he said tightly.

She positioned herself at the knob, ready to throw her weight in.

"One, two, three!"

They both grunted. William tried to force the broom-stick through the opening. Desiree planted her feet against the door and pushed against the wood paneling. "Come on," he groaned when the broom handle began to crack near the center.

Desiree propped her hip next to the knob and shoved her shoulder against the jamb.

With a shriek of its own, the door flew back from the jamb. Desiree fell into the hall. William came down on top of her.

The floor was wet. She realized it was sweating. She gasped and choked when her lungs filled with black smoke. She looked sideways, toward the swinging doors into the tavern and nearly screamed.

Orange flame flickered, throwing moving shadows across the walls. She could hear the hiss and roar of it, the sound of more glass shattering...

"Come on!" William scooped her off the floor and set her on her feet. He took her arm and made a break for the garden door.

It opened for them. They nearly mowed down the person on the other side.

It was James. He took hold of Desiree, pulling her out of the smoke. "This way!" He motioned for William. "Come on!"

"Shooks." Olivia threw her arms around William once they reached the inn lawn. "What happened? What started it?"

William tried to answer and coughed on the smoke in his lungs. Olivia pounded on his back.

Desiree took a breath of clean air and coughed, too. Briar was there, draping her in a blanket and offering her a thermos. "It's water." She rubbed Desiree's shoulders as she drank. "You got out. Thank goodness."

"Kennard," William grunted. His voice was like rocks. He took a second thermos from Cole. Sirens wailed in the distance. He turned to look at the tavern then at the small crowd gathering. "It was a setup."

"Liddell?" Cole asked.

Desiree nodded when he looked to her. "I—I think so."

"Yes," William confirmed.

"Fan out," Cole said to James. "See if we can't catch him."

"Oh, Liv," Adrian said, grabbing Olivia close. "The tavern."

Desiree was still fighting for breath, but she turned to watch. That same eerie orange light was licking in the upper windows now, in the apartment. The whole building was going to go, she thought, even as the sirens closed in and flashing red strobes joined the light show. She looked to William.

He'd dropped to the first step of the gazebo. Mavis was there. She crouched down beside him as they watched the structure steadily get swallowed by the well-laid blaze. He was panting still.

Desiree watched him lower his head, his chin on his chest. Then he looked around until he found her.

She saw sorrow. A clutch of fear. Fatigue. Above it all, though, she saw relief.

I'm sorry. The entreaty blazed through her. Her eyes filled. His tavern. The legacy of so many before him. By morning, it would all be gone—because she hadn't left him and the rest of them well enough alone.

Chapter 13

"It's gone. Everything's gone. The tavern, the flower shop, the bridal boutique…" Olivia's voice was like the knell of a grim bell.

Desiree lowered her head. She didn't want to listen to the conversation from the next room, where Olivia was conversing long-distance with her husband, Gerald. William was with her. She was pretty sure their other son, Finnian, was on the line as well.

They'd brought her to the Leighton orchard. It was tucked away, just out of bounds of Fairhope's city limits, kept away from the main vein of Highway 181. The house was buried in the midst of the orchard, down a dirt lane smoothed by time and family traffic.

She and William had been checked out by paramedics at the scene. After a while, they'd given them the okay for medical release. No one had been hurt in the flame-up. Officer Rolls was the only one sent to the hospital. It seemed Liddell had hit him with a brick before torching the place.

Desiree and William were interviewed by police. Another exhaustive round of questions. After, Olivia had grabbed them both in a solid hold. "Let's go home." She'd sounded so weary Desiree hadn't argued.

The tavern and apartment weren't the only casualties of the fire. Roxie Strong's bridal boutique was now lying in the ruins of Adrian's flower shop. The inn had survived, even if much of the glass of the greenhouse in between hadn't survived the heat.

"There'll need to be an investigation," William was saying in the next room. "But the police are pretty certain it was arson."

Burn. Desiree dropped her head onto her folded arms on the countertop in front of her.

It was her fault. All her fault.

"Insurance will pay for damages," Olivia continued, "but the rebuilding process…" She sighed. "I can't think how long it'll take…"

"I'm coming home now." Desiree could only guess that was Gerald's voice on speakerphone. "I'm about to get on a flight. It'll be after dark before I'm home, but I'm coming."

"Me, too," said another voice. "It's peak travel time for the holidays and I'll have to sell my left nut for a seat, but I promise, Mum, I'll be on the redeye to Pensacola."

"Just be safe," Olivia told them. "I want my boys in one place. For a little while, at least."

"You can count on it."

"Liv?" Gerald again.

Olivia answered, "Yeah?"

"I love you."

It took Olivia a moment to answer. Her voice sounded strained. "I love you, too."

Desiree pushed up from the seat at the counter. She did her best not to make a sound as she reached for her coat. It still smelled like smoke. She shrugged it on anyway and braced herself for the predawn freeze as she pushed through the door to the back deck.

The trees did nothing to cut the chill. It was the wet kind of cold. There was only a hint of light in the east. Still, Desiree could see the cloud cover above. She shivered. Her teeth chattered. But she left the deck by way of the steps and started across the dry grass of the yard.

"Dez."

She stopped, cursing to herself. She hesitated before turning back to the house.

There was light enough to see William's face. The shadows on it, the plain fatigue. The fuzz of a beard growing a shade darker than fair. The bruising, growing darker still. He frowned after her. "What're you doing out here? You should be upstairs, resting. Mum just went up."

She didn't have a reply. She couldn't be here too long. Didn't he see that? Didn't he see that everything she touched became plagued by the decade-long streak of bad luck she had going for her?

When she stood with the distance between them, unmoving, he deflated. "Don't go anywhere."

Desiree waited, dancing a bit on cold toes. They were growing stiff even through her boots. She wished she'd thought to grab her scarf or a pair of gloves.

The door to the deck opened once more, admitting William in his plaid jacket. He turned the collar up and came down the steps to her. "Let's do this, then," he muttered.

"What?" she asked as he bypassed her for the orchard.

"It's a walk you want, I assume. The orchard goes on for a mile. I don't want you getting lost, so let's go." When she didn't move, his breath plumed thick in the night. "Dez. I'm not letting you go off alone. You know that. You don't need to be alone right now, and after last night, I don't feel so much like being alone, either. We don't have to talk. Let's just walk."

She let out a shuddering breath. Then she set off after him. He waited for her to catch up, then matched his stride to hers.

They passed under the first branches of the pecans whose stark, naked branches reached for one another against the dim sky. Desiree shivered more, burrowing deeper into her sweater.

William shrugged off his jacket. He dropped it over the line of her shoulders and raised a brow, lest she argue. She thought about doing so anyway, then gave in, slipping her arms inside the warmth of his sleeves.

The inside was lined with wool, she found. It stole the chill. Folding it across her torso, she hugged the warmth closer. Hugged him closer. The scent of him. Had the collar been drenched in it? It curled up her nostrils. She closed her eyes, trying to wring his essence over the panic.

Leaves crunched underfoot. They had to pick up their feet to keep from tripping over roots. The trees were resting for winter, yet their twisted roots writhed across the hard pack.

The frigid air should've slapped her around. She'd hoped for clarity. But the storm inside her was past the point of breaking. No amount of cold was going to bring her back at this point. She walked hard beside William, who remained silent. The storm walked with them, undiverted, even as the sky lightened and the organized rows of the orchard fell into untamed slopes and dips. She was exhausted by the stress. She couldn't bear to weigh what she'd cost William and his family anymore, but it stayed with her, too, growing heavier and heavier. By the time William slowed, she was grateful. They'd made it to a clearing. The pecans had been choked out by a stand of oaks. He stopped at a tree and touched the wooden rungs of what must've been a ladder. There was enough light to trace where it led but too little to distinguish what was beyond it.

Desiree placed her hands on her hips and nearly bent over double, trying to collect herself. The storm was at a tipping point. It'd be best if she were alone when its noise reached the point of overtaking her completely.

"There used to be a little gulley here," he said, looking around. "Finnian and I would come and throw rocks in it. This was always the best time of year. You don't have to worry about snakes or ticks. There wasn't a day in winter we weren't out here, poking sticks in the mud. Skipping flat rocks. Marking trails. Here we could just be boys. It made us feel more grounded, I guess."

Desiree straightened. She was beginning to feel the stitch in her side. She was breathing heavy. Her emotions were coming through the inhalations. She gritted her teeth to stop the weakness from bobbing to the surface.

He ran his palm across a mossy wood plank leaning against another trunk. "We had a fort. One of the big storms knocked it down over the last few years. We built it ourselves with hammer and nails. I'm shocked it lasted as long as it did…" He turned to her, as if realizing she hadn't said anything in some time. "You all right?"

She started to lift a hand, then stopped, pressing it to her ribs. She was going over the edge.

She heard his steps coming at her, across the rocks. "We hiked far at a fast clip. You should've told me to stop."

"It's not…" The words hitched. She stopped talking.

He studied her. Then he touched her, gentle as birdsong. "It's happening again. Like that night at the tavern."

She couldn't deny it.

"Talk to me," he said. "I can help."

"No," she refused. "You can't."

"I can take it," he promised. "You've lived with it. I can't begin to understand what kind of guts that takes. I'm strong. Maybe not as strong as you…but if you'd let me, I'd like to carry some of it. Or at least help whenever it gets to be too much."

She released a breath. It fell like a sob. She wondered it wasn't a scream.

"You haven't needed anyone," he went on. "I get that. You can go on, if you want, carrying it all. But I'm here. You see? There's someone here for you now." He touched her chin, just a little. "Dez. You don't need me. You are who you are because you survived. I don't want to take what you are. I'm just here for you to lean on."

"So…what?" she asked, at a loss.

"So…" He lifted his shoulder in return. "Lean."

She eyed his chest and felt her brow furrowing.

He tapped the line of his shoulder. "Right here."

She wanted that. Wanted him. She looked at him, the sincerity, and fought to breathe through the pain. She saw possibilities there. She'd begun to see dreams. Finally, something for herself that didn't involve fear and anxiety. She toed the line of temptation, wanting it all. Wanting to believe her place was here, with him.

She rocked back, stumbling away. She fought through the halting words coming up her throat. Truth. She'd give him truth and then he'd see, as much as she did, how much she didn't belong. "You…you want to know—how I know—he's dead? Eric. Or Radley. Whatever his name was."

He frowned in answer.

She elaborated quickly, purging what she'd hidden from him. What she'd tried hiding from everyone. "It wasn't his health, like people seem to think. It wasn't even some old gambling debts he'd let fall into the wrong hands…"

He shook his head. "You don't have to—"

"It was me," she expelled. She was shaking inside his jacket, under the kind beam of his gaze. "*I* killed him."

William lapsed into silence. Deathly silence. She knew it was the breaking point for them, whatever they had, and she could no longer look him in the eyes, so she backed away farther, roaming the small site. She raised her voice, managing to find it again. She carved it out of herself. "He found me again, after I bought the house by the water outside Chicago. It'd been so long, I thought he'd forgotten or gotten busted for something. I got home after dark one night and walked to get the mail. He came at me with a knife. I told him I didn't have anything for him. I didn't keep cash on me anymore, because of him. I didn't keep portable things of value. He wanted me to get in my SUV instead, to drive us both away. South, he said. He wanted us to go south. He wasn't wearing a seat belt, so at the end of the drive, I braked hard. His head hit the dash. I tried to get out. He used the knife…"

William had gone still. Desiree closed her eyes instead. "I don't remember getting out of the car, or how. I can remember being on my hands and knees in the drive. I remember bleeding, smelling blood. He was hurt. I must've done something else, maybe jabbed him with the keys or something. It didn't stop him. He was like a bear, madder for being in pain. I knew if I stayed that way, on my knees, it'd be over. Or he'd get me back in the car and…from there, I don't know. All I do know is… I'd left a shovel near the end of the drive. I'd wanted to plant something, for spring. It was the first time I'd planted something. Dared to put down roots. I saw the shovel blade in the beam from the headlights. I didn't know what I was going to do when I picked it up. My mind shut down and my gut took over…"

A dry sob shook her. Still, she kept going. He'd hear this—this nonviolent man. He'd hear what she was capable of. "I still hear the sound in the quiet. I see him—just a shell. Nothing he did in life ever terrified me more than he did lying there. Because I saw what he'd made me. Feral. Scared enough, desperate enough, to take a shovel to his head. To drive me to commit murder."

She waited for him to speak. When he didn't, she fought her gorge. "Now you know."

"That you survived?" he said quietly after the space of a moment.

"That I killed."

"For survival." He walked. Not away, she found when he was in front of her. His eyes, hemlock and fierce in the dull light of oncoming day. "Dez, you have to know it was self-defense."

She nodded, twice in a jerky fashion. "I know that."

"So would you have had it the other way, you dead or still trapped?"

She shrugged, raising her hands to her face. She was shocked to find it coated with cold tears. She licked the salt off her mouth, wiped the wet dripping from the point of her chin.

"What happened next?" he asked gingerly.

"I didn't dig a shallow hole in the woods, if that's what you mean."

Something ticced over his face. Something he quickly choked down. "I meant, what did the police have to say about it? You went to them."

"I went to them."

"And they ruled it self-defense, didn't they?"

"They investigated," she said. "I had to leave town after, start over somewhere else, but they let me off. No charges."

"You see?"

Not as plainly as he did. How could her tears feel cold on her face when they burned hot behind her eyes?

"And the fact that you went off and started over again... I don't know how you did that."

"I'm not sure I was successful," she admitted, hating the tears for working their way into her voice. Her breath hitched again, and it felt like a mountain rolling over on her chest. "I was rid of him, but he wound up staying, the way he planned. He never left me."

"Have you told anyone but the police about this before?" he asked quietly.

She shook her head, swiping at tears, staring at the wet on her fingertips, shaking her head at it, too. "They wanted me to talk to a counselor, but..."

His voice dropped into the quiet. "Jesus Christ." He stroked her hair.

She opened her mouth to tell him no and couldn't manage it. She vibrated like the string of a violin stretched taut enough to break. His feet moved closer over the rocks between them. His arm came up around her front, slow. It lay warm across her collarbone and cradled her opposing shoulder. Slow, he pulled her into him. "Come here," he whispered.

His brow came to rest against the side of her head, his face in her hair. She didn't feel him breathe. She held her breath, too. Her heart rabbited. For a moment, she didn't know if she would flee from him or cave.

Bit by bit, she leaned. Her head tipped against the wall of his shoulder, seeking refuge. His head lowered until his lips pressed against the nape of her neck.

They stayed that way, together.

A giant wave of emotion swept forth. "Why're you doing this?" she wondered. "Why don't you run? You're good. You're such a good man, William Leighton. *Why* are you still here?"

He lifted his head. She felt his hand underneath her chin, bringing it up. She resisted for a moment, not wanting him to see the devastation. She felt devastated all over again that he'd choose her still.

He scanned her features, then his fingers feathered across her cheek, wiping the mess. "You have trouble standing up against everything's that happened. You do it, but it isn't easy." That thing ticced over his face once more. She saw what it was this time—anger. "And nobody's had the cojones to stand up for you. You've forgotten what it looks like when someone does. That's what I'm doing. I'm standing here for you."

"But why?" she wanted to know. "I don't deserve you."

"You're wrong." He repeated it for good measure. "I stand for you because that's what you do for the people who matter. For the ones you love."

She stared at him, shock painting her white. She could feel it in her lips. Blinking away the little black spots floating in her vision, she realized he meant it.

He didn't blink. "I love you."

She closed her eyes once more. He was there, too, on the backs of her eyes. A gift from an otherwise cruel life.

She accepted it. It was like touching the sun. Hesitant at first, she realized that it wasn't forbidden. He'd given it freely. Then she pulled that warmth he offered inside her, tucking it away into the recesses of her soul, where it spread light into fissures. His lips touched the point of her cheekbone. Her hands rose, seeking him. She reached for his face.

She felt stubble, heat, and wanted to melt into the safe friction of both. His mouth touched her own. She didn't step back; she absorbed him as his hand came around to cradle the small of her back, edging her in closer.

The smell of ash lingered on both of them. The night's trauma felt like more than a shadow. If Liddell Kennard had had his way, they'd have burned with the tavern. They'd survived only to watch the structure fall to ruin.

Exhaustion fell away in another clutch of survival. Desiree found herself standing on her toes, gripping the front of William's shirt to confront him. If she let go, she'd step right back into ruins. She stayed fused inside the warm circle of his arms. She felt too raw for comfort, but she wasn't sure it was comfort she wanted at this point.

What she wanted was to be seen, for him to see what

was now open. He'd taken all the ugly things keeping her heart wrapped up tight. It'd come unraveled. Inside, it didn't look like the crypt she'd feared. Free from restraint, her heart was wide-open and spread out like a banquet.

He made a noise in his throat as her lips parted, allowing him to venture deeper. The kiss built until she began to understand that he was as unfiltered as she was.

She accepted him as he'd accepted her. She might not be able to say it as he had. Not yet. But this, she found, she could give.

This she needed.

She realized her hands were in his hair, tangled up in messy waves. She flattened them against his scalp, then his cheeks. "I wish I'd known you first," she murmured as he caught his breath. "I wish I'd known you at all, before all this."

Tipping his mouth to hers again, he grazed it across, a thorough brush of a kiss she felt all the way down to her toes.

She caressed his face. "I brought all this on you and your family. I know it was my coming here that caused the fire. I'm sorry."

"You had nothing to do with that. They're going to catch Liddell Kennard. He'll pay for what he's done, and it'll be over. You'll be free."

She let out a sound of disbelief.

"You belong here," he told her. "You don't believe it yet. But this is the place where you belong. James and me and the rest of us will chase every Kennard out of state until you feel safe and certain enough to put down those roots you've always wanted to again."

"Do you really think that's possible? That that could be me?"

He released a quiet laugh. "I don't think, honey. I know."

That blind faith. His unwavering devotion to the vision of her that he saw... She could almost see it, too. As he lowered his hands to grip hers between them, she watched them meld together, his pale, hers dark, her wrists lost beneath the cuffs of his oversize jacket. She held him tightly. Was this what it was like—to know she had a choice?

She hoped she could be brave enough to make it when the moment came.

She ran her thumbs over his knuckles. "You're so cold."

He offered her a rueful smile that was so William she had to smile back. "Will you come back with me now? Officer Picks won't happy when he finds out we went off without him. And I don't like the idea of Mum there without me. We could both use a little rest as well."

They could both use *a lot* of rest, she thought. She nodded.

His hand spanned the small of her back as they trudged back the way they'd come. She wedged into the place against his side, letting his arm circle her waist completely. Shields down, weapons down, she raised hers to his back in return. The woods passed by slower as day brightened under the stern brow of the cloud blanket. She didn't mind so much. It was like being alone in the world.

She was accustomed to being alone. Admittedly, she'd never much liked it. Then again, she hadn't thought she'd had a choice.

Choice. She leaned her head against his shoulder. Placing her hand on his navel, she let her eyes rest, trusting him to lead.

She'd told him everything. He'd given himself in return.

I love you.

The way he looked at her... The way he said those words...

For once, she didn't mind the solitude. Not as long as it meant being alone in the world with him.

Chapter 14

"There's a car coming up the drive," Officer Picks observed from his post at the front window of the Leighton house. "A taxi, by the look of it."

William rose from his crouch behind the curved home bar where he'd been taking stock. He knew his Christmas duties and he knew them well: keep the libations flowing and stay out of the kitchen. He set down an old bottle of what might have been bourbon at some point and moved to the kitchen door. He planted a hand on each jamb, leaned in and caught the attention of the ladies drinking Bloody Marys on either side of a brawny teak table. "Dad's here," he said.

Olivia was up like a spring. She patted her silver-tinged curls as she crossed the kitchen. "How do I look? Oh, never mind. Me first!"

William had his first chuckle in days as she shoved him

to one side of the doorway. He nodded to Desiree. Lifting a hand, he gestured her through. "Ma'am."

"You can stop being the gentleman." Her eyes dodged his as she added in an undertone, "I'm already yours."

His heart did a wet, happy roll. *Well. She said it, didn't she?* "Are you?"

She slanted another look at him from underneath her lashes. It nearly launched him through the roof.

He inhaled carefully, making sure his mother wasn't looking. Desiree might be his, but he wasn't sure she was ready for any public displays of affection. Especially not the kind he was thinking. Both Picks and Olivia were glued to the front window. Ducking his head, he landed a kiss on Desiree's mouth.

He meant it to be quick, all things considered. Then he felt the quick sigh rising from her. He felt her hand lift to the line of his jaw. He tilted his head, gentling the glide of his lips over hers, and watched her brow crease with all the pent-up emotions he'd felt, too, living in close confines.

He could hear the car pulling up and broke away with reluctance. Her hand balled into his shirtfront in response. "As if I wasn't all tied up enough inside…"

There was more in her stitched brow than ardency. "You look nervous," he noted.

"Your father…" she muttered.

"You're worried about Dad?" William asked. "Compared to Mum, he's a genuine pushover."

"Yes, but…it's who he is," she said. Olivia flung the door wide, squealing as the man came up the porch steps. Desiree took a steadying breath. "He's not just your father. He's…you know."

William studied her. It struck him. He began to smile again, warmed by his affection. "You read his book."

Her chin lowered. He watched the crown of her head bob.

He lifted his hand to frame her cheek, bringing her face up to his. He'd seen her shaken. He'd seen her pissed off. He'd seen her righteous. She'd let her guard down in the woods, so he'd even seen her soft. What he'd never seen or anticipated was Desiree the fangirl. He pecked a kiss to the tip of her sweet nose. "All the more reason to meet him face-to-face."

No sooner was William's father through the door, bearing all signs of a rushed and bedraggled traveler, than Olivia dived at him. He caught her with a grunt, dropping his heavy suitcase with a bang. He shrugged his computer case off his shoulder. William grabbed it before it could hit the floor, trying to ignore his mother's legs wrapped firmly around Gerald's waist.

Officer Picks cleared his throat. "I'm going to try to catch the driver, ask him if he saw anything off between here and the highway."

William nodded understanding. It'd been six weeks since his parents had seen each other. He could stomach their good returns; that didn't mean anybody else should be forced to watch.

They were kissing now, making agreeable noises. William glanced at Desiree and saw that her eyes were round, her lips parted. "Any minute now," he muttered.

She blinked. "Should we...*do* something?"

"Like throw things at them?" he asked. Gerald was now swaying with Olivia slumped over his torso like a heavy blanket. "I think we'd have better luck with an atom bomb."

"We could leave."

"They'll be done in a minute." He crossed his arms, shifting his feet. "Finnian used to pelt them with spitballs."

"Did it make any difference?"

"Not really," he mused.

Desiree made a thoughtful noise.

William squeezed her hand. "We'll give them another thirty seconds…"

"Before what?" she asked.

He winked. "Before we go make some hot cocoa."

Her answering smile softened the contours of her sharp-angled face. It softened him. He stuffed his hands in his pockets, because she didn't do PDA. He and Finnian had cringed through the better part of their childhoods at his parents' affection practically every time they bumped into each other. Like Desiree, he'd never been one to mark his territory over a member of the opposite sex. Suddenly, despite the proximity to the people who'd given him life, he felt emboldened to do so.

With a groan, he stepped into their collective bubble. He gauged which one would be more likely to come out of the fog fastest. His mother was likely to take a blind swing at him if he intervened, so he reached up and tapped his father on the neck. "Dad? Dad? It's William."

"Mmmph?"

"William," he said again. "Your son. Remember, thirty years ago? C-section. Squalling newborn. They took out Mum's insides, put them on a table. You fainted…"

"Bloody hell," Gerald said as he blinked his way out of the haze. "William!"

He grinned as Olivia's feet finally slid back to the floor. "Hey. You nearly drowned."

"There're worse ways of dying." Gerald clapped him firmly on the back as he embraced him. He rocked. Although they were both the same height, Gerald rocked him like a youngster with newly scraped knees. "My boy. How are you?"

William heard the concern in his father's Hertfordshire voice. There was little more comforting than the polished vowels of Gerald's vernacular. After half a life in the States, his recent decades on the Southern Gulf Coast, he still talked like an Eton fellow. "Fine."

The urge to tell Gerald everything the man didn't know pushed up his throat. The extent of the damage. How the tavern distillery and stores for the house brew had been destroyed along with everything else. Gerald had nurtured the project from infancy. Leighton Lodge had been his first real contribution to the Lewis family business. William wanted to tell him that though the fire marshal was still investigating, they knew it to be arson, and though they could identify the suspect by name, he was still at large.

He could go through that moment with Gerald—and no one else—when he'd thought he might go down with the tavern and how it hadn't been that that terrified him—it was that Desiree was trapped there with him. He wanted to tell Gerald that was when he knew he loved her…as much as his father loved his mother.

He hadn't thought such a thing was possible.

Later, he reckoned. Later, he and Gerald would find a quiet moment to share what needed to be shared. Until then… William pulled away. "There's somebody I'd like you to meet."

Gerald sparked to the third person in the room. "Desiree, is it?" He took the hand she raised to shake his and promptly bent to kiss the back of her wrist. "It's a pleasure, really. Especially as you've enchanted my eldest."

William aimed an apologetic look over his father's shoulder.

Desiree was speechless. Gerald's hand draped over the back of hers. Her eyes were crater wide. William watched, alarmed, as she blinked several times against a wet veil. Her throat moved and she said, quietly, "I'm happy to meet you, Mr. Leighton."

He beamed at her. "Call me Gerald, love. We're happy to have you for the Christmas holiday."

"I feel like I'm intruding—"

"Our dungeon is your dungeon," he said, patting her wrist. "I assure you."

"Unless you stumble into the fun dungeon by mistake," Olivia quipped.

"Mum," William said with a shake of his head.

Gerald chuckled. "Any word from Finnian?"

"He's renting a car from Atlanta," Olivia explained. "There's bad weather between Georgia and here."

"I'm sure he'll be all right," Gerald assured her. "Finnian's been through worse scrapes."

William pinched the skin between his eyes. "No worse than wandering into the hell that is Olivia and Gerald's fun dungeon."

"There is no fun dungeon," Olivia clarified. After a beat, however, she added, "Just don't go in the attic. You might find our—"

"Fa la la la laaa!" William sang off-key, plugging his ears. He opened his eyes, hoping Desiree hadn't sought the closest exit.

Her eyes were wet still, but mirth creased her features to perfection. Her mouth bowed with laughter. Unplugging his ears, he caught a drift of naughty laughter and grinned.

By God, he was lost to her. Good and lost.

"I'll be happy to have all three of my men under one roof," Olivia noted, joking aside. She kissed her husband square on the mouth before bending down to right his suitcase. "Until then—Shooks, Mama calls for another round of Bloody Marys."

"On it," he said as he handed Gerald his computer carrier.

As the older couple made their way up the stairs, speaking in low tones, William saw Desiree discreetly wipe the tears of mirth from her cheek. "All right?" he asked.

"Yes." She smiled in return. "He's wonderful."

William glanced up the stairs. "He's the best of us. They'll be up there awhile."

Desiree's mouth formed an O. "Will they?"

"It's been six weeks," he noted. "A lot's happened. It'll be *hours* before we see them."

"I…" She cleared her throat. "Should we leave, then? Do you think they'll want privacy?"

William snorted. "Nothing's going to bother those two. I'll drop this in his study. Then you and I can skip the Bloody Marys and get straight to cocoa." And, just for good measure, he followed the urging over the space between them and slid his mouth across hers in parting.

"Dez?"

She shot out of sleep, blinded by dark and the grip of fitful half dreams. The image of flame died on the backs of her eyelids as she groped to orient herself. "Wha—what is it?"

"Shh." Hands took hers. William's voice smoothed over the pall, as if to calm a spooked horse. "Hey. It's okay. It's me."

Desiree remembered. That she had spent another night at the Leightons'. That she was sleeping in his bed because he'd taken the couch downstairs. She glanced toward the windows. It was still night. "What time is it?"

"A little after midnight." He tugged on her hands. "I need you to get up."

"Why?"

"I'll tell you. Or, I'll show you. Just get dressed, as warmly as you can, and meet me by the front door."

He was whispering, which meant his parents were still asleep. "Are you sure nothing's the matter?" she asked.

"It's going to be great," he said, switching on the light. "Trust me."

She held up a hand to stave off the beam of the low-wattage bulb.

"Huh."

Squinting at him, she saw him standing between the door and the bed, his hands on his hips. "What?"

"This is how you look when you wake up," he assessed.

She dropped her feet to the floor and paused, fighting the urge to reach for her hair. "I guess."

He gave a faint nod. "Okay."

Desiree saw the flash of heat in his eyes before he studiously turned and left the room. She felt heat as well, not all of it in appropriate places.

Surprised at herself, she smoothed her hands over her face. *This is his parents' house, Dez. This is not to the time to revive your long-lost fantasies.*

The house was a bit chilled, she noted. The temperature must have dropped. Dress warmly, he'd said. She rooted through her bag until she found a thick pair of socks and corduroy slacks. She put on her wool-lined half boots, the ones she'd worn the night she'd failed to steal the Trans Am. She pulled a plum-colored sweater over her head then she bound her hair to her head and pulled on the trapper-style hat.

He was waiting, as promised, near the front door. As she came down the stairs, going slow so her hard-soled heels wouldn't knock against the treads, he broke into a wide grin. "What's going on, Dimples?" she murmured.

"Come here first," he said, holding up her jacket.

"We're going outside." She frowned. When he motioned for her to do so, she turned with a sigh. "It must be freezing."

"A little below that, actually," he offered, helping her into the sleeves.

"You're happy about this," she gauged, pivoting to face him again. She buttoned the toggle buttons on the front of the coat, one by one, giving him a grim look. "You're a freak."

He laughed quietly. "Gloves."

She looked down to see that her gloves were already in his hands. "You know how much I hate the cold," she said, lifting her hand. He nudged one glove on, then took the time to separate the fingers into their individual pockets. She could've done it faster, but she was still a touch lethargic. And she liked his head bent over her hands, making sure she would stay warm.

"It'll be worth it," he ventured, finished with the first. He swapped it for the other. "Here's the plan. I got a text a few minutes ago from Finnian. He's driving up any minute. I've told the new officer on duty what's happening. He's in the kitchen, sampling tomorrow's Christmas vittles. Finnian doesn't like the cold, either. So we're going to surprise him."

"With…?" Desiree asked.

In answer, he opened the front door. At first, Desiree was shocked by the solid wall of cold. Once she'd sucked in her breath, though, it rushed back out. Rain was falling, silent, thick.

That isn't rain, she realized with a start. "It's…snowing," she breathed.

He opened his mouth in excitement. "How 'bout that? Snow. On the coast. On Christmas Eve." He took her hand and pulled her onto the porch. "Come."

She pressed the folds of the hat against her cheeks. "Snow's lovely and all, but isn't there a fire inside?"

"Here's your bucket," he said, passing her a silver tin loaded with…

"Snowballs." Things began to sink in. "William. We're not doing what I think we're doing. Are we?"

He picked up a matching bucket. "Pick a base. I'll start from the bushes there. Once he launches into counterattack mode, you start throwing, too. He won't know what hit him."

"What if he starts throwing in my direction?" she asked as he crept down the porch steps.

"Careful," he said as she descended the first step. He held out a steadying hand. "They're slippery. And don't worry. I'll make sure his attention stays on me."

There was a light in his eyes. As many days as she'd known him, she'd most always seen a light in him. But this one was downright impish. "Huh."

He stopped, letting the snow dust his shoulders. It got caught in the line of his lashes. "What?" he asked.

She smiled at him a little. He'd made her do that a lot

lately, in spite of it all. Smile. She placed her hand on his brow and wiped the snowflake away with the pad of her thumb. "This is how you looked when you were a kid."

His mouth turned tender at the edges. He tilted his head as she lowered her arm to support the bucket. "Pretty sure I never thought of a girl this way when I was a kid."

How exactly was he thinking about her? she pondered. Like she'd thought of him upstairs under the gleam of need he'd aimed at her for a few shining seconds?

They heard the sluicing of tires through puddles. Desiree looked around to see headlights starting to peek through the trees.

"Take cover," William urged before he made for the shadows.

She trudged in the opposite direction. "What have I gotten myself into?" she thought out loud. She found a place behind a redbrick planter and hunkered there. The car lit up the front of the house, cutting a wide swath through the darkness, the brakes squeaking slightly as it came to rest. The engine ran for a minute more before its rumbling ceased. The headlights went out at the sound of the driver's door. A curse blew through the night. Something about "a yeti's bollocks."

She heard the first of William's snowballs hit. Or, rather, she heard Finnian's surprised grunt. The second and third came shortly thereafter, one wet splat after another. "What the—" The rest of the sentence was muffled, probably because the guy got pegged in the face. "*William!*" came the rallying cry. "This means war!"

"Now!" Desiree heard William call from across the yard.

She fit the first snowball into her glove and stood up

from behind the planter. She aimed for the figure hiding behind the passenger's side of the sedan, her side. It hit him in the back of the neck. He sprawled across the snow, surprised.

She ducked when he squinted in her direction. "What is this? Two against one? No fair!"

A fat snowball broke apart on the front of the planter, spraying her with ice. "William!" she shouted.

"A girl," she heard Finnian say. "You brought a *woman* home, brother? For Christmas? I'll be damned." He grunted as he got pegged again in succession from William's side. Desiree heard his voice again, closer. "I bet I find her before you do."

"Oh no," Desiree muttered. She backed away from the planter and the bucket, grabbing a snowball for good measure. She slunk farther into the shadows.

As she neared the line of the house, a beam of white light spilled across her, lighting up the snow-crusted yard. She froze, caught in the act of escape. Finnian, puffing clouds of crisp air, came up a few feet short. His cheeks were frosted red. His hair was wet, and he was panting. The light struck him full in the face. He narrowed his eyes, trying to see her under the stream of the motion light. Shielding his eyes with his hand, he grinned. "Hello, poppet."

She saw the dimples. Heard the drawl. It wasn't as deep, but the eyes…they were the same. The brow. The length of his face, his chin. The lean figure. Her jaw dropped. "You're *twins*?"

Before Finnian could answer for himself, William came out of nowhere, plowing into him. They both crumpled to the snow. "Go, Dez!" William urged as they wrestled on the wet ground.

She took off, teeth taut together. Her pulse was in her ears. Her face was frozen, and the snow had soaked through her gloves and the knees of her slacks. As she rounded the house, she felt the keen sense of joy chasing her. She ran a bit faster as it caught her up and she giggled with exhilaration.

She'd forgotten what it was like to play.

Still…*twins*? How had nobody told her? Or *had* they told her and she'd just forgotten?

"Everything okay?"

Another light hit her in the face.

"Sorry," Officer Caten said, lowering the beam. "I saw someone running. You all right out here?"

"Yes," she found herself saying. "We were just…"

He nodded away the rest when she couldn't find an excuse for the silly grin only just fading. "Good." He shuffled his feet on the planks of the back porch. "Thought you'd like to know, just a while ago I heard from Rolls's wife. They've let him go home."

"He's all right?" Desiree asked, voice lifting.

"He's going to be fine," Caten confirmed. "He even asked after you, said he'd be shadowing you again soon, if necessary."

"Thank you." She fumbled over her own staggering relief. "Thank you," she said again.

He nodded. "You better scoot. I hear one of 'em coming round the house."

Desiree heard footsteps and took off running in the other direction. She stepped high to keep from tripping in the snow. Still, her half boots sank all the way in, and snow crept into her socks. Willing herself to get to the front door first, she rounded the last corner of the house—

—and collided with someone else. Her speed carried her over his front until they were lying in the snow with her planted on top.

"Jesus," he wheezed. "You know how to knock the wind out of someone."

"William?" She peered at him to be sure.

"Yeah?"

She smacked his chest. "Why didn't you tell me about you and Finnian?"

"What about us?"

"That you're identical? Literally identical!"

"I thought everybody knew."

She drew her hand back to whack him again. He laughed. "Okay, okay! Yes, he's my identical twin brother, only he likes bad country music, deep-sea diving, bottlenose dolphins and men. The last in tights. Like, tight tights."

"I get it," she said. "You're the same but different."

"Very different."

His hair was askew. He still had that twinkle in his eye. He looked like Christmas, she realized. The thought was odd, but it held.

The twinkly warmth and his smile tapered off, slowly. His voice strummed from low, really low. She felt it vibrate up his chest as he said, "You're still on top of me."

"I know," she said back. Then she dropped her mouth to blanket his.

It was a wet kiss. His mouth was cold. Only his breath was warm. She felt hers wash against it as his tongue encountered hers. She was kissing William in the snow. The need she'd seen in him wound tight inside her and moved to her extremities.

She might not need a fire to keep her warm. He'd just about do it for her.

His hands cupped each side of her waist. Her navel snug against his, she planted her knees in the ground, sliding a bit up the long length of his torso.

He made a sexy noise in his throat. She wanted to lower her mouth to the line of it but confronted his scarf and frustration instead. There was no limit to the surprises of this day. "You're trying to make me forget."

"What?"

"That somebody tried to get the both of us killed."

He tugged her hat down over her head before using the low face flaps to bring her mouth back to his for a soft repeat. "It's clearly not working."

"It's working," she murmured. She tugged at the knot of his scarf and growled. "Were you a Boy Scout or something?"

"Or something."

"If I could get to you..."

He waited, eyes shining as they pinged back and forth between hers. His breath plumed between them, warm in the frosty air.

She smiled at him. She doubted there was a more patient person in the known universe. She could feel his body tightening. She could see his pupils widening. "I'm not sure I should say," she settled for finally.

His head dropped back to the snow. He closed his eyes. "Maybe not. I'm about to come unglued as it is."

Maybe she'd like to see that.

Maybe? Hell, she'd fight her way to the front of that ticket line.

She *definitely* shouldn't say that. Certain her pupils were dilated, too, she perused his features. Long bones, more narrow than wide. Strong chin, wide mouth, Roman nose. There was a hairline scar near his ear, she saw for the first time. His stubble glistened in the slant of the porch light. He'd forgotten to shave again.

She lowered her mouth to his jaw, hesitated only a moment before she placed her kiss there on that white mark so old it had nearly faded away altogether.

His groan deepened into his chest. "Dez."

"Don't." She shook her head, nuzzling the ridge of her nose against the place beneath his ear where the smell of him was greatest. She shivered, deep in her bones, because heat sparked there now.

Whatever he had to say, she'd melt. Whatever he asked, her answer would be yes.

For William, it'd all be *yes*.

"That's a first. You caught her before me."

Desiree jolted. William's hands held her hips steady. Together, they both glanced around to see the figure coming out of the dark.

"What the hell happened to you?" William asked Finnian.

"Oh, this?" Finnian reached up to his brow where a large cut was weeping blood. "There were rocks in those balls you threw at my face."

William hissed. "I'm sorry."

"Sorry you aimed at my face?" Finnian said, dabbing the mess. He managed to look casually perturbed.

"No," William replied. "About the rocks."

"Once Mum sees this, she'll rethink all that misplaced affection she feels for her eldest. Some of it might trickle down to lowly ol' me." He eyed Desiree. Their sprawled forms together. He raised a brow. "This would make her right proud. No, no." He waved a hand when Desiree started to get up. "The hunted becomes the huntress. Very modern of you, Miss…"

Not this again, Desiree thought as she reached down to extract William from the snow. "My name is Desiree, and you're Finnian."

"Ah, good. Reputation proceeds me." His smile. It tipped farther up in one corner than William's, giving his face more of a roguish bent. Despite the gash on his temple, his eyes held a naughty light as they scanned her from head to toe in a way that made Desiree question whether William had told the truth about the men in tights. "You haven't fallen in love with this simpleton, have you? Once his noble intentions wear in, he's a dead bore."

William took turns wiping the snow off himself and Desiree as she did the same for him. "Let me go ahead and apologize for him in advance," he muttered to her. "Baby brother thinks he's the life of the party."

"A knight's only as good as his discarded morals."

Desiree pointed at his head. "You'll need to get that clean."

"Are you a nurse?" Finnian anticipated as he fell into step with them. "Please tell me she's a nurse," he begged his brother.

"She won't be yours," William informed him. Still, his arm fell around Finnian's shoulders. "Mum'll be glad you're home. She worried."

"Worry's a mother's plague not even ours could duck. The slippery minx. How is she, in spite of it all?"

"She needs a decent laugh."

"What're prodigal sons for?" Finnian patted his brother's back as they climbed the steps to the front door. "Did I mention it's bloody good to be home?"

William laughed at Finnian's raffish appearance. He ruffled his overgrown hair and pushed him into the warm house. "Go on before you bleed to death." Then he held out a hand for Desiree. "Shall we?"

There were snowflakes caught in his stubble. She sighed at him. "Yes."

Chapter 15

Desiree changed into a fresh set of pajamas. They were the black thermal set she only reached for on cold, cold nights. She stuffed her feet into a pair of woolly socks and hoped her toes would return to room temperature by morning.

Sitting on the edge of the unmade bed, she ran her hands over her head. When she felt how unruly her hair was, she reached for the scarf on the bedside table to pile it up out of the way.

The latch on the door clicked. Her hands lowered as William moved through the slight parting of the door.

She noticed first that his nose was red and that he sniffled a little. "Are you all right?"

"What?" He stopped. "Oh. Fine. Are you okay?"

She nodded silently. She wasn't able to articulate what she felt as she watched him go to the dresser against the far wall in his wet, rumpled clothes. "William."

"Huh?" His back to her, he quickly gathered the front of his shirt and pulled the length of it over his head.

His back was slender, his spine long. His skin was smooth. She dug her toes into the rug and told herself to look away. She didn't. "Your family…" When he groaned at the implications behind that statement, she smiled. "I like them."

He glanced over his shoulder, shooting a grin at her before turning back to riffle through the top drawer for a fresh shirt. "The feeling's mutual."

Gathering her thoughts, she shifted her focus to his feet. They were bare. He'd need to cover them. "At first, I felt like an impostor. Here. At the inn. Then… I don't know. I guess it was the tavern. It made me feel more at ease with myself. I felt the same way in the apartment. But only after you told me it was mine…"

He'd turned to her again. "I'm sorry you couldn't stay longer. It suited you."

"Finish getting dressed," she advised. "You need to get warm."

He went back to poking through his dresser. He found a pair of pajama pants that looked the right size and shut the drawer. Then he walked in the direction of the bathroom.

"I don't mind if you change here," she told him.

He paused a few steps short of the bathroom, surprised. "You're sure?"

"It's your room," she said with a shrug. "We're both grown-ups." When he didn't move to change, she turned and faced the other direction. "Here. Is this better?"

He let out a half laugh. She heard the way it quavered. Was he really still that cold? Thankfully, she heard some rustling as he undressed the rest of the way. She smiled a little to herself. "You do realize the male body is no mystery to me."

The laugh strengthened, digging deep in a quiet way as not to alert the parentals across the hall. The bed dipped on the other side, and she knew he'd sat to put on his socks. "Maybe I'm modest."

She remembered how he had blushed in front of her eyes once. She wondered if he were blushing now, if the blush spread lower than his face.

His weight lifted from the bed, she felt. He walked around it where she could see him. "May I?" he asked, gesturing to the space next to her.

She nodded, pressing her lips together when he lowered to the spot. The sweater was in his hands. She waited as he fit his arms through the sleeves. They were muscled, just enough, and dusted with more fair hair. He tugged it over his head and pulled it over his chest. He had a nice chest, flat with a hint of abs below.

Her navel flared enough to make her toes curl again. She licked her lips, needing to finish what she'd started. "It was you." She took a deep breath and met his gaze. She was nervous and jittery. It took her a second to realize that for once it was in a good way. "The tavern. The apartment. They had you in common. Nothing else. You put me at ease, even when I knew I was better off with my guard up. You made me remember what it was—to ask myself what I want."

"Did you get an answer?" he wondered.

She did a turn about his handsome, noble features. Her eyes burned with something at the back of them. Surprised, she closed her eyes and looked away.

He took her hand. After a moment, he whispered, "You used to pull away when I did this. Or jump like the damned. Not anymore." He slid the palm of his other hand over the back of hers.

She shuddered. Again, not from cold. Though his fingers were chilled. The skin of his wrist was pebbled with gooseflesh. He'd lain in the snow, she recalled. "You're still cold," she told him. "Are you sure you're all right?"

He didn't answer right away. She looked to him. "William?"

"I'm fine," he said, still looking at the way their hands fit together.

She wasn't convinced. Her hand left his, only to lift to the shoulder of his sweater. She tugged, drawing him into her. "Here."

"Mmm," he hummed as her arms wrapped around him and they embraced front to front. Then tighter as he wrapped his arms around her. They stayed knit together.

"Warmer?" she asked after some time.

"Don't move," he murmured against the skin of her neck.

She didn't. "William."

"Yeah?"

She thought over her words. She nodded, certain. "You're not going."

"Where?"

"Back downstairs."

His grip loosened a bit, enough for him to lift his head. He scanned her, his lips parting. "I'm not?"

She started to shake her head. Then stopped. "Unless…unless you want to go."

"No," he said quickly. "No. It's just…" He took a breath. "If anything happens, I… I'm not planning on anything happening, but…if it *does* happen…"

"You're adorable," she blurted when he remained flustered.

He dropped his head. "I'm sorry. What I'm trying to say is… I want you to be sure."

Desiree swallowed. He was serious. "I haven't been this sure about anything in a long time. I haven't wanted anything this much, for myself, in longer."

"No regrets?" he asked.

"No regrets," she echoed. She watched him and the emotions he was trying to hide. "William, please. Kiss me."

He nodded swiftly, eyes like hooks. She felt them, deep. He tipped his open mouth to hers.

"Come here," he said in a guttural voice.

She gasped when he tugged her into his lap. She turned her knee, parting her legs over his lap. He gave her the high ground. She threaded her fingers through his hair, kissing him as thoroughly as he kissed her. His fingers dug into the skin of her waist where her shirt parted from the waistband of her pants.

As her chest buffered against his in the closeness, she felt his arousal beneath her. Her thighs bloomed with sensation. It forked through her so swiftly, she might've panted.

Thank God! She'd been terrified to go down this route. She'd failed here with others, with the few men she'd chosen as an adult. She'd never felt open enough. Safe enough. This was a safe place. Here, with William, there was no safer place on Earth for her to be who she was. What she was. To want. To need. To accept.

The danger was out there, somewhere. She was still afraid of it. But he was right. She couldn't take cues from everything but her heart. Not when it was this loud.

Oh, his hands. The glide of them. The sureness that spoke of where his needs were at—right in step with hers and climbing. They teased, smoothing the exposed skin at the small of her back. They were firm. They knew where they wanted to go. But they were tender. Through them, she knew precisely what he wanted from her. And yet, he held back, as if he were afraid of spooking her all over again.

Chivalrous to the end.

Not tonight, she thought. She placed her hands on the wide plane of his shoulders, taking her lips from his. He made a sound of protest. It halted when she took the hem of her thermal shirt, pulled it up and away.

He kept his eyes on hers, but she felt his body tighten like a drum. When she raised an expectant brow, one of his dimples showed. He nodded, straightening to pull the sweater over his head.

He was so lean, she felt pear-shaped by comparison. There was hair on his chest, darker than the rest on his body. It triangled across his pecs and crept in a tight line to his waistband. There was gooseflesh there, too, she discovered, over every inch of him.

His palm cruised the length of her spine, bringing her back to him. Skin to skin, he brought the smoldering wave of the kiss back, cupping the nape of her neck. Deep. Sweet. Molten and slow. Like an old B. B. King song.

His teeth nipped lightly in the center of her lower lip. The need turned into a fire tornado inside her, and she fought for breath.

"Sorry." He shook his head slightly. "Sorry."

There was a stir beneath the heat. Escalating it. Fitting the framework of his face between her hands, she fished his lip into her mouth. She suckled, tilting her head until his arms hardened around her.

He went down on one elbow. A chuckle warmed his mouth.

She sought it, sought the warmth. "Don't turn the tables and get shy on me," she told him.

"I'm just trying to keep from spontaneously combusting." He stiffened. "Oh."

The syllable drew her back. "What?"

He pressed his lips inward. Then he held up a finger. "Wait here?"

"You're serious," she muttered.

"I'll come back," he swore. "You just..." He lifted her, positioning her so her back was to the pillows at the head of the bed. "Right there. Wait for me. Okay?"

"Not really," she answered. Still, she sank into sheets that had gone chilly.

William scaled to the bed's edge and over, lithe moves that told her all she needed to know about how loath he was to leave.

"What're you looking for?" she wondered out loud.

He scooped up the pants he'd discarded on the floor, digging through the pockets. He made a noise when he found it.

"Oh," she said as he held up the condom. "That may be useful."

"I believe so. Remind me to thank Finnian later."

She frowned. "What about Finnian?"

"Nothing," he said quickly. He tore the packet neatly along the top. His feet faltered. "Christ," he started.

She fought the urge to cover herself. His eyes were round. "What is it?"

"Look at you."

He breathed it like a prayer. She licked her lips again. "Get in the bed, Dimples."

"Uh-huh," he returned with a tight nod, already untying the drawstring of his pajama pants.

She laid her head back against the pillows, watching him undress. His thighs were long from hip to knee. His calves were muscled. She found where the hair on his navel rivered down to. As he went to a knee on the bedspread, she lifted her foot.

He took the hint, tugging at the cuff of her pants. One side loosened, then the other, and he pulled off the rest of her thermals.

He fit her like a blanket. She accepted his weight as her proportions melded to his. His legs were longer by several inches. He might've been slimmer in some places. He was hard where she was soft, square where she was curved, pale where she was dark. Still, they fit. An unsung jigsaw.

"Is this okay?" His eyes were knit shut, his temple resting against hers.

She trailed the rounded edge of her nails across his ribs, tracing them as she'd once traced steel-core strings. She wondered if he'd sing just as brightly as her fiddle. "What do you think?" She smiled when he drew his head back to gauge her.

He smiled back, softly. He touched a kiss to the corner of her mouth. He shifted over her, his knees sinking into the mattress. The packet was still in his hand. He narrowed his eyes, tipping it toward the light.

"Are you...reading it?" she wondered out loud.

"Just checking," he said absently. He discarded the foil and gingerly went to work making a tent for his erection.

By the time he was done, she was wet with anticipation. She felt it between her legs and sent up more thanks that these things worked still. Shivery, she flattened against the sheets as his hands came down on either side of her head. He touched her hair as he lowered his mouth to hers. "Tell me when you want me to stop," he told her, kissing her.

"I won't want you to stop," she whispered back.

He swore. His hips flattened to hers. Her legs spread. He was shivery, too, she found, holding him as his touch spanned to the point where she was wet. She bucked a bit off the bed. "Oh, God," she sighed. Her palms were raised, she realized. Drawing them around his waist, she brought her knees up, her pelvis with them.

He fit to her, using his hand to guide himself. She made a noise, a small one. Before he could pause, she wrapped him tighter with her arms until they were meshed together completely, as one. She dropped her head back as his breath shuddered across her face.

"Dez."

"I'm good," she assured him.

His lips cruised the top side of her collarbone. The music of his voice transferred to the bone, driving his vibrations deeper. "This is it. This is how I—"

"Come unglued?" she finished, already moving. With him. Against him. The old rhythm of lovemaking was easy to pick up again but harder to define. Raking her fingers through his hair, she dragged his mouth back to hers. "I want to watch."

He rocked against the nest of her thighs, hemlock eyes going marble jade in the space of a downbeat. "Mmm."

It grew difficult to watch. Because watching William Leighton come undone set her on the same path. The sensations twined and rooted deep in her navel and thighs. They climbed up her torso, wrapping around her rapid-beating heart. It squeezed until the air came short. Not from fear, or panic—from sheer emotion. Exertion. The finest exertion. What had started out as clumsy and sweet had taken on a new life and intensity.

She came. The miracle of it budded deep. She pressed her hand against her belly as the length of his counterglide strengthened. She pressed, harder, as her toes curled into the balls of her feet and her nerves went off the grid.

At first, she thought it would flare down, slink back. Safer that way. But she turned her gaze back to his face, bringing him into focus. There was sweat on his temple and a furrow in his brow. His eyes were shut tight. He said her name once, then again.

She loved this man. Everything about him. Everything. Her demons hadn't chased him off. He'd seen what they were, and he'd stayed. He'd rooted himself beside her, stood his ground, for her.

She'd forgotten that it wasn't all bad—loving someone. Not everything about it hurt.

She let go of the past. She let go of the hurt. She let go, period.

She could fly, she found. They both could, in tandem.

After, she wasn't sure either of them came back down.

Chapter 16

William was fairly certain he was dreaming. For one, he was in the tavern. For another, "Somebody to Love" wasn't crooning from the jukebox. There was a man on-stage, karaoke mic in hand, and he could've been Freddie Mercury's twin.

Third, Desiree was there. Smiling at him. Only for him. William grew hot thinking about what that smile entailed. Later. When there wasn't a crowd of people or space between them.

William groped for his collar. He *was* hot. Absurdly hot. The bar scene wavered. He fought to bring it back into focus but sank into a confused haze.

He woke in a sweat that normally only supplemented nightmares. He sat up in bed, letting the sheet fall to his waist. The air of his childhood bedroom was a shade too cool. It clung to the perspiration on his skin, bringing on a racking chill.

"You talk British in your sleep."

He attuned himself to the warm spot on the bed next to him. Reaching over, he touched the curve of her hip. Relief flooded him. It'd been real. She was here. Nor had she left. "Do I?"

A hand grazed across his back. "It's crazy how much you sound like your dad."

"You like that, huh?" he ventured. A headache nibbled at his brow. He lowered his face into his hand to massage it.

"What's wrong?"

"Nothing," he dismissed. He fell back to the bed, slowly, so he could sprawl next to her. Turning into the shape of her, he buried his face in her hair. "Let's go back to sleep," he rumbled as he drew her against his chest.

"William."

"Hmm?"

"It's Christmas morning."

"Oh," he remembered, "that."

"Don't you like Christmas morning?"

"Honey, right now, I like living in this spot with you."

Her hands streaked over the skin of his back, nails skimming so lightly he shivered and swore as exhilarating weakness coursed through him. Her lips caressed his throat. "I like waking up in William Leighton's bed," she murmured in return. "Especially when he's here to warm it." Her middle hugged close against his as she arched her neck on the pillow to receive his kiss.

He'd never thought he was much good at kissing. Then she sighed. Broke away for a breath, then came back for more and lingered, lids closed. He tilted his head, lifting his hand to her cheek. His fingers spanned through her hair as he took them one step further into oblivion.

Oblivion felt fluid with Desiree. A boat bobbing over the depths of a generous sea.

Anchor line was all the way out. The tide was yanking him down with it. Down, down, down to the rocky bottom, where he didn't mind dwelling. Not if it meant staying in bed with her.

The bedroom door swung open without preamble. "Rise and shine, Shooks!"

"What the—" William would've fallen out of the bed had Desiree's arms not been around him. "Mum!" he shouted in horror, flicking the top sheet to cover Desiree's body.

Olivia, already dressed in her Christmas morning staples—chunky-knit sweater, tartan skirt and boots—grinned from ear to ear. "Oh, please. Like I didn't know the pair of you were in here copulating."

William covered his face with his hand and dropped his head back to the bed. "Jesus Christ," he groaned.

"To your credit, Desiree," Olivia went on, unperturbed by his discomfort, "you're not near as loud as the first girl he smuggled into this room. Margorie Bolton made sounds like a dying turkey. Gerald woke up in the middle of the night once ready to fire up the oven for Thanksgiving."

Both William's hands cloaked his face now. "This is it," he mused. "This is what dying feels like."

"Mavis Bracken was more discreet. Either the pair of you were better at hiding things or she didn't find you near as impressive."

Any minute now, William would shrivel into a mortified husk.

"You think a mama doesn't know?" Olivia asked, sounding more smug than admonishing. "I'd have made every one of 'em breakfast if you'd have had the balls to bring them downstairs instead of sneaking them out Finnian's window."

William grabbed for the sheet. "Let me in," he said to Desiree.

She made a noise under the covers. A sob? "Dez," he said, alarmed. Looking to the door in accusation— "What've you *done*, woman?"

"She's laughing at you, you fool," Olivia said. "Now the both of ya make yourselves decent enough for a full Scottish breakfast."

Olivia left, and William tossed back the covers. "Dez?" he said again. She was curled in on herself, face hidden. He touched her shoulder gingerly. "Hey…"

She snorted. Then she broke—and not in the way he'd feared. A cackle bolted into the air as she flopped on her back. "*Dying turkey!*" she squealed then rolled the other way, convulsing with laughter.

William pursed his lips. He got caught up, however— in the tidal wave of her mirth. Amid the charm of her naughty-pirate chortle. He slunk against the pillow, arms over his head, grinning in spite of himself. "Go on, laugh it up," he invited.

She obliged him, choking on amusement until she was nearly blue in the face. She turned back to him, eyes tearing, muscles slack. "That felt good." Propping herself on her elbows, she scooted up to his mouth. "I haven't laughed like that in…"

"It looks good on you." He grabbed her chin and brought her lips to his. "Tastes good on you, too."

They kissed until they were both breathless. Finally, she asked, "If we don't come down, will she come back for us?"

"It's likely," he muttered, regretful. He tuned his ear toward the Jack-and-Jill bathroom that connected his room with Finnian's. "Doesn't sound like Finn's grabbed the shower. You wanna…"

She was already bouncing out of bed, a ball of energy he couldn't tear his eyes off. She stopped, however, at the door. "Will we really have to thank him? Finnian?"

William righted himself slowly, throwing his feet over the edge of the bed. Any bouncing and he was sure his head would loll right off. He worked his neck, turning his head and stretching it. "Yeah, probably."

Her eyes narrowed. "You'll have to explain that one to me someday."

Someday, he thought as she moved out of sight. His smile stretched broadly across his face. If he wasn't mistaken, that was a promise for tomorrow.

Desiree washed as quickly as she could, knowing the brothers shared the bathroom. She did her best by her hair, choosing to pull it up when it didn't behave itself.

Her body was electrified. Her mind was buzzing. She grinned as she went about her minimal makeup routine. Her reflection grinned back, shining and regal.

She hadn't had a Christmas in so long, she'd thought it wouldn't mean anything. When she emerged into William's bedroom and discovered he was no longer in bed, she went to it and placed her hand on the sheets.

She could still smell him. Herself. Them, together.

With a pang, she realized she couldn't recall any feelings of Christmas with Mercedes. There were memories, so far away in time they'd faded not in color or spirit but sensation.

Her Christmas with William thus far had blazed with

delighted fervency. She'd remember every bit of it. He hadn't made her forget; he'd made her remember what she was—a woman alive. A woman enflamed.

She'd never forget this night with him. Their first. Ever.

She dressed in the best outfit she had to hand—the same she'd worn to dinner at the Brackens'. As she moved her scarf around, something slipped out of its fold and fell at her feet.

The envelope from James.

Desiree knelt on the floor, heart knocking. She lifted it, reading the curvy lettering. *Mr. James Bracken.*

She flipped it over. She tore the seal carefully. It had gone soft with time.

She'd forgotten her mother's stationery. Watercolor peonies encircling lined paper. As she unfolded the sheets and confronted Mercedes's words head-on, her hands shook. Sitting on the bare floor, Desiree folded her legs in front of her and bent over the pages.

She started slow. Her mother's voice rang through her head. As Mercedes rolled out her confessions, Desiree read faster and faster. The signature at the end hit her true.

Yours forever,
Mercy

Desiree exhaled sharply. She pressed her hand to her stomach. A sob moved against the inside of her, and she held it in by sheer will. She swiped at her face, smearing wet tracks.

Mom. The call bubbled in her mind, breaking on grief's surface. *Mom, why didn't you tell me?*

It wasn't anger she felt, or blame. Her mother had loved a man. Mercedes had loved James Bracken, as much as Desiree thought she might love William Leighton. And she'd let him go.

Desiree shook her head as she wiped her face again. She riffled through the pages, scanning the words again. Her mother might've come to peace with a life of disappointment. She might not have had another choice.

But her daughter might.

Screw Eric Kennard, or Radley Kennard. Whoever that bastard had been. Screw Liddell and Osias and all the rest of their family. She had a chance here. If she could let go of her fear…she'd have the choice her mother hadn't.

Desiree folded the letter and placed it back in the envelope. She put it on top of her overnight bag. After breakfast, she would call James and arrange a meeting.

It was Christmas. No more secrets. No more unspoken things.

Desiree finished dressing and mopping up her face. She made sure it didn't look as if she'd been weeping before she took the stairs down to the first floor, following the smells of cooked sausage and spices.

She stopped on the last step, wondering for a brief moment if she'd wandered into an alternate universe.

"Happy Christmas," Gerald greeted as he walked to her with a steaming mug. He wore a Santa hat, a wide smile remarkably like his son's…and a kilt. "Eggnog?"

Her mouth was wide-open, she realized. She took the ceramic, trying not to stare below his waist. "Erm, yes. Thank you."

"This way," he said. There was a twinkle in his eye,

if she wasn't mistaken. "We're in the den. Did you sleep well?"

Desiree followed where he led. "Yes. I…" She trailed off as they entered. Olivia and her sons were gathered around the tree, having a heated debate over the gifts that skirted it. Desiree couldn't help but gawk. While Olivia wore pointy elf ears, the twins were wearing light-up Santa hats and kilts to match Gerald's. "Oh," she said in surprise.

"Is something wrong, love?" Gerald asked.

She shook her head quickly. "No. It's…" She lifted her hands in indication. "Kilts."

Gerald chuckled. "Christmas tradition, on my mother's side. She was half-Scots. And speaking of tradition…" He handed her a red headband with felt antlers. "This one's more Liv."

"Yeah," she weighed, placing them on her head without further question. "I feel that."

Gerald squeezed her shoulder. "Manners, everyone," he called to the others. "Manners!"

"She's peeking!" Finnian complained.

"You're just as bad," Olivia chided him back.

"They're fighting," William said, holding each back by the shoulders. He saw that Desiree had joined them and raised his voice. "All right! All right! She's here, so the both of you, sit!"

"Gerald, light the drinking lantern," Olivia commanded as she and Finnian moved to the couch in acquiescence.

"Already lit," Gerald informed her. He produced his own eggnog mug.

Desiree glanced around. The others were holding mugs, too, and watching her with interest.

Gerald cleared his throat. "It's customary for the guest to drink first."

Desiree nodded. She narrowed her eyes at William, whose shoulders were raised in a half shrug. Lifting the cup to her mouth, she tilted it. She coughed. "What the hell is that?" she asked, holding the mug away from her as the sour taste slid down her throat.

"Lewis eggnog," Finnian informed her. "It's as old as the margarita mix."

"Only we can't serve it at the tavern," Olivia explained. "It's—"

"Deadly," William said. He walked to Desiree. "I wanted to warn you, but they told me not to."

"It was a test," Olivia said cheerily. "You passed!"

"Great." Desiree said, blinking. As if that would clear the raucous taste. She thrust the mug into William's keeping. "Take it away?"

"Yep." He took the mug and, grimacing, downed the remains. "Ah. Now it's a bloomin' holiday."

Finnian tossed his eggnog back with little effect. "*Nollaig chridheil agus bliadhna mhath ur.*" He winked Desiree's way. "That's Gaelic, poppet."

"For 'A merry Christmas,'" Olivia translated, raising her empty cup.

"'And a happy new year,'" Gerald chimed. He set the empty mugs aside as William led Desiree to the couch. "The guest also gets the first gift."

"Gift?" Desiree froze. "Oh, I didn't expect any—"

"It's from all of us," Olivia intervened, passing her a long, cylindrical package wrapped in green, trimmed with scarlet ribbon.

Desiree wondered what to do with it. She looked askance at William. He gave her a nod. She licked her lips, then started ripping. There was a box underneath the paper. She found the opening on one end and drew out the long metal item inside. "It's a bat," she said, a bit puzzled.

"Is that Glinda?" Finnian asked from the opposing couch, where both his arms spanned the back cushions.

William groaned, hunching over his knees. "Mum…"

"What?" Olivia asked. "Every lady's got to have the protection she needs."

"Glinda's been in our family for years," Finnian told Desiree.

"Longer than the pair of you," Gerald said with a fond smile. He turned it on his wife. "She's practically part of the family."

"Would you like me to take her away?" William asked Desiree.

"She's fine," Desiree said. She gathered the softball bat to her chest, snagging Olivia's eye. William didn't want her to think about the threats outside these walls, but that didn't make Olivia's gesture any less thoughtful. It was an unspoken gesture of support from the Fairhope woman Desiree had found it hardest to bond with. "Thank you. You barely know me…" She sought William. "Well, most of you. It's not every day you meet people who'd take someone in. Especially for the holidays. You've made me feel…"

Gerald dipped his head. "Every bit as much a part of the family as Glinda, I hope?"

Desiree nodded briefly, then buttoned her lips, because her emotions were bobbing on the surface again.

William leaned into her. His arm went around her back, and he rubbed her opposite arm.

Gerald lifted a package from underneath the tree. "This one has your name on it as well."

This one had been wrapped with a bit more care. The bow was tartan, like the men's kilts. A bit numb, she opened the package with care. "It's a book," she said, unable to curb a smile.

"First edition," Gerald told her. "I'm told you enjoyed the latest Rex Flynn novel. This was the first book I wrote for our intrepid time traveler."

Desiree flipped to the title page. It fell flat with the smell of libraries and bookshops, signed with: To Desiree, whose journey has brought her just as far as Rex. May you find peace for the rest of your days.

She cleared her throat, bringing the binding together with care. She hugged the book to her middle, trying to find the right thing to say. They'd touched her. Between Olivia's bat, Gerald's book, William's generous loving, Finnian's ridiculous charm and the welcome they'd collectively given her…she was beyond touched. "This is the best Christmas I've had…probably ever. Thank you, again." Her eyes rose across the coffee table to Finnian.

He lifted his hands, rueful in his relaxed pose. "I didn't get you anything. My brother's an arse and didn't tell me you'd be coming." He smirked, eyes twinkling slyly. "I suppose a kiss will have to do."

"Stay over there," William snapped before Finnian could move.

"Afraid she'd like it better coming from me?" Finnian asked, brows v-ing knowingly. "Like Margorie. Less boisterous, of course."

William groaned. Desiree turned to William and said discerningly, "He's not gay."

Olivia exploded in laughter. William raised his gaze to the ceiling, feigning interest in the texture.

Finnian shrugged when Desiree sought him again. "Not the first time he's been so threatened by my mere presence he's taken up the art of storytelling."

William handily pointed out, "Technically, you did have that three-way in college."

"Oh, yes." Finnian broke into a fresh grin. "I hear they're still repainting the freshman dorm."

"And that's my boy," Olivia mused. She gave a present to her husband. "For you, Shakespeare."

It took some time for them all to clean up the mess of gift giving. Desiree's stomach was tight from laughing. As a family, the Leightons were a hot mess. She'd laughed enough for crying and wheezing. "They're crazy," she murmured to William as his parents escaped into the kitchen to put the finishing touch on Scottish breakfast.

"Yeah," he said with a nod. "It's a wonder I turned out so rational and levelheaded."

"Every Lucy needs her Desi," Finnian opined from across the room. He dropped his chin and eyed Desiree. "But Lucy's far more fun. Come on, Dez. Give us the kiss of Christmas cheer."

William reached for the back of his neck and shook his head. "You're incorrigible."

"It's on my warning label," Finnian admitted.

William took her hand. "I have to tell you something."

"Oh?" Her heart thudded. He was wearing his serious face again.

"I bought you something for Christmas, but it got burned up in the tavern." His hold on her tightened. "I'm sorry."

"Your family...what you've all done for me—it's enough, William. I can't begin to imagine how I'm going to reciprocate."

He watched Finnian leave the room, arms full of gifts. He placed his hands on her arms. "Dez. You should stay here. I don't have to be the reason. I'm fine if I'm not. But everybody needs a home, and I...*we* want this to be it for you—Fairhope. Once they catch Liddell Kennard—and they're bound to, with the warrant out for his arrest—and everything calms down, I hope you'll see as much as we do how much you seem to fit here and that you have a place here."

The temptation to say yes—to give up all her inclinations toward a nomadic life—was stronger than she'd have thought a week ago. It would be so easy, she realized, to say yes to him. To admit that she wanted to stay. So she wouldn't have to say goodbye to him. She licked her lips, trying to keep her pulse even. "I'll think about it."

He scanned her face. His softened as understanding dawned. "You will?"

She nodded. "Yes." Willingly, she went into his arms. His head nuzzled against hers, and his chest rose and fell on a relieved breath. She clutched him tight and closed her eyes as he dropped his head to her shoulder. She wanted to tell him more—how much this time with him had meant to her. She wanted to tell him what she felt. She wanted to go on with him, just like this.

He shivered from the toes up.

"Are you all right?" she asked, realizing goose bumps had risen to the skin of his arms again.

"Better now."

"William," she said, reaching up to his brow. "You're warm. Do you have a fever?"

"I'm fine," he assured her. "Let's break fast with the others, shall we?"

"You lied. You're not fine."

"I don't need to be fussed over," William said. He saw the bedcovers. After the walk up the stairs where Desiree had, embarrassingly enough, had to support him so he wouldn't keel straight over, it looked like salvation. He didn't so much get in bed as collapse on it.

He was hot, and cold. The product of a fever, his mother had resolved after cornering him with a thermometer. He'd been marched up by the two of them after only one round of bangers and mash.

Not a moment too soon, he found. He ached, everywhere. His head was on fire. He tried not to moan as an involuntary shudder wracked him. "Bloody hell," he swore fervently.

"He needs another blanket, I think," Olivia gauged even as she tugged the coverlet up over him. "Desiree, toss me that quilt."

"Don't let Finn eat the trifle," he muttered.

"Just like a man," his mother tutted as she fluffed the pillow under his head. Her scent washed over him, familiar. "Puny and petulant in a sickbed."

He frowned. "Don't know what you mean."

Her palm swept across his brow, sweeping his hair back. "You need something for the fever."

"I need Christmas trifle."

"I'll send it up."

"Trifle?" he asked hopefully.

She pecked a kiss to his damp brow. "Meds."

William turned on his side, bringing his knees up toward his chest. He ducked part of the way under the coverlet. If he could just get this shuddering to stop… maybe he'd feel half-decent enough. Enough for Christmas trifle.

A weight settled onto the bed next to him. Someone stroked his hair. "I should've seen the signs," Desiree murmured.

"Signs?" he grunted.

"Last night. You were chilled, even after you got dressed and we were…after we were together."

"I'm fine. I'll be fine. After nap." He hissed through his teeth as the aching in his bones drove deeper. "Nap'll make all things better."

"You can hardly speak." She cradled his head and brought her lips down to his.

He turned away at the last second. "No. Don't want you to get sick, too."

"I think we're past that point." She kissed his cheek anyway. "Do you want me to stay or go? Which would help?"

"Stay," he groaned. He couldn't keep his eyes open anymore. The light from the windows was staking his eyes. "You're staying." He shrank nearer and nearer to the point of fuzziness. The chills slunk away as warmth flooded the line of his spine. Her hand fit into his, and he realized that she'd curled against the line of his back. The web of sick fatigue pulled him in, and, with her there, he let it.

Chapter 17

"He's resting better now, I think," Desiree said, leaning on the island in the kitchen for support. She'd stayed in bed with William for much the day. He'd slept fitfully. "I think his fever's coming down. Maybe it's just wishful thinking…"

Olivia offered her a plate of grapes and cheese. She was dressed to go out, having thrown a fur-lined coat over her garb. "You've done well by him."

Desiree shook her head. It had been years since she'd taken care of anyone but herself. Memories of her mother's sickbed weren't far from her mind, however. "I wish I could say he'll be feeling better tomorrow."

"I think he will," Olivia said, popping one of the large black grapes into her mouth. She swapped it from one side of her mouth to the other. "We've been cooped up inside this house long enough, I'd say. If it were the flu, either me or you or both of us would be laid up in bed, same as him. And Leighton men may act like babies when they're sick, but they don't stay down for long."

Desiree hoped Olivia was right. She took a sip of water and picked at her plate.

Olivia patted her wrist. "Put something in your stomach. You'll feel better." She stuffed a thermos filled with the poisonous eggnog into a large tote. "I'm sorry to leave, but the quiet'll help him sleep longer."

Desiree eyed the kitchen table, where a cluster of gifts waited to be taken out to the trunk of the car. "Another tradition?"

Olivia nodded. "It's custom to make the rounds. We draw names, the four families. Whoever's name we draw—the Savitts, the Brackens, the Strongs—we visit on Christmas."

"It's nice," Desiree decided. She sank her teeth into one of the grapes. The juices spilled into the creases of her mouth, earthy rich. "Who'd you draw this year?"

"Brackens," Olivia said. She capped a dessert plate with a clear plastic top to protect the red velvet cake Gerald had prepped after breakfast. "I'd ask you if you'd join us…"

Desiree shook her head. "I'll stay. Someone should be with him."

"Is there a message you'd like me to take?"

Desiree found herself smiling around the remains of the grape. Subtlety was not Olivia's strong suit. Desiree had to admire the attempt. She thought of her mother's letter to James, what it had revealed. Thinking it over, she tore a cube of cheese down the middle. "You can tell James…"

Olivia stopped what she was doing. Her stare fixed on Desiree.

She licked her lips, tasting grape juice there. "Just tell him I've read it and that we should talk."

"At the first opportunity?" Olivia wondered.

Desiree felt her brow knit together. "No, I... I'm not in as much hurry as I was before. Whenever he can get away from his family. I know they've got a lot going on, and I don't want to intrude."

Olivia tipped her head. "Did you ever think they might want your intrusion? Why else would they have invited you to the Farm to begin with?"

"I don't know," Desiree said. "I'd just... I'd like to speak to him. Could you tell him for me?"

"Of course I can," Olivia said. She smiled. "So. You're staying."

Desiree downed one part of the cheese cube. She savored it, choosing not to meet Olivia's pointed gaze. Desiree saw what was behind the question. She saw the mother and shrugged, unable to answer for either of them.

Olivia weighed her with eyes wiser than one might have expected, as full as they were with mischief. She started packing things again for the Brackens. Voice down to a mutter, she said, "He's been waiting, you know. I have been, too, in a way. The day William finds the one he's been waiting for...we all knew that'd be a red-letter day."

The one. For William. Desiree swallowed cheese and forced herself not to look away from Olivia's discerning gaze.

He's been waiting...

She frowned. "If it is me, I'm not sure I was worth the wait."

"Don't sell yourself short," Olivia admonished. She jumped when something clanged to the floor. Bending, she picked up the butter knife and dropped it on the island between them. "What's that old wives tale? Drop a knife, a woman's coming?"

"A man," Gerald said, entering with a blast of cold through the door to the patio. He went to the table and gathered another load of gifts into his arms. "Drop a knife, a man's coming."

"Right," Olivia said. "If you drop a fork, it's a woman. If you drop a spoon—"

"It's me," Finnian said, entering after his father. He stomped the icy sludge off his shoes on the mat. "I'm the spoon."

"Wrong again," Gerald said, nudging by his son to get back through the door. "Drop a spoon, a wee babe's on its way."

Olivia raised her brows at Desiree as she placed the knife in the sink. "We'll be glad it's a knife. I'm too young to be a grandmother."

Desiree's mouth worked in denial. She settled simply for, "Okay."

"Speaking of the hairier sex," Olivia continued, "I just spoke to Officer Caten. He says there's a new officer who'll be joining us this evening. Officer Bell, I think was the name. I don't want you to get spooked by an unfamiliar face."

"Thank you," Desiree said. "When can we expect him?"

"Within the hour, I think," Olivia said. She slung her purse from the counter behind her to the island. It clipped Finnian in the ear. He yelped. "What do you keep in there?" he said, rubbing the side of his head. "Rocks?"

"Yes," she said, pulling the hood of the coat over her head. "Don't you remember me threatening to chuck them at you if you didn't mind yourself as a lad?"

"No," he said, face screwed up.

She winked at Desiree. "Must not have listened. Take care of Shooks. We'll be back after while."

"I will," Desiree said. When Finnian didn't follow, she asked, "You're not going with them?"

He scowled after his mother. "And ride in the car with that? Fuck no. Alas, I am meeting someone. You'll be all right with Officer Who's It? I could wait." When she only grinned at him, his hand went dramatically to his chest. "Ms. Gardet, are you simpering?"

She rolled her eyes. "You know what I think?"

"I'm *dying* to hear."

"I think you're just as noble as he is," she said and raised her eyes in the direction of William's bedroom. "You just don't want to be."

"Aren't we perceptive?" He tipped two fingers to his brow in salute.

Desiree jerked when a clatter came against the outer door. Flattening her hands against the counter, she sighed. Would it ever stop? The wariness?

Finnian went to answer it. "What'd they forget, do you reckon?"

Desiree frowned. She craned her neck toward the window over the sink. She'd thought she'd heard Gerald and Olivia's car leave already.

An icy chill skated down her spine. Before she could give it a name, Finnian yanked open the door. "Officer Bell, I presume."

"Mr. Leighton?"

"One of them, yes."

"I'm going to need you to step outside," Desiree heard the voice on other side say. "We found something we'd like you to take a look at."

"Me?" Finnian glanced back at her. There was a question in his eyes.

Desiree took a step toward him. Then another. Why didn't this feel right? *Don't go*, she thought.

Finnian reached for his hat and gloves. "Shouldn't Miss Gardet accompany us?"

"I don't think that's necessary." When Finnian eyed him, taking his time putting on his gloves, the officer added, "It shouldn't take but a minute."

Finnian sniffed. He looked to Desiree. "Sit tight," he said and winked at her before exiting through the exterior door.

Desiree felt nailed to the floor. She made herself pry her feet up and go to the window. There was the officer, shorter in stature but wide in the shoulders, trudging from the yard into the orchard with Finnian jauntily in step. She waited until they were lost to the trees. Looking down, she saw her knuckles white on the rim of the sink.

In the sink was the knife Olivia had dropped minutes ago. She wrestled off a shudder. With one last check of the yard, she made herself leave the window.

She went up the stairs. The house was so silent, it pressed heavy against the tunnels of her ears. She'd lived alone for years. Since coming to Fairhope, however, the only time she'd spent in solitude was her brief stay in the tavern apartment. Her room at the inn had been quiet, yet the promise of others sleeping close by had hung in the air. The dingy motel she'd stayed at before she'd tried

stealing the Trans Am had had paper-thin walls and in-
discreet neighbors.

Silence, that old trusty companion, had become
strange to her. Restless with it, she paused outside the
door to William's room.

Still resting, she thought when she heard no noise.
She turned the latch as silently as possible and peered in.

He slept askew across the mattress, half in and half
out of the covers—the indecisive pose of someone either unaccountably troubled or deeply uncomfortable.

He'd been the latter up until an hour ago, when he'd
turned one final time onto his stomach and sunk into
concentrated repose.

She couldn't see his ribs rising and falling. She moved
from the door to the bed. Laying her hand flat on his
back, she waited a beat.

His lungs rose against her hand, then back down. This
close, she could hear the minute sound of a snore. She
closed her eyes at the falling away of his exhale. Just
sleeping. She felt the press of his foot against her thigh.
It was off the bed. She thought about tucking it back into
the bed. Wary of waking him, she simply flicked the top
sheet over his bare heel, then adjusted it so it covered
the skin of his back. She didn't want him waking up to
another unshakable chill.

"Dez."

She stopped. *Damn it.* She'd woken him after all. "I'm
not really here," she whispered. "Go back to sleep."

He inhaled, shoulders rising as it dug deep. The exhale came on a sigh. "Don't go away."

She tried to repress a grin. He was talking in his sleep.
The British ring of the words told her so. Leaning down,

she pressed a kiss to the center of his spine. "I'm just downstairs," she murmured, unsure if he could hear.

He made a noise. "Don't leave."

She froze. Relaxing her hold on his shoulders, she frowned.

His toes moved and his spine lengthened, stretching before he slumped, limp once more. "...hurt like hell..."

Desiree touched her cheek to his back. The skin was hot and clammy under her cheek. She closed her eyes. He expected her to leave.

He'd asked her to stay. She'd demurred. Deep down, he'd taken that to mean that she wouldn't. A thousand knives made piecemeal of her heart. "I don't want to go away," she confessed. "I don't want to leave you."

He didn't reply right away. Then, more sleepily, "Don't."

She bit the inside of her lip hard. Her emotions were about to crack. They'd be seared over the iron-hot mess that was all that remained of the reservoir of her defenses, the one he'd obliterated with kindness and patience. With honest eyes, boyish grins. Dimples. He'd boiled it down like wine in a saucepan. Raw and fine.

She heard a tune in her head—a silvery thread floating from the past. Something she'd played when she was alone. For herself. The music had never been about her. She'd learned it to appease her mother, then to impress the authority figures around her. To crook a precocious finger at the man who was her tutor. To drown the sound of her stepfather's voice through the thin walls of their house after he crawled back to her mother the last time.

Only occasionally had she played for herself alone. And then, only one song.

She found herself humming it, tentatively at first then

keener. It was the song she'd wished Juilliard could have heard her play when other pieces, more complex, had been chosen for her: Sibelius's "Valse Triste."

Though thusly titled, it had never been a "sad waltz" for her. The way the notes lifted and fell then lifted, rising in pitch again and again... The notes had rung over the Florida marsh and made her feel as if she could go places. Bigger and better places. Happier places. It encapsulated hope.

Once she'd lost her future, she'd stopped playing it along with everything else. It'd been so long since she'd been afflicted by hope, she'd thought she'd forgotten the piece entirely.

Her fingers itched for the bow and fingerboard of her instrument for the first time in years. As she hummed, she found herself going through the stopping of strings, each upbow and downbow...

She hadn't been able to play for herself since Mercedes's death. But maybe, one day, she'd play for William. This man who said he loved her.

Something rushed past the window. She looked to it, expecting to see more snow, falling fast. Her heart stuttered when she realized that it was smoke, rising.

She went to the sill. It was thick, and growing thicker. She craned her neck, trying to see beyond the pane. It wasn't coming from the house. More, the driveway.

She looked to the bed. William was still passed out, belly down on the bed.

She left him there, muttering, "Finnian" as she rushed to the door. She took the stairs down to the first floor two at the time, nearly tripping on the last. She burst out of the front door, calling, "Finnian!"

The black smoke hit her full in the face, making her retreat into the house.

She paused before she could close the door completely, lifting the collar of her shirt to cloak her mouth and nose. Squinting, she saw the cause of the inferno. She moaned as the flames licked from the windows of the Trans Am's cab. The heat and smoke made her mother's name on the license plate writhe in a sickly dance.

Desiree saw a figure laid out flat in the center of the driveway. At the sight of his orange ski cap, she let out a cry. "Finnian!"

Another figure wavered through the smoke column, striding through it as if he were immune to the heat. Desiree's legs locked, and her gorge rose. The lumbering walk was too much like his brother's. His skinhead had the same shape, round at the top and nearly flat on each side.

Olivia and Gerald were gone. William was sick in bed. It was a good bet Finnian was worse off. The Leightons lived far enough out from the nearest highway. The smoke wouldn't be visible to passersby right away. Neighbors were just as remote.

She was alone with her worst nightmare.

Desiree closed the door, having the sense to lock it and the dead bolt. She tripped in the direction of the phone.

It was old-fashioned. Rotary style. Her jaw shook. She bore down on the trembling.

She thought of James first. Her phone in her bag upstairs. She couldn't remember his number.

She dialed 911 instead. "There's a fire," she told the operator, pressing her back to the wall. She watched the door. The windows. "I don't know the address. It's at the Leighton orchard. Somewhere off Highway 181, I think."

Glass shattered. He was coming inside. "Send someone," she begged the operator. She left the phone hanging by the wire as she retreated into the den. The wide glass doors leading out onto a nice brick-lined veranda drew her attention.

William. He was upstairs. Alone.

She eyed the distance to the stairs. If she could draw Liddell away from them…away from the house…

She unlatched the sliding glass door, testing it to make sure the jamb hadn't frozen in the cold. It budged enough. She braced her hand in the opening, waiting.

Liddell came around the corner. His scanning eyes seized her. He grinned. "There you are."

She shoved the door open and made a break for the tree line across from the veranda.

He was on her heels. "You ran from Rad, too. He always caught you. Didn't he, mousy?"

He was playing with her. Taunting. She kept running away from the house. Away from William. Finnian.

"Faster, mousy. I'm on your ass now."

He was getting closer. And closing the distance still. What was wrong with her legs? The snow wasn't that deep. Her boots felt like they were lined with lead.

"What's the matter? Don't you wanna watch the show? Gonna be a hot one."

She heard him chortle. Like her stepfather used to chortle when she tripped or broke something by accident.

Her eyes fell on a solid rock on the ground. She dived for it. Its cold face fit to her palm. She dug her fingers into the crusty dirt, prying it from its resting place. She whirled, pulled it back and beaned it.

It hit him in the face. His head whipped back, feet flying after it. He hit the hard pack with a thud.

She should've kept running. But she stood, breathing clouds into frigid air. It raked her throat and froze her lungs until they tweaked inside her chest. Still, she watched the blood rise against the gash on his forehead. It smeared dark against his fingers as he raised them to his face. "What the hell?" he growled.

"You're sick like him," she found herself saying. "You're *all* sick."

His eyes flashed. He was wounded. He was pissed. But he was also impressed. She saw it feed the dark light in his eyes. He lumbered slowly to his feet, wavering a bit but not enough to stumble. Taking a leering step, he came at her again, slowly. "You don't know a thing about my brother." He raised a finger at her. "You got him painted a villain. Just like Adrian Carlton."

"Adrian Bracken," Desiree corrected him, though she didn't know why.

He spat in the snow. "Adrian Kennard, more like. She lied to divorce him. He tried to give her a home, too. He tried to make something normal for that bastard boy of hers. And all he got for his trouble was a busted-up face and a prison sentence."

"And all you and the rest of his family's had for him since is excuses," Desiree said. "Your tribe's one big excuse, from what I understand."

His steps quickened enough for her to back away in retreat. "He tried to do right. He wouldn't have laid a finger on you had you stayed with him after your mother bit the big one."

"He'd have brought me here," Desiree pointed out. "He'd have brought me to you and your father. What then?"

Another sickening grin cracked across Liddell's

bloody face. "Oh, we'd have taken James Bracken's pound of flesh. Out of you, that is."

"For what?" she asked, trying again not to be sick on the slushy white canvas. "What was it all for?"

"If not for Bracken, my brother'd have been free," Liddell said. "He wouldn't have had to change his name, live one step ahead of the law... Those of us left behind never could touch the son of a bitch. Hell knows we've tried. Till we got the call from Florida from Rad about Mercedes. About *you*. James Bracken's own flesh and blood."

"Is that what you'll be taking from me now—James's pound of flesh?" Desiree asked. The trees were getting thicker. She was no longer in the orchard. She'd gone the wrong way. If not for the smoke wafting from the house, she wouldn't know which direction to keep him moving away from. Still, panic rose to her throat.

She was beginning to realize there was no way out of this. Out of his grasp. He was surer on his feet. She'd hit him in the head with a rock, and he still stalked her like a hunter through the woods.

Buying time. That's all she had left was to buy more time.

"That and more," Liddell said. He licked his cracked lips, looking her over in a way that drove a lance straight to her bones. "You see, I know about you. I know what happened when he found you outside Chicago."

Desiree's back hit a tree. She tried sidestepping it. Her feet got tangled in the aboveground roots and she staggered.

He dived. His fingertips bit into her triceps, and she shrieked. Up close, his gaze was even more terrifying. Gray, metallic. Not silver. Shrapnel. His grip tightened on her, and she bit her lip to keep from making another noise to entice him. Tasting blood, she blinked the tears from her eyes.

"I know all about you, mousy," he said. He spoke through his teeth. "I know you were the one who killed my brother."

She hissed. It was hard to think over the panic that had brought numbness to her knees. "You're mistaken—"

The backhand cracked across her face. Her head snapped sideways as pain split against her cheekbone, blinding. Squeezing her eyes closed, she waited for the next.

He didn't hit her again. Instead, he started to yank. "The police sealed the report. But I know. They tried to cover your ass. Paint you up like the victim. But really, you whacked him. With a shovel to the head. You murdered my brother in cold fucking blood. And you call me sick."

She dragged her feet as he marched her back toward the smoke. The house. *Not the house.* There weren't any sirens. No flashing lights. *Not yet!* A sob wheezed out of her. She wanted to retch. Instead, she played her last card. "P-police will be here. I c-called them. You'll need to get me away from here."

"Police will have to catch us both," he said through a mean grin. "Come on, mousy. Let's go for a ride."

He frog-marched her out of the woods, retracing their steps across the slushy ground until the house came back into view.

She saw with horror that the fire had spread to the cherry tree close to the house. She saw the chaos of flame and cinders falling on the roof of the front porch. That gable above it…how far was it from William's room?

He yanked her around hard so her attention was on the

direction he was taking her. She nearly fell over Finnian's supine form. She saw his blood in the snow and could've wept if she'd known how through the fear.

Liddell shoved her toward a battered pickup truck. "Hands against the door."

She shook her head. She didn't want to be tied. She *would not* let him tie her up.

He planted his hand on the back of her head and shoved her against the passenger door frame. "I said, 'Hands against the door!'"

"Hey, Kennard."

Liddell turned. So did Desiree. She gasped at Finnian. He was unsteady on his feet, but he was standing. "Take this, ya ruddy bastard."

A snowball broke across Liddell's nose. He hollered, hands rising to new gashes. Finnian had taken a leaf out of William's book. There were rocks inside.

"Dez, run," Finnian rasped. There was blood around his mouth, more on the collar of his jacket. He leaned against the front of the pickup, imploring. "Run, Dez. Run!"

She started to take off. The end of the driveway beckoned. She staggered forward, Finnian's plea heavy on her ears...

What the hell was she doing? Running away from the closest thing to a family she'd had in over a decade? Once Liddell cleared the ice away, he'd overtake Finnian again. The man was already sagging toward the ground. Over the men's heads, she saw the porch roof had been lit and the flames were climbing toward the gable above it.

Not this family. *Not mine.* She sucked in a great breath and charged.

She took Liddell down on a flying leap. She dug her

knee into his back until he cursed. Planting both hands on the back of his head, she mushed his face into the snow and held on as his arms flailed.

It wasn't enough. But time was all they needed.

He rolled, flinging her off him. She scurried, searching the ground. No more rocks. She shrank into the smoke, hoping he'd lose her.

He kept coming. Surprised, she sidestepped him. The heat of the car's inferno was enormous. It melted into her, searing.

She didn't hear him coming. She wasn't sure she saw him, either. But just as it had in the marsh house with Radley, something told her to *duck*.

She went onto her haunches. Liddell went clean over the top of her and he tumbled headfirst just as Radley had into the mirror.

Only this time, it was the flames.

She covered her ears to the screaming, rolling out of the way as he staggered about. His clothes were alight. His arms covered his face and head.

"Dez!"

She looked around at Finnian. He was on all fours, near the pickup. "They're coming!"

Desiree shook her head. She didn't hear the sirens. She looked to the house. The porch was groaning. *The gable.*

She came to her feet, taking several steps toward the house.

"No, Dez!" Finnian warned. "They're coming!"

Not in time. Not enough time. "William." She went around the house. She'd never be able to get through the flames to the front door.

The glass door, she remembered. Her boots scraped across the bricks of the veranda, toes catching. She kept herself upright and went sideways through the gap in the sliding door.

The smoke was in the den now. A warning to turn around. She ignored it, using her collar to cover her nose and mouth. The smoke thickened as she ran through it, wetting her eyes as she moved toward the front.

The stairs. They weren't far from the door. She could hear the fire now. Glass creaked. The windows wouldn't hold up long under the heat.

The foyer was ablaze. She held her breath. If she could just get to the banister.

Closing her eyes against the smoke, she groped for it.

Her palm, slick with sweat, found the wooden knob on top of the banister. She gripped it, dancing around it to get up the stairs as fast as possible.

She could hear the smoke alarms in the upstairs hall. She fell on the first door.

It was open already. She couldn't see through her tears.

She hit the floor on all fours. "William!" she screamed.

Was that a cough? "Dez. Over here."

"Oh, thank God," she cried, moving across the floor of his bedroom. Her hands fell over the softness of pillows. She knocked them out of the way, her hands falling across skin. "William," she said in relief, draping herself over him.

"What's happening?" His voice was small, hoarse and riddled with confusion.

"Outside." She placed her hands on either side of his waist. Straining, she could make out his profile. She passed a hand over the curls on his brow. They were pasted to his feverish skin. "There's a fire. William, you have to help me."

He cursed then coughed at the smoke. "You go. I'll wait for the responders."

"No!" she shouted. "You're all I've got! Now help me, William, so you and me can walk out of this building together!"

He grunted. At first, he didn't move at all. Then he slowly lifted himself to sitting.

She positioned herself underneath his arm and pushed up with her legs. Together, they got him to his feet. His weight was on her as much as his own legs. They took several stumbling steps toward the door.

The foyer would be even hotter now. But there was no other way. "This way," she gritted, lurching the both of them in the direction of the stairs.

"No," he argued, digging his feet in. He planted his hand on the wall to bring them up short and to keep himself from overbalancing. "We can get out the back…"

She went with him, to the door to what must be Finnian's room. There was a large picture window across from the bed.

William planted his hand against it. Sweat ran down his face. She could see it now plainly, along with the exhaustion sitting on his brow. "It's not locked. Push."

She pushed up from the sash. The pane swung out from the sill.

"Squeeze through," he bade, his hand on her arm.

"You first," she persisted. When he shook his head, she nearly growled at him. "Don't argue with me, William Leighton!"

He groaned at her. "Same time," he said.

They took turns nudging each other out the window. Neither of them were sure-footed on the deep pitch of the roof below. Ice was the enemy. It made them slip.

William fell over her, his weight coming down on her

hard. The breath went out of her. She realized, though, as she opened her eyes that he'd saved her, just barely, from going over the near edge. Turning her face to his, she saw that his lips were near blue. He was panting like a steam train, and his lips were trembling. She placed her hand on his cheek. "Stay with me, Dimples," she told him firmly. "Okay?"

He cracked a smile. It faded off into the smoke-smudged air. He closed his eyes, and his brow dropped to hers. "I believe…that's my line," he murmured.

The sound of sirens pitched over the roar of fire and alarms. She linked an arm around his waist, looking around wildly. "I don't see a safe way down."

"There used to be a ladder…"

"Not anymore. We'll have to make a jump for it."

"In this state, I'm more likely to land on my head than my feet," he admitted. Shivering, he carefully moved his weight off her. "You'll have to go. Jump, Desiree. You can tell them w-where I am. There's enough t-time for that."

Just enough, she estimated, her pulse rattling against her ears. It might make sense. It might be the faster way. The safer way. "But I don't want—"

"Go," he said. If he'd had any strength, he'd have pushed her toward the edge. "Go on."

She whimpered. Then she planted her mouth over the panting line of his. She took the taste of him with her as she leaped from the ledge and hit the ground running.

Chapter 18

The waiting room of the hospital was overcrowded. Desiree was surprised to see it packed with familiar faces.

James was the first to see her. He got up from his chair and crossed the room in a swift gait. "Dez. Thank God!"

"I'm fine," she began. Whatever else she'd meant to say fell away as he wrapped her tight against him. "I...oh."

"They wouldn't tell us anything," he said, holding her close for a second. He stepped back, bracing his hands on her shoulders. Scanning her, he frowned at the cuts and bruises. "You're all right?"

She nodded, unable to give voice to the soreness. She felt so heavy, everywhere. "The doctors were warier of smoke inhalation than anything else, again. But I'm fine. I'm fine."

She said it twice because he was still searching. He rubbed her arms up and down. "It all comes back to me and the Kennards. I'll never be able to express how sorry I am for all this…"

She held up a hand to stop him. "They weren't right. Radley. Liddell. None of them were right. I'm not sure it wasn't their nature or the way they were brought up… Something was twisted inside them both." She pressed her lips together, measuring James's face. All that was familiar in him all of a sudden. "We tried to stop them. Both of us. In our own ways. They tried hitting us back, harder, and lost."

His eyes were sad and so blue they looked watery. "You lost a great deal of your life to their games. You might've lost a good bit of your spirit. I'll do whatever it takes to help you move on."

She licked her lips, looking around at the others. Adrian smiled at her, a few paces behind her husband. Mavis and Gavin were there, in the corner. They watched her, concern and curiosity as plain on them as it was on the others—Harmony, Bea, Briar and Cole.

Desiree found herself seeking Cole more than the others. "Is he…?"

"Liddell?" Cole finished for her. He jerked a shoulder. "He's suffering, but he's alive."

"He'll wake up to a heavy guard," James assured her. "And he won't be slipping out of jail time like the last round."

She nodded. It was enough. It had to be enough. "What about the house? The Leightons'?"

"From what we understand, it's not as bad as what happened with the tavern," Adrian explained. "There's damage, but it isn't total. More than anything, Liv and Gerald are concerned with your well-being and the twins'."

"Have you heard anything about them?" She hadn't seen William since she'd watched the responders load him and Finnian into the first ambulance.

"Not much," James stated. "I'm sure they're all right."

"Tell that to Liv," Adrian muttered. "She's tearing up the hospital's bureaucratic tape as we speak. I would be, too." She looked from Desiree to James. She placed her hand on his back. "This one was half-sick worrying about you."

Desiree eyed James. She told herself not to look away. There was no way of knowing whether Mercedes's letter had survived the fire. There was no telling how long Desiree would remember the words to it, exactly, if it hadn't. She swallowed the knot in her throat. "I read it."

James blinked. "The letter?"

She nodded. "This morning." She peered at the windows. It was difficult to believe she'd read it less than twenty-four hours ago. The sun was just now starting to come up. "I don't know if the Leightons told you before they were called back to the orchard. But we're going to need to talk about some things."

He nodded, too. "Okay."

It was that simple? He was so big and strong. Not weak. And he cared. He cared about her. Nothing of what her mother had written would change that, one way or the other.

Adrian had sensed the weight of what was between them and had moved away toward Briar and Cole.

Desiree worked herself up to the truth. "She wanted you to know," she said quietly.

James listened, bending his head toward hers. She saw the truth strike him, as deeply as it had her.

"She wanted to tell you about me," Desiree contin-

ued. "But she knew you were recovering from alcohol-
ism. She knew you'd find your way. She wrote it down
plain—'You were the strongest man I ever knew.' She
wanted to make sure you found it. I guess she thought
you finding out you had a kid so soon after you left
would've sent you off course again."

His jaw moved, and his brow knit. "She should've
told me."

"Everything would've been different if she had," Desiree knew. "You'd have come back."

He nodded, his eyes unwavering. "I would have."

"You wouldn't have Adrian," she weighed. "Or your
family. Everything you've made. She knew, by the time
she wrote you. She knew what you'd made for yourself.
She said it made her rest in her decision not to tell you."

He blew out a breath and lowered his head. "Ah,
Mercy."

She forced herself to go on, reciting the rest. "She
wanted you to know she was proud of you. She wrote
that she was proud of me, too. Proud of herself for raising me into what I was."

"What you are," he amended. He smiled at her, a
crooked smile she knew.

She'd seen it in the mirror. She sighed a little. "So
you're my father."

He beamed then and put all her fears to rest. "Yes."

"I'm glad," she found. Her lips warmed, moving hesitantly to match the smile on his. "I wasn't sure I would
be. But I'm glad it's you."

"You'll need to meet Kyle when he comes."

"Yes," she said, trying to wrap her head around the
fact that James and Adrian's son, the Navy SEAL, was
her half brother.

"I meant what I said," he murmured. "You've got a place here should you decide it's right. Me and Adrian… we'd love nothing more than for you to stay."

Her hands had threaded together. She unwound them, trying to put her feelings into words.

"Sadists! Damn you! Where've you stowed them? Some dirty back hallway with rusty scalpels?"

"Liv." Gerald hastened to calm his wife. "That's not the reason."

"Why else would they not let us see our own off-spring?" Olivia seethed. Her hair was a mess. She was pacing raggedly. "Why else won't they tell us what's going on?"

"I'm sure they've got them a nice room and they're taking good care of them," Gerald assured her. He looked imploringly at the others in the waiting area, trying to steer her in the direction of the crowd.

Briar came to his rescue. "Olivia. Don't you remember when Gerald had his concussion? It was *hours* before they let you see him."

"It's bull," Olivia said. "I haven't seen them. I need to see them."

"And you will," Briar told her. She grabbed her cousin into a hug and held her in place. "You will."

Olivia seemed to deflate. She grabbed onto Briar like a lifeline. "They're all right, right? I need somebody to tell me my boys are all right." Over Briar's shoulder, Olivia eyes searched the others. They landed on Desiree. "*You!*"

Desiree braced herself as Olivia released herself from Briar. The frantic woman came at her, eyes wide and red-lined. Desiree held her breath.

Olivia grabbed her face in her hands. "What'd they

do to you? They didn't hold you hostage, did they? Did they stick you anywhere? Brainwash you into a cult?"

Desiree tried shaking her head and found she couldn't move. "Um, no?"

"Good." Olivia embraced her hard and held.

Desiree had never noticed how much smaller Olivia was. She felt the steel core that made up Olivia's resolve. She drew from it, pressing her brow to the woman's shoulder and gathering the offered warmth like the necessity it was.

"Mrs. Leighton?"

Olivia released Desiree. The doctor standing in the doorway looked sturdy and compact, yet he was no match for this mommy. "What's been done with them?" she demanded. "Let's have it!"

He cleared his throat and glanced around the room. "May I speak privately with you and your husband?"

"No." Desiree found herself chorusing with everyone else in the room.

The doctor's brows shot to his hairline.

Gerald took pity on him. "We're all family, Doctor. Go on."

"Well, then," the doctor said, beginning to look amused at least. "Your sons are both in stable condition."

"What does that mean, exactly?" Olivia milled her hand in rapid circles. "Spell it out plain. No fluff."

"Finnian has a moderate concussion," the doctor obliged. "He's conscious. There's a little amnesia surrounding the attack, but he seems to be doing well."

"Eating the Jell-O or not eating the Jell-O?" Olivia wanted to know.

The doctor smiled. "Eating the Jell-O—vigorously. Also causing mayhem among my nursing staff."

Briar nudged Olivia. "Apple. Tree."

"What can we say? He's a card."

"He was bleeding," Desiree mentioned. He touched her neck. "I worried he might've been—"

The doctor nodded away the rest, serious again. "Yes. He does have a stab wound. The police say a box cutter was most likely the culprit."

"Great Scott," Gerald uttered, blanching.

"Luckily, no internal damage was done," the doctor announced. "He should be on his feet within the next few hours, though we'd like to hold him overnight. Your other son—"

"William," Gerald murmured. He and Olivia had drawn close. Desiree wondered if they knew that both their hands were tangled together in a tight knot.

"Yes, William," the doctor said. "We've been monitoring him closely. He has a flu-like illness. I understand that started sometime this morning."

"Last night," Desiree spoke up.

"His exposure to the smoke and the cold may have aggravated the condition. His lungs are fine. His heart's fine. He's managed to get some rest and is awake again. But we would like to keep him overnight, too, as a precaution."

Olivia breathed a sigh. "Looks like we'll be camping out here."

The doctor made a noise. "Only two visitors to a room at a time. Visiting hours are posted—"

"Thank you, Doctor," Gerald said, noting the fighting gleam returning to his wife's eyes. "May the lady and I see them now?"

Not even the force that was Olivia Leighton could get past the strict visitors' policy. It was an hour later when

Desiree could make her way to the recovery ward. She looked for the room number. Administration had directed her to this hallway with its textured white walls and floor so clean it sheened under the lights.

Her stomach was in knots.

Passing by an open room, she heard a whistle. Doubling back, she peered inside.

Finnian was laid up. His head was wrapped, and there was a bandage on his neck. Still, he was propped up, and various snacks littered the bed. His grin was lazy and lopsided. "Aren't you a sight for sore eyes?"

"How are you?" she asked.

"Bloody knackered," he said. "But not done in."

"I'm happy to hear it. I hear the nurses have taken quite the liking to you."

"I'm inclined to let them keep me," he mused. He laid his head back, closed his eyes. "There's someone else, though."

"Dr. Charles?" she asked, pointing down the hall where she'd met the man.

Finnian pursed his lips. "Nice eyes but too short. He'd have to wear heels. Imagine."

Overcome with an unbidden laugh, Desiree clapped her hand to her mouth.

"Dr. Charles might've had his chance had Bronny not popped by to see me. She's got eyes, too. Goddess eyes."

"Bronny." Desiree narrowed her eyes. "Who's she?"

Finnian peered at her with one eye. "Jealous?"

She tilted her head in answer.

The lopsided grin fractured off. "A rogue can dream, eh? She doesn't like me to call her Bronny anymore. She's one Bronwyn Strong now."

"Any relation to Ines?"

"Her elder sister. Probably shouldn't be telling you this. She's my wife. Er…ex-wife, presumably."

She couldn't help it. She reached up, pulling the covers higher. His hospital johnny didn't look at all warm. She smoothed her hand over the edge of the pillow. "Ines was your sister-in-law. William never said."

"He doesn't know."

"What?" Desiree shook her head, eying the drip next to the bed. Was he still concussed? "How would your own brother not know you were married?"

Finnian caught himself. His legs shifted under the sheet. "Now I've gone and said too much. I'm usually a locked vault."

Who covered it all up so well with his charm. Desiree smoothed his shoulder. "You saved my life. It was foolish. You were hurt. He might've—"

"All's well that ends well, poppet," he told her kindly. "No thanks necessary. William would have have done the same for mine."

When he reached up, she linked his hand with hers. "Thanks *is* necessary."

"I'm not unconvinced you didn't save my life," he said. "I know you saved his. *That* was foolish."

"If he'd stayed there a moment longer…the smoke. The floor could've given way before the responders got in. They might not have been in time. I'm not sure he could've left under his own power."

"You're a bloomin' hero, Desiree Gardet, and you licked the Kennards while you were at it."

She frowned at the mention of Radley, Liddell and the rest. "We'll see."

"Future plans?"

She demurred. "I'll tell you mine if you tell me more about Bronny."

"You were looking for him just now. William." He jerked his chin, changing the subject skillfully. "He's just across the hall. Tell him to enjoy his spoils."

She found a smile and leaned down to touch a kiss to his bandaged head. "If your lady comes back, would you like me to tell her?"

"That I cut a dashing figure fighting a villain in the snow?" His head bobbed as he closed his eyes and turned his head away in repose. "Aye. She seems to think I'm a right cad, as is."

"I'll put in a good report," she assured him.

"And no one the wiser," he requested, placing his finger to his lips.

"Not one," she promised. She stared at him for a moment, his face so like his brother's. Yet different. She adored him all the same. "I'll send someone to check on you."

"The one with ribbons in her hair," came his sleepy murmur. "Mary Elizabeth. Or was it Mary Louise?"

"Incorrigible," she rued. As he began to drift, she left him to his rest and crossed the hall to the opposing door. Unlike Finnian's, it was closed.

Desiree gripped the handle and paused. The knots were back, clutching listlessly.

She took a breath and turned the knob. The door swung in silently.

William wasn't upright. Neither was he moving. . She watched the pattern of his vital signs on the heart monitor, gauging them for herself.

She thought he might be sleeping. When she closed the door behind her, though, his head turned on the pillow and his gaze, a bit hooded, fell on her. The corners of his mouth lifted. "There she is."

He was still hoarse. Approaching the bed slowly, she tried for a smile. At his side, she clutched the bed rail. "You look better," she observed.

His smile grew. He closed his eyes, however. It was a minute before he spoke. "If these body aches would leave off, I'd say I was feeling improved." When she hovered, uncertain, he looked to her again. He scanned her face. This time he saw more. With him, she was an open wound, as always. A fissure grew between his eyes. "It's all right. Everything's all right now. It was you who set yourself free. I told you you were strong."

She shook her head. She didn't feel strong. She didn't feel fixed. She wasn't even convinced that one of Radley's brothers wouldn't wriggle loose and come after them all again. "Liddell made a mistake. It was me he wanted. He should've left you and Finnian alone. I would've gone with him if he hadn't put you at risk."

His entire brow wrinkled. "Thank goodness he did."

She heard the dreadful undercurrents in the statement and swam against the cross tide of her emotions.

He saw her. Always what was underneath. He lifted a hand. "Come here."

Screw the bed rail. She scaled it, curling against the solid line of him. He pulled back the sheet. She heard his indrawn breath. "Let me," she whispered and arranged the sheet as he lay back down. She lay beside him. The great thunder drum of his heartbeat was audible when she pressed her ear to his side. She listened to it thump, heavy at first. When it began to settle and his breathing slowed once more, she held very still.

It was a grateful silence on his part. She was tortured

by the what-ifs and what-might-have-beens. She hadn't
had time to contemplate them all. She hadn't let herself.
The smell of him, the press of him brought it on. She
struggled. They came to a boil. Her chest released an
exhale on a shudder.

"All right?" he asked.

She nodded. "I didn't think I wanted this. I thought
the only thing I knew how to be was alone. That was
the choice—the only choice, for a long time. Until... I'm
not sure when exactly, but I realized there was another.
I don't have to be alone anymore. And I don't want to
be. Gerald told me that when he and your mom went to
the Brackens', James had your old truck ready. It was
his gift to you for Christmas."

"Which means," he uttered, "that if Liddell hadn't
burned the Trans Am to a crisp, it would be yours at long
last."

She was silent on the point of the Trans Am.

"I'm sorry, honey," he murmured. "The one thing you
want out of all this...it's ruined."

"I thought so," she said, down to a whisper. "Somehow, I thought the old car would give me all the answers
I needed. Somehow, I thought it would fill all the empty
pockets of my life. But that was before."

"Before?"

She could hear his pulse quickening again. Laying
her hand over the center of his chest, she said, "We can
talk about this later..."

"Dez, please."

He breathed it. Rubbing that spot over the center of
his chest, she said quietly, "I thought it would be a relief.
But all I could hear was you when you said once you'd
wait for me—to decide whether it was right for you and

me to be together. You'd wait so I'd never have to wonder whether or not it's right, I'd just know."

"Do you?" he wondered.

"I do."

He exhaled in a tumultuous burst. "Dez."

"Seriously," she said, eyeing the screens with his vitals. "Mary Elizabeth is going to come kick me out any minute…"

"Screw Mary Elizabeth," he said. "You're staying."

"I am staying," she replied. "I'm staying with you." Raising her head, she braced herself on her elbow so she could see his reaction. "I love you. It didn't take the possibility of losing you to know. I knew last night when you touched me. When you took me slow. I knew it was right, and I knew that I love you."

"God, that's good stuff," he said, closing his eyes. "You have no idea."

"I do, actually," she said. She kissed his shoulder. "Because knowing made me feel at peace."

His hand spread warmth over the back of hers. "Do you want to know when I knew?"

She nodded.

He threaded their fingers together, then brought hers to his lips. "You asked me if you could look at me. I watched you open up. To that point, you'd worn distrust like some women wear Manolos. I watched your eyes open up and worlds unfold. I'm pretty sure I'm still lost in there somewhere."

She grinned at that.

"You felt safe enough with me to do that," he said. "If you had left…" He took a moment, playing with her fingers, fanning them against his. "You'd have taken a chunk of me with you."

He touched the back of her neck. She understood the bidding and brought her lips up to his to brush. His unsteady breath mingled with hers, and they lingered.

"Oh, God," she whispered as those worlds he'd talked about bloomed.

"Yeah," he agreed with a quick nod. "The medical brigade's definitely coming."

She rested her cheek on his shoulder. *Later*, she promised both of them. There would be plenty of time for that later. "She told me to take your hand."

"Who?"

"My mom. When we met, I heard a voice. You held out your hand to help me out of the car, and it said, 'Take the man's hand.' I used to hear it all the time here and there after she died. I wasn't sure if it was really her communicating over time and space or wishful thinking. Those thoughts stopped coming to me through the years. Until you held out your hand. It didn't make sense. She never wanted me fraternizing with boys... She always said there were better uses of my time. But she told me to take your hand. Do you believe in that sort of thing?"

"I do now," he told her. "Maybe it was her—who led you here."

Desiree thought of all the connections—the Trans Am. James. The letter. The voice. The feeling of belonging living on the bay had brought her. Taking William's hand finally...and finding home. The mess with the Kennards had been superfluous. She'd wound up exactly where she was meant to all along. "There are things still uncertain. My stuff is in Wichita."

"We'll get it."

"I shouldn't live with you. At least not at first."

"We'll figure it out."

"I have a cat. He's ornery."

"I have a dog," he groaned. "He licks."

"Himself?"

"Himself," he weighed, "others, the rug, the couch…"

She opened her mouth carefully. "We'll adjust."

"Everything'll work out."

It was the first time she believed it. Despite all the extraneous details, she believed—in the power of her and him. In her own power.

"I'll love you, Desiree," he swore. "All the days of your life."

He would. She knew it like she knew the Leightons would rebuild their tavern, like she knew he would recover. Like she knew she'd love him in return. Always.

It wasn't too late to make her own, she knew, too. It hadn't been too late to decide what was right for her, just as Mercedes said she would. Desiree had made her choice, and she'd chosen well. She'd found the last good man, and she wasn't letting go.

* * * * *

COMING NEXT MONTH FROM

⊕ HARLEQUIN

ROMANTIC SUSPENSE

#2231 AGENT COLTON'S SECRET INVESTIGATION
The Coltons of New York
by Dana Nussio

Desperate to redeem her career by capturing the Black Widow killer, cynical FBI agent Deirdre Colton seeks help from principled rancher Micah Perry who's among the murderer's collateral victims. First she must stop whoever is threatening the widower's life and that of his toddler son.

#2232 CAMERON MOUNTAIN RESCUE
Cameron Glen
by Beth Cornelison

When rescue volunteers Brody Cameron and Anya Patel are trapped by a landslide, they discover not only a mutual attraction, but also evidence of a serial killer's lair. When they become the focus of the killer's wrath, they must join forces to save their lives and find their happily-ever-after.

#2233 ON THE RUN WITH HIS BODYGUARD
Sierra's Web
by Tara Taylor Quinn

Posing as a married couple on an RV vacation, bodyguard McKenna Meredith and wrongfully accused fraudster Joe Hamilton face danger and death from multiple unknown sources. As their perilous road trip continues, they learn to see past their obvious differences—but with their lives on the line, it may not matter.

#2234 COLDERO RIDGE COWBOY
Fuego, New Mexico
by Amber Leigh Williams

Because of a tragic accident, Eveline Eaton's modeling career is at an end and she must return home to the town she escaped from over a decade ago. It's hard to heal, however, when she begins to sense that something or someone is stalking her—and the only person who believes her is Fuego's silent cowboy, Wolfe Coldero.

YOU CAN FIND MORE INFORMATION ON UPCOMING HARLEQUIN TITLES, FREE EXCERPTS AND MORE AT HARLEQUIN.COM.

HRSCNM0423

Get 4 FREE REWARDS!

We'll send you 2 FREE Books plus 2 FREE Mystery Gifts.

FREE Value Over $20

Both the **Harlequin Intrigue®** and **Harlequin® Romantic Suspense** series feature compelling novels filled with heart-racing action-packed romance that will keep you on the edge of your seat.

YES! Please send me 2 FREE novels from the Harlequin Intrigue or Harlequin Romantic Suspense series and my 2 FREE gifts (gifts are worth about $10 retail). After receiving them, if I don't wish to receive any more books, I can return the shipping statement marked "cancel." If I don't cancel, I will receive 6 brand-new Harlequin Intrigue Larger-Print books every month and be billed just $6.49 each in the U.S. or $6.99 each in Canada, a savings of at least 13% off the cover price, or 4 brand-new Harlequin Romantic Suspense books every month and be billed just $5.49 each in the U.S. or $6.24 each in Canada, a savings of at least 12% off the cover price. It's quite a bargain! Shipping and handling is just 50¢ per book in the U.S. and $1.25 per book in Canada.* I understand that accepting the 2 free books and gifts places me under no obligation to buy anything. I can always return a shipment and cancel at any time by calling the number below. The free books and gifts are mine to keep no matter what I decide.

Choose one: ☐ **Harlequin Intrigue Larger-Print** (199/399 HDN GRJK) ☐ **Harlequin Romantic Suspense** (240/340 HDN GRJK)

Name (please print)

Address   Apt. #

City   State/Province   Zip/Postal Code

Email: Please check this box ☐ if you would like to receive newsletters and promotional emails from Harlequin Enterprises ULC and its affiliates. You can unsubscribe anytime.

Mail to the **Harlequin Reader Service:**
IN U.S.A.: P.O. Box 1341, Buffalo, NY 14240-8531
IN CANADA: P.O. Box 603, Fort Erie, Ontario L2A 5X3

Want to try 2 free books from another series! Call 1-800-873-8635 or visit www.ReaderService.com.

*Terms and prices subject to change without notice. Prices do not include sales taxes, which will be charged (if applicable) based on your state or country of residence. Canadian residents will be charged applicable taxes. Offer not valid in Quebec. This offer is limited to one order per household. Books received may not be as shown. Not valid for current subscribers to the Harlequin Intrigue or Harlequin Romantic Suspense series. All orders subject to approval. Credit or debit balances in a customer's account(s) may be offset by any other outstanding balance owed by or to the customer. Please allow 4 to 6 weeks for delivery. Offer available while quantities last.

Your Privacy—Your information is being collected by Harlequin Enterprises ULC, operating as Harlequin Reader Service. For a complete summary of the information we collect, how we use this information and to whom it is disclosed, please visit our privacy notice located at corporate.harlequin.com/privacy-notice. From time to time we may also exchange your personal information with reputable third parties. If you wish to opt out of this sharing of your personal information, please visit readerservice.com/consumerschoice or call 1-800-873-8635. **Notice to California Residents**—Under California law, you have specific rights to control and access your data. For more information on these rights and how to exercise them, visit corporate.harlequin.com/california-privacy.

HIHRS22R3

HARLEQUIN
PLUS

Try the best multimedia
subscription service for romance
readers like you!

Read, Watch and Play.

Experience the easiest way to get
the romance content you crave.

Start your **FREE TRIAL** at
<u>www.harlequinplus.com/freetrial</u>.

HARPLUS0123